Vivienne Vermes is a writer and actress of Irish and Hungarian descent who divides her time between Paris and London. She has published four collections of poetry: *Sand Woman*, *Metamorphoses*, *Passages* and *When the World Stops Spinning*, and has performed her work in festivals throughout Europe. She is winner of the *Piccadilly Poets'* award, the *Mail on Sunday's Best Opening of a Novel* competition, as well as *Flash 500s* prize for short prose and the *Paragram* national competition for best poem and "petite prose". She has taught creative writing in universities in Transylvania, and runs a writers' workshop in Paris.

As an actress, she has played roles in a number of French films, including *Les Trois Frères*, *Le Retour* and in *Les Profs 2* in which she portrayed Queen Elizabeth II. Her voice also warns passengers on the Paris metro to "Mind the gap".

The Barefoot Road is her first novel.

The Barefoot Road

Vivienne Vermes

Matador
9 Priory Business Park,
Wistow Road, Kibworth Beauchamp,
Leicestershire. LE8 0RX
Tel: 0116 279 2299
Email: books@troubador.co.uk
Web: www.troubador.co.uk/matador
Twitter: @matadorbooks

ISBN 978 1788038 638

British Library Cataloguing in Publication Data.
A catalogue record for this book is available from the British Library.

Printed and bound in the UK by 4edge limited
Typeset in 12pt Minion Pro by Troubador Publishing Ltd, Leicester, UK

Matador is an imprint of Troubador Publishing Ltd

To my parents, Miklos and Josephine, and
my grandparents, Jenö and Annushka

PROLOGUE

Before it happened, nobody could have imagined it. After it happened, many denied it. Others said it would never happen again.

It was a still night in June. The river flowed, black and untroubled, through the village with its long straggle of houses. Under the roofs, the villagers were asleep, lost to their dreams – fragments of laughter or terror, bits of memory and pieces of history interwoven behind wooden walls.

At the bend in the river, a woman was singing. She sang quietly, not wishing to disturb the families of her people who had settled down for the night in their tents, or the tilting makeshift shacks that were their homes.

She sat watching the flow of the river. As her own song ebbed away, she listened to the water lapping against the riverbank.

Then another sound. Footsteps. A twig snapping. Voices. A shout. Whoever was coming was not alone. And whoever they were, they cared nothing for stealth. Lights, now, through the bushes, coming down from the mountains, advancing along the towpath, bobbing torches, a necklace of flames.

The woman sat paralyzed for a moment. Then she hoisted her skirt and ran in the dark, tripping over the roots of trees. She wanted to warn her people.

They were already awake, some of them, stumbling out of doorways, emerging, sleepy, from behind the flaps of tents: children crying, mothers clutching shawls around them, as if folds of threadbare fabric could protect them; a shuffling, dazed group, ripped from their dreams, startled, not knowing which way to go. They were trapped, caught by the black arm of the river that curved around the land they lived on.

The men came. An angry red-faced mob with clubs in their hands and hoe handles under their arms. Torches thrown into open doorways. Fire, spreading quickly from shack to shack, indifferent in its hunger for wood or rags or flesh. Screams. The woman watched from the trees. She wanted to run away. She wanted to run towards.

She saw the dark shape of her sister holding a bundle in her arms. Her hair fell loose over her shoulders, almost hiding the baby girl she clutched to her chest. She turned in circles. Her mouth was open. She ran to the river. The men were upon her. Her sister fell to the ground.

The woman ran from her hiding place. Time slowed down, almost stopped. Images, frozen, that would later turn themselves inside out in her dreams; the torch of a hand on fire, the odd flames, the black burning stalks of fingers; her young cousin lying on his back on the ground as quiet as a leaf, his eyes looking up at something very high in the sky, before a boot came down to imprint itself on his head, again and again, until he had no face.

She ran towards her sister, even though she could no longer see her. She had disappeared, buried under the bulk of the men. But she could see the baby on the ground, as if tossed aside, insignificant as the pale rags she was wrapped in, moving her arms in little jerks, seeking safety in the air itself.

She ran to the infant and covered her with her body. Her face was on the earth. Then her head twisted sideways. The smell of alcohol. Mouths on her face. The thickness of smoke, the crackle of fire. A strange sound wrenched from her throat. The heavy plash, again and again, as the river received the flotsam of the dead and dying.

At dawn, an eerie smoke rose from the charred wood that flaked off burnt walls, fluttering in the wind like the wings of dying bats.

The few who survived gathered whatever belongings were left to them and followed the river downstream. They walked, hungry and dazed. They clung to the belief that what had happened to them here would not happen elsewhere. Even while they knew it was not true, they held on to this belief. The young woman carried her sister's baby in her arms. When it began to cry, she drew her hair down to cover it, just as her sister had done.

In the village, rumours spread, then subsided, even though on that night the river ran red. They didn't see the colour of the water. It was dark, and anyway the village, although close by, was upstream. Where they lived, the water did not change colour. Some said that the people who lived down by the bend in the river chose to leave. They did not hide their relief, for now their community, free from outsiders, could return to its preoccupations of sowing and harvesting, the producing of infants, and the anointing of the dead.

They thought they would live, so, in peace, just as the numb and bereft ones thought they would find another piece of land, another bend in the river.

They did not know, they chose not to know, that a hunger lay under the earth. It would sleep for a while, a generation perhaps, until, fed on old blood and fear, it would rise again, claiming the land, and the people who lived on it, as its own.

1

Paraschiva bent down to catch the bad hen, the one who had pecked half of the feathers off the cock's throat the day before. The bad hen's time had come, Paraschiva decided. She had already planned the slippery red stew she would make with peppers and onions and gobs of fat as big as dogs' paws. Spring would soon be coming down from the mountain, the first snows were already melting on the peaks. A late-winter stew, thought Paraschiva, for some warmth in the belly to balance the wet of the land-thaw on the skin.

But her back went. Again. Leaning down to scoop the hen up, Paraschiva heard the now familiar crunch where some inner fluid had dried up or turned into old crystals. Bent double in a warped right angle, her one bright turquoise eye watched as the bad hen stalked through the open door of the barn, fluffing its rear end into a defiant gold-brown crest, and then disappeared into the yard for another day of pecking, bullying, and life.

Paraschiva, immmobilised with the pain that shot darts like firecrackers down her old thighs and knees all the way to her feet, closed her one eye and exhaled deeply. This, then, was the breath of age. "Yaaaagh!" she spat onto the floor of chicken pellets and calf turds.

"Pavel!" she bellowed, and the sound bounced out of the barn, around the yard, and off into the hidden roots of the pine trees.

"PAVEL!" she yelled again. A scuffing of feet from across the yard. It was her son, with his forty-year-old face and his child's mind. Pavel, whose heart seemed to talk to itself in the middle of the night, telling him to be kind to whatever he cradled in his big hands, and not to answer back to the barbs of a world that did not understand him.

Paraschiva glared at him. He first frowned, then, grinning, shuffled alongside his mother. She looked at him out of the corner of her eye. He was enjoying the game, his face lit up with morning light and mischief. She thought of scolding him. Then she thought better of it. He was Pavel, her son, with his mind that saw the soul in all things, yet could name none of them. And she was Paraschiva – hen-throttler, stew-maker, healer, witch and mother. He was her fate, as she was his. He gave her a lop-sided grin, then with infinite care placed himself in a pose that perfectly mimicked Paraschiva's, with knees slightly bent and back locked into a horizontal curve like a billhook, so that mother and son formed a perfectly ridiculous duo, like two half-people waiting for the day to begin; until a magical click released Paraschiva's back, when the bad hen had already plucked the remaining feathers from the cock's throat, and the early spring sun, surprisingly strong for the season, was beginning to warm the milk that Paraschiva had laid out on the table for breakfast.

She stood, now gratefully vertical, watching the road that led from the village, her crooked fingers splayed like old fishing hooks hung out to dry, waiting to catch the wind.

She had walked around the yard a dozen times, fed the chickens, stroked Pavel's head in her lap, looking for ticks, and mumbled odd curses through her teeth.

Curse the funeral, curse the fact we have to die, curse the fact we have to live, curse the night and curse the day. And God love Ioan Trifoi, but let him be on time for once. Otherwise she might just get back into the ancient brown dress that had worn so thin and light that it felt like air or muslin, and was so full of holes that it showed glimpses of her old skin, and was like wearing nothing at all. She pulled angrily at the white sleeve of the blouse that was closed tight around her wrists and neck, then sighed and looked out across the bright patches of green that spotted the mountain sides, little pieces of brilliance in amongst the dense black of the pine forests, and, higher up, the grey teeth of the mountain ridge and, higher still, the gleaming white of the peaks. Paraschiva had always resented the mountains, which is why she spat so often, in rage at this landscape, with its walls of serrated rock that had sawn off something in her soul.

She had come from the plains on the other side of the peaks, had been brought here as a girl by her father, on his wild quest for a tawny-haired tinker woman with the longest legs that had ever wrapped around him. Demented, he had loaded a cart full of books, some on the healing powers of medicinal plants (he had heard there were no doctors on the other side of the mountains), seventy bottles of apricot brandy, and his beautiful ten-year-old daughter with the blue-green eyes. He had left his wife and sons to their keening and had set off across the mountain, obeying the fire in his belly that was the one thing that seemed truly stable in a world where frontiers, laws and languages had a habit of changing with the seasons. Passion. That, he trusted. And he had three of them: his daughter, his bottles, and the girl with the amber skin.

He died a month after they had trundled into their new land. Holding a bottle in one hand and the reins in the other, he fell off the cart and broke his neck on the night of a full moon in May. Paraschiva had wailed a ululation that echoed up and down the valley, a crazed, discordant song that brought the villagers out of their beds and halfway up the mountain. They buried him there, where he fell, and later placed a small unpainted wooden cross by the side of the road. The small girl with the thin arms and turquoise eyes, they had taken to the house of the mayor, who was used to dealing with strays, drunken deaths (of which there were many, especially, for some reason, on the nights of the full moon) and objects lost and found.

Paraschiva had stayed there for two miserable years, resisting, to the best of her girl's power, all attempts to teach her the language or customs of a place where people trussed her up in ridiculous tight-cuffed dresses. Then nature came to her rescue. In a season it transformed her body from a brittle, skinny, sparrow-like thing to a rippling form of flowing curves. From the moment Paraschiva discovered that a provocative sway of the hips, arch of the back, or cat-like stare could be used as effective weapons of insurrection against the mayor's efforts to institutionalize her, or the village women's attempts to domesticate her, she flaunted them fully, until the village boys and young men took to prowling around the mayor's house like crazed dogs.

This provoked much discussion and division amongst the villagers. The mayor's household could not contain her, and no other home wanted to invite such trouble under its roof. So when Paraschiva took herself off to live in an abandoned wooden house high up the hill, a good hour's ride away on bad and rutted tracks, the village breathed a sigh of relief.

First, she checked on all sides that no human habitation cluttered her view, then understood that, apart from staying alive, her main preoccupation would be to get used to the pockmarked faces of the crags that bit into her sky. She never did. Instead, she started to spit, and never stopped.

By the age of sixteen, she had acquired a cow, three goats, a dozen hens and many household repairs in exchange for her favours. Below, in the long straggling village that lined the river banks, heads waved and tongues wagged, and for a while there were calls for action, followed by silence.

For Paraschiva had sent each of her lovers back down into the valley with not only satisfied loins, but with mouths brimming with stories: Paraschiva was a witch, and whoever called for her harm or removal would undoubtedly end up in a wolf's jaws, or worse, be slowly eaten alive from the inside by the small snake spirits that entered every orifice.

Satisfied that the rumours had grown from stories fit to frighten children into tales of terror that would keep the adults away, Paraschiva settled down to the serious study of medicinal plants, interspersed with the milking of cows, the scattering of corn for the chickens, the raking of hay and the annual bale-making – a task she most hated, for then she was required to call on the help of the Brumarus, a family from the village, and, year after year for three weeks, she was plunged daily back into the chitter-chatter, the gossip and the communal meals that she so detested.

It was Ivana Brumaru, a woman with hair that fell like limp yellow rags down her back, with a body as grey and stodgy as an old winter potato, who carried back the tales of Paraschiva's astounding promiscuity: she had slept with every man on every mountain peak, from the village to the frontier; she had had six children by the time she was eighteen, and had mashed each one into pig fodder. Some believed the stories, and trembled. Others discounted them, and laughed out loud. But most of the village shared one belief: that if Paraschiva's body belonged to the devil, her hands were guided by angels.

For Paraschiva had discovered arts other than those practised between sheets, or out in the fields. She had become a healer. She could poultice an arm or leg wound that was vicious and raw, rubbing it with crushed garlic and dock leaves so that the limb looked like it should be laid out on the table; in a miraculously short space of time the skin would be clear and smooth as a baby's bottom. She could lance abscesses, set fractured bones, pull teeth, anoint arthritic joints with her own odd, invented salves and ointments (she would shamelessly mix honey and belladonna, garlic and milk curds) so that word spread quickly, from village to village, that not only could the woman with the strange blue-green eyes curse, and no doubt kill, she could also heal.

Each week a villager or two would wind their way up the rough hill path, through Paraschiva's big wooden gate and into the yard, and would sit, trembling with fear and reluctant gratitude, as Paraschiva spat and glared and swayed her hips and laughed, mocking the frailty of these humans who came to her, fragile, not only in flesh, but also in spirit.

By the time she had reached early womanhood, the wagging of wild tongues had all but died away. It had become clear that Paraschiva, in all her vicious beauty, had brought to the village some strange demented blessing.

As the years passed, the villagers became so accustomed to Paraschiva the healer, they almost forgot about Paraschiva the woman. It was only when a traveller from another village would dare to ask what had caused her to lose her left eye that she would turn away so that only the most invasive of strangers would notice that her good eye had filled with tears.

Now she squinted down at the bend in the road, her brow furrowed with displeasure at the thought of the day ahead. First, she had to go to the funeral of Alina, who, by general consensus, had long outstayed her welcome to this world, and had died peacefully in her sleep at the age of ninety-six, her eyebrows still joined in the middle of her head in a permanent frown of judgement against the earth and all who moved on it. The relationship between Paraschiva and Alina had been like the sound of a sharp stone scraping across ice. Yet here was Paraschiva, trussed up in black skirt and white blouse, with buttons and bindings, feeling like a donkey in harness. Paraschiva had to go to the old hag's final party, if only for the sake of Alina's granddaughter Irena, whom Paraschiva had saved from eternal infertility by prescribing a daily intake of several pints of explosive home-brewed beer, which had the effect of rendering Irena loose of tongue, leg, and thigh, thus freeing up her womb to conceive two sets of boy twins and a girl in the space of a few years, five gifts for which Irena showed her everlasting appreciation by offering Paraschiva the devoted adoration of a handmaiden, visiting her three times a year with a cartload of flowers, grapes, rock-hard homemade wheaten cakes, several boisterous children and a bottle of tuica to which Paraschiva had taken an instant and lifelong liking.

She could do with a glass now, she reflected, rubbing the place where the tight waistband cut a red ridge into her flesh, announcing that another year had yet again added lard to her body, and that she would soon have to die herself if she was ever going to fit into the wooden coffin that was waiting for her in the shed, in among the hanging bacons and sacks of potatoes.

She cursed, and launched a kick at a passing chicken, then comforted herself that at least it was Ioan Trifoi who would drive her down into the valley and back, and that, of all the people except Pavel and one other, it was Ioan Trifoi she loved most, because he had a face that seemed permanently about to break into a smile at some inner joke that only he had access to, and it was Ioan Trifoi alone, in the whole valley, who could make Paraschiva's sides ache with laughter.

It was Ioan Trifoi who had built her a huge wooden gate with an overhanging bat stencilled out of the wood so that the night stars shone through the spaces of its wings on the portal. She went to it now, sliding the latch, and opening the heavy wooden doors to let in the full view of the valley, with its winding bright dust road that reminded her of that other country beyond, where the plains stretched just as yellow, but where the roads were straight, and the horizon was unbroken with its promise of freedom.

2

Ioan Trifoi woke in the middle of the night haunted by a dream in which a slim blonde girl with a bright blue kerchief that matched her eyes stood in front of him, smiling and very still. He reached out his hand to touch her, and, as if in answer, she removed her headscarf which connected miracuously, as if by a magic thread, to all of her garments, and in one winsome move the clothes slid off her body and she stood in front of him, naked and shining, with a fleece of gold between her legs that matched the sheen of her hair.

In his sleep, she slid like a ghost so that her body was under his, and his hand touched the golden juice of her, and he entered her, as if searching through hay to find the dark wet earth beneath.

He woke up to his own moaning, and found himself looking into the sleepily startled eyes of Magda, his wife of twelve years, whose round face gleamed white as the moon, whose folds of flesh he was now pumping with his hands.

Magda sighed contentedly, and thanked heaven quickly, in her half-sleep, for a husband who had given her a fine child, who had built their home with his own hands, who worked hard day after day, yet could still reproduce the passion of their first night.

She snuggled some of her weight into the dip where his ribs hollowed away into his waist, sighed, and went back to sleep, with a light but irritatingly irregular snore that kept Ioan Trifoi awake until dawn, and only then did he return to the yearning place of his dreams where Magda stood in front of him as she once was, gleamingly white and full of mystery, eighteen years old, his one and only bride.

He was awoken by the morning sunlight streaming onto his face. He jumped out of bed, and cursed. He was going to be late. It was the day of the funeral and he had to be up the hills and back by midday, to collect an old woman whom he loved, and bring her down to the troublesome world of people, their living and dying.

At the other end of the village, Father Diaconu was whimpering and sweating under a mound of damp and twisted sheets.

Every demon from each abyss of his tormented soul bounced up to meet him like a blazing volley of fiery cadavers, each one set alight to announce, in flame, the sins of the priest.

He dreamt he was standing in his familiar place in the pulpit, conducting his usual sermon of reward and punishment. Suddenly a baton appeared in his hand and he began to conduct the congregation as one might an orchestra. Row upon row of innocent, upturned faces became his instruments of pleasure, and, when he raised the baton in his right hand and the bible in his left in a crescendo, all the stiffly starched women of the village raised their crimped black skirts up to their waist, turned their backs to him, and bent over to reveal, each one, the splendid cleft pear of a backside, waiting for consumption by Father Diaconu, and him alone.

While the music played on magically, changing from something classical and grandiose to a rustic jig, Father Diaconu, having miraculously shed half of his body's blubber, pranced like a satyr from backside to backside, entering each cleft with virile abandon, and leaving each dry old maid or village virgin groaning with passion hitherto unknown.

When Father Diaconu woke up, he hid his face under the pillow. He would confess his sins. He would flagellate himself. At that thought the sheets began to bulge again with the excitement of his nether regions, so Father Diaconu did what he always did on such occasions (and there were many), he burrowed around in the bottom of the wooden wardrobe, thrashing around under his priest's robes until he found what he was looking for. He set the bottle of tuica on the table, took down a tumbler, and proceeded to drink glass after glass until the stars had faded and the first cocks were crowing, by which time the priest who should have been preparing to officiate Alina's passing was lying on the kitchen floor, so close to the embers of the fire that it was a miracle that the straggling hairs of his beard were not singed by the coals. Father Diaconu lay, a great heap of white flab, alcohol and sin, totally incapacitated, and unable to perform a single of the day's duties.

Ioan Trifoi's horse went slower than anyone else's in the village for the simple reason that not only did he never beat it, but he crooned to it as it walked along, which caused the horse to swish its tail, sent shivers of pleasure down its neck, and had the effect of slowing it to a soothing amble.

So it was that, lulled by the smooth sun of the March morning, the clopping of the horse's hooves and the sound of Paraschiva's throaty cackle as they exchanged jokes and gossip, Ioan Trifoi's cart arrived late at the church to find a red-faced, restless congregation, caught between fury and embarrassment, anxious to bid Alina her final farewell. One of the more spiteful of the village women, who had a long nose to match her tongue, hissed: "The old hag has the last word, even on her way to hell." And another, more generous soul replied: "It's not her fault if Diaconu got there first."

For the priest's inert form had been found by a tearful Irena who, unable to exact anything from him other than an unintelligible dribble about "arses afloat on the river of flames" had given up and returned to the church, her eyes red and bulging with tears.

It was in this state that she flung herself on Ioan Trifoi as he got down from the cart, at which point he closed his arms around the sobbing female mass of grief and shame.

Throughout his charmed life Ioan Trifoi had learned that, in all troublesome situations, there were only two outcomes: either there was a solution, in which case there was little point in worrying; or there was no solution, in which case there was no point in worrying at all. So, while he stroked Irena's shaking back, he breathed deeply and waited for inspiration.

When it came, he passed her gently into Paraschiva's waiting arms, motioned to her to follow him, and walked into the church, down the aisle and up into the pulpit. Finding the bible inconveniently closed, he said a quick prayer, and opened it at random.

The congregation shuffled and nudged one another. Irena looked up at Ioan expectantly, while Paraschiva smiled her one-eyed smile in encouragement.

Ioan Trifoi cleared his throat and began to read:

"Thy two breasts are like two young roes that are twins, which feed among the lilies."

That the pinched and puritanical Alina should be sent on her way to an unspoiled world with such lascivious words sent a ripple of mirth along the lines of mourners. The men in the front pews exchanged glances. Behind them, at the back of the church, the women's chins began to wobble like so many plates of jelly.

Yet not everyone laughed that morning.

In a corner of the old church, near the altar, under a faded fresco of a ladder leading to heaven, with human forms tumbling off every rung, plummeting down into a river of fire, Radu Surdu stared straight ahead, his eyes deep-set in his unnaturally small head. He stood up and inhaled deeply, which had the effect of expanding his chest and raising his shoulders so that his neck disappeared into the barrel of his torso. He glanced along the pew and noticed with satisfaction that around him some fifteen villagers had remained sober and stone-faced, immune to the contagion of laughter.

Among them was Elena Barescu, a widow for the past fifty years, who had never forgiven God for snatching her handsome husband from her the day after their wedding. She had been menstruating on their wedding night, and, having waited three years throughout a long engagement, they decided to be patient another two days, so their dream of union would be realized to perfection. It never happened. He died the next day when a mysterious cracking sound, like that of a rifle shot, went off inside his head, and his brain flooded with blood. Elena had never pardoned God for this act of sin. Nor could she forgive herself for calling God a sinner. Within the confusion of her heart, she sat wedged into her pew, with the pinched mouth and crumpled brow of those who live a life of unresolved conflict. In some hidden corner of her mind of which she herself was only dimly aware, she thanked Radu Surdu for allowing her to remain as tight and closed as a barn door frozen shut, solid with ice, in the dark of winter.

So when Radu Surdu stood up, Elena joined the group of villagers who followed him down the aisle and out of the church, along the straight road that led into the centre of the village. They walked in twos or threes in stiff solemnity, presenting, to an outsider, the sobriety of a funeral procession. Only something barely perceptible about Radu Surdu's walk – a movement that was a fraction too sharp, there where the heel cut too heavily into the dust – betrayed the fact that his feelings were not entirely caught up in grieving for the dead, but with the anger of the living.

3

Pavel held up his fingers and watched, with fascination, as the sun, now high in the sky, filtered through the skin where the fingers joined, turning it into a luminous pink and orange membrane, like the web of a duck's foot. He parted his fingers, letting the sunlight fall through them, blinding his eyes. Joining them again, he watched how his skin once more became a filter for the light.

Then he got bored.

It was rare that Paraschiva left him alone for the best part of a day. Gleeful at first, he had run around the yard, the big boots he hardly ever removed kicking up the dust. Then a disconsolate, angry Pavel did a familiar round of vandalism: he stuck his dirty hands in the milk churn, smeared butter into his hair, plucked two tail feathers out of the cock (later he would blame the bad hen) and contemplated urinating into the well, remembering, just in time, that the well was sacred.

Then he got sad, and went out to the far fence to talk to Luka.

Luka was neither a wolf nor a dog, but something in between, with a wolf's narrow muzzle, thin white needles of teeth, and a dog's liquid eyes, that seemed to be forever watching and waiting for Pavel, and release. Paraschiva kept Luka on a short chain, which he strained against all day, walking in semi circles, backwards and forwards, first one way and then the other, going slowly mad with the wolf in him pulling towards freedom, and the dog in him attached to the home of the old crone who had not slit his throat when a farmer had left him, a skinny jumble of bones and grey fur, in a bundle outside her front gate.

Pavel and Luka exchanged greetings in what had become, over the years, a ritual of gestures. Luka hunkered down, squatting in the dust, while Pavel spread himself flat on his belly, propping his head in his hands, his face close enough to feel the hot vapour of the animal's breath. They sat thus for long minutes, perfectly immobile, like some strange grey-brown sculpture almost indistinguishable from the dust.

Then, as if triggered by an invisible signal, they moved swiftly in unison. Pavel, in one quick gesture, detached chain from collar, and man and animal loped off with the fast pace of those who know where they are going. Neither slowed until they reached the edge of a copse, finding cover under a canopy of leaves that sheltered ferns, bracken, roots and an army of small living things, all involved in the quiet, munching, never-ending struggle between the eater and the eaten.

Light spilled in patches over a narrow track that led down to the valley where the dark overhang of the spruces gave way to the sharper outline of the beech wood, now tinged with the earliest spring green. They paused there for a moment. Then, as if by consensus, they turned their backs and made for a gap in the undergrowth, to where some trodden leaves gave the barest hint of another way, one that led steeply up through the ferns, quickly lost itself in a warren of brambles and continued, hardly visible, until it disappeared altogether, lost in the density of the pines.

When Father Diaconu heard the first moans of wind rattling the tiles on the roof, he shuddered, sure, with his first clear thought of the day, that God had sent him the scraping of dry bones as a punishment for his sins. He remembered the neglected, dead Alina, and, in a vision from hell, imagined her puffing, dragon-like, all the way from church to breathe into his mouth a fiery blast of reprimands.

In the deceased woman's house, at the other end of the village, an uneasy calm had descended on those who had earlier shared in the morning's mirth. Around an oval table laden with plates of chopped pork fat dusted with garlic and paprika, mouth-size pieces of suckling calf, butchered only the day before, wheat cakes, courgette and marrow pies, potato bread and baked apples, the guests picked at the food respectfully, sipped discreetly at their tumblers of tuica, and mumbled polite lies about Alina's generosity, her sharpness of thought and purity of spirit.

In a corner, sitting under a stag's head whose glassy eyes looked out as if from another world, sat Paraschiva, unaware that in the dim late-afternoon light the antlers were casting long and spiky shadows across her, so that her face looked like a full moon seen through the branches of a blackthorn bush. This ghostly apparition did not, however, deter Irena's children, who gave the room its only animation, moving backwards and forwards between Paraschiva and Ioan Trifoi, hoping for a story or a song.

Gabriela, Irena's only girl child, lay across Paraschiva's lap, as if with some private knowledge that she owed her being to the old woman's special skills and, with her brown curls spread over Paraschiva's knees and hanging halfway to the floor, she fell fast asleep.

Paraschiva stroked the child's frail arms that were flung out, half-graceful, half-awkward, in a gesture of abandon so trusting it was almost wanton. The child had a glow about her, Paraschiva thought. She was beautiful, yes, but then so were most of the children in the village, with their ruddy cheeks and hair that turned chestnut or blond in the summer sun. Gabriela had something else about her – some combination of a child's mischief with the luminosity of an ageless spirit – that gave her a shining quality. Paraschiva feared for her, as she feared for all those who shone too brightly.

As if to reassure herself, the old woman began to hum gently, rocking the sleeping child on her knees, letting the sound carry her over the mountains and back to the plains, to a wooden house and a hog in the yard, to her own mother, cradling her with the same fears and tenderness, until the memories fell over her like water.

She was brought out of her reverie by a loud and fruity belch, which began in the cavernous stomach of Barbu Temeru and erupted on the gathering with all the resonance of an old bugle calling disheartened troops to battle. As if on cue, the solemnity of the gathering dissolved with a shuffling of discreet, yet purposeful movement. Barbu Temeru lumbered to his feet and moved his bulk across the room to fetch an old cloth bag that hung off a peg on the wall. Opening the top of the bag, he pulled out a stained and battered violin, and looked at it with the smile of a long-lost lover.

Alina's three old cousins made the sign of the cross quickly over their shrivelled bosoms and prepared to leave, mumbling excuses about getting home before the storm, already in their minds relishing their walk back through the village, during which they would exchange tirades against those who dared to mix death with dancing.

Barbu Temeru tucked the old violin under his chin and began to pluck each string in turn, twiddle each knob and scrape the bow across the neck, producing a cacophony of jarring chords, part of a painful process that passed for tuning.

Ioan Trifoi downed another tuica and got to his feet, shaking out his legs as if to be rid of the day's ceremony of death, or of their lifelong daily walk towards their own dying. He tilted his head upwards to where the light shone down from an oil lamp, so Paraschiva, from where she sat in the penumbra, could see the gleam in his eyes that always preceded his dance.

He was not handsome, she thought, in fact, without the light in his eyes or the spring in his step, he could sometimes look quite ugly. His nose was too big for his face, his hands were too large for his arms and his hair was ruffled up and out and all over the place, as if he had just got out of bed and run his hands through it, which he usually had.

Yet when she looked at him, standing there in the pool of light with that glint in his eye and spring in his step, it was as if he possessed some piece of sun that transfixed her with its warmth.

In her long and multi-coloured life, Paraschiva had only ever met one other who had radiated such a light, and he had long since disappeared into the dark.

Ioan Trifoi waited, his head held high. His posture was ready, impatient even, but already the light was dulling in his eyes.

The violin should by now have been tuned. But all that Barbu Temeru could produce was an empty sound that scraped around the room.

He laid the bow across his lap and placed the instrument on the table, putting it down carefully, as if it were some injured animal. The violin was a victim of last autumn's equinox flood, on a night when a river of mud had flowed down the mountain and swamped Barbu Temeru's shed in a torrent of sludge, branches, and dead animals. He had woken up to find the entire winter rations of cured ham, flour, chickpeas, potatoes and salt, awash. The villagers immediately rushed in with help, and soon his kitchen table was creaking under enough food to feed himself and his family.

They were out of harm's way. There would be no bare cupboards, no begging from door to door, and the hearth would not go cold. The damage could be undone, the winter kept at the door. The ordinary things – the boards, the hinges, the rabbit hutches, the stable doors – they would all, in time, be replaced. Barbu Temeru counted himself an almost lucky man. It was in the extraordinary that he felt unlucky. For he knew the violin to be a fragile, speaking thing, a teller of tunes from beyond. He knew, too, that the delicate wood of the violin could never be fully repaired. With coaxing, it would play out a tune. Villagers would continue to move to its rhythms. But its sound was crude compared to the whirling notes that used to spiral into the air. Long gone were the fingers of the people who had the skill to restore it. And long gone their music.

Now, on a darkening March afternoon, Barbu struck up a discordant tune, and Ioan Trifoi danced to it. But both men held in their hearts the memory of a more stirring music, and a more spirited step.

4

Up in the hills, the woods were singing. Twigs clicked against each other, tiny drumsticks bruising the early spring buds. Pavel half walked, half ran up the path, his back bent low, his eyes on the ground, with its thick twisted roots that burst out of the earth like the deformed knuckles of a giant.

From time to time he stopped, cocking his head to the trees, listening. For Pavel knew that if you waited long enough, the forest would speak its own sounds. Luka was far ahead, already up where the pine trees stopped in a line, where beyond were the rocks, and above them the snows, now made dangerous by the first protracted bursts of sunlight. Pavel remembered the sounds of other early springs – the whistle of the cracking ice, and the colours – the blue and black veins that streaked and suddenly widened. Once, he had seen a great frozen mass become dislodged, topple and crash its way down, flattening rocks and trees in its path, like a huge uprooted tooth.

Pavel was not afraid of the mountains. His fear and discomfort came from all that went on in the valley below. He rarely went into the village: if Paraschiva tried to make him walk down the dust road that led to the houses, he would curl into a ball in the dirt, his arms linked around the trunk of the elm by the gate, and refuse to move.

Standing with his back against the rough bark of an alder, watching the clouds fill the spaces between the criss-cross of black branches, Pavel laughed, then scratched his head and set off at a faster pace, jumping over boulders, spluttering with joy when he slid on mud or slapped the soles of his boots down hard on the surface of a puddle.

Today, Paraschiva had left him. Today, Pavel had been angry and was so no longer, for today Pavel was free and would take his freedom to the forbidden top of the mountain. He laughed ever more loudly as the path climbed upwards. He didn't care that his laughter drove away the small animals that sometimes came close to him. Today nothing would quell Pavel's glee, for his was the joy of the bad child.

He walked until the sun was directly overhead, a pale disc, visible and then invisible, swathed by scarves of grey cloud. High above him, he could see the peaks appear and disappear in the thin mist. He caught sight of Luka standing immobile on his familiar rock, his head turned to the way that led through the mountain ridge. Then the animal vanished with the mountains, hidden by the falling grey veil. Pavel walked faster now, his legs driven by an old fear, that one day he would reach the wolf's rock, and find it bare and empty, with Luka gone through the crack in the mountains, into the dark pass, away from him and the farm and the chain. This was a fear that bit at Pavel's heart, leaving him hungry and clawing at the straw on his bed at night with the terror of being left alone in an empty land, where no one, not even Paraschiva, could share his unspoken language.

Pavel broke into a run, even though on one side the rock sheered away into a steep tumble of stones. He ran until his lungs ached with the wetness of the air, until the sudden slash of a late-winter wind sliced sideways through his clothes. He would get to the wolf's rock and then return, quickly. He knew the paths well, he could soon be back at the farm, sitting by the fire while the March winds groaned down the chimney.

Above him, the sun disappeared in the thickness of a new layer of cloud. When he got to the rock, Luka had gone. He called out, and his own voice came back to him, bouncing down from the dark grey wall of stone. Here was the lonely impenetrable place of the heart. Pavel scrambled to the top of the rock where Luka had stood, and hunkered down. Far below him, the pine trees moved their branches in the mist. He let out a low whistle.

It was answered by four short barks, and Pavel's world jumped up. The dog was nearby. The barking came louder now, furious, interspersed with angry growls. Pavel looked to where the sound came from, there where the rocks fell away on three sides, leaving a bowl, its brim now edged with a white lace of cloud. He ran with his heart in his legs, scrambling down, clutching at the fragile whip of a branch that barely held his weight, falling over the wet sides of rocks, scratching his calves where he slid on a pile of scree, landing sharply with a howl of pain and joy. There where the cloud cleared, he ran to bury his face in the fur of the dog's neck. But the dog broke away, would have none of the greeting. Luka's lips were curled up, his teeth bared, the whites of his eyes gleaming. He rushed away from Pavel, ran five paces, his tail sweeping, stopped, ran back, barking. The wolf-dog danced his alarm for Pavel, and Pavel followed with his eyes.

In the deepest hollow of the rock bowl, he could see the old blackened trunk of a pine tree, long since blasted by lightning. And there, in among the twisted mass of roots, he could see a scrap of red flapping in the wind. Tentatively, he walked towards whatever it was that fluttered on the ground in some dance of its own. He stopped before he got to it, when he saw that the red thing was wound around a shoulder, and the shoulder was attached to a body, and the dog's bark was so wild because the chest of the body was bare and alive, and breathing.

5

Paraschiva and Ioan Trifoi rode in silence through the village, each lost in their own thoughts.

"Rain," was the only word Paraschiva said, lifting her head to a sky that had grown as dark as a donkey hide. She left her head where it was, raised up to the cloud, as if too tired to bring it back to its usual place on her neck, feeling the first drops watering the wrinkles on her skin.

Ioan Trifoi hummed softly beside her – an old quiet tune, for her, for the horse, for himself, to relieve the spirits on a day full of the dead.

They passed through the long straggle of the village, the road lined with dark wooden houses under their fringes of slatted pine roofs, each home vying with its neighbour for size and importance, some with the owner's name carved into the wooden portal. Behind windows, oil lamps were being lit, casting shadows on the faces of children lured to the table by the smell of roasting pork.

With the sound of the cartwheels crunching round on the dirt road, Paraschiva thought of the summer, and the autumn, and the winter ahead, and thought again, in her own revolving circle, of the coffin in the shed, and of Pavel, and of what would become of him after she had gone.

"When I die," she said, in a voice distorted by the upward stretch of her throat, "I would like you to read at my funeral."

They stared at each other for a moment, then broke into laughter at the memory of Trifoi's attempt to officiate.

They were still laughing when they passed Radu Surdu's house. It was one of the most imposing in the village. He had built it using all the local labour, from this village and the two neighbouring ones, over three long summers.

"May all his teeth fall out and down his throat and may he choke on them," Paraschiva spat out the words in an incantation and sent them, with her breath, to the front window where a light illuminated the shadows of heads. "And may one tooth stay to rot in his gum, and give him toothache." She finished the curse with satisfaction.

Ioan Trifoi chuckled at the old woman's invective. He patted her knee, which he had sat on as a child. He loved the old woman, especially in her wickedness.

Paraschiva turned her good eye away from the window, to block out the sight of the house. But the sound carried. Above the noise of the wheels of the cart jolting across the ruts in the road, Ioan Trifoi could make out the voices of Alina's cousins, full of complaint and piety. There would be reproaches and reprimands for the funeral fiasco. That much was certain. Father Diaconu would be chastised at a communal gathering, and would, as ever, make a whining lament. He would, as always, go away with the sharp looks of Radu Surdu's followers at his back. But nothing more. The simple truth was that the village needed its priest, and Father Diaconu was the only one with whom they had been blessed, or cursed. He was their lot, and Radu Surdu could complain and whip up as much spite as he liked, but so far his demands for a replacement had come to nothing. Maybe that was why his eyes burned like little black winter grapes.

Ioan could hear his voice rising now, drowning out the others. He could make out isolated words: "… inevitable… subversive faction … intolerable… incisive action…" Words which the villagers never used. Words which, Ioan Trifoi felt certain, they would not even understand. Radu Surdu was not a dangerous man, he thought, just a crippled one. Beaten with a lead pipe from the age of three by a father who hanged himself, and none too soon. The whole village knew the tales of madness of the Surdu house. Ioan Trifoi could not like the man, but nor would he condemn him.

Paraschiva pulled her shawl tightly around her, yet still felt the rain seeping through.

"A man without veins," she said. "Not enough blood in his body, nothing beating in his chest, so he needs to take hold of other people's hearts."

Ioan Trifoi put his woollen jacket around her, to shelter her old shoulders. Then he groped in the back of the cart and, from under a blanket, pulled out a brown felt hat the shape of a flowerpot with a black tassle hanging down. He plopped it on her head. It would keep her dry, and, more than that, it would make her laugh, and there was nothing Ioan Trifoi liked more than to hear the old woman chuckle, for it made him forget the cold that cut at his heart when he thought of the day he would have to bury her.

6

It was alive, of that Pavel was certain. The chest was rising and falling, but irregularly, in spasms. The eyelids were blue and flickering, the hair around the face matted and hanging in clumps, like pieces of dried moss.

It was alive and yet it smelt of death. He knelt beside it. It frightened him. He had met death before, many times, had seen it in men and animals; its smell was familiar to him, he did not fear it. But this creature was living, yet with its odour of decomposition. A whimper rose from his throat, but no sound came. Beside him, the wolf-dog had stopped barking. Pavel looked from Luka to the strange human heap in front of him, then to the mountains above and felt his world closing down.

He looked back to where it lay, with its irregular breathing, trying to stay alive.

It was a woman. Her breasts were exposed to the air. Brown breasts, the colour of the river. The bare torso rose out of the torn pile of clothes. From the waist down, she was swathed in layers of ragged cloth, stained red and brown with dirt and dung and blood. Pavel wanted to cover her up, or uncover her.

Get rid of this half-and-half creature, half-clothed, half-naked, half-in-life, half-in-death. But the breasts fascinated him. The brownness of them, with their swell and the rise of the darker brown of the nipples. He wanted to touch them, and he wanted to run away from the smell he could not understand, flee down the mountain to Paraschiva and lay his head in her lap. He did as Luka had done, ran four steps forward and three steps back, while the wind rose and brought in more clouds across the mountain ridge above him.

For a second, a gust lifted the red shawl beside her and he saw what lay underneath. It was small and blue and perfectly formed, and the life had gone out of it.

He understood the death-smell and knew that he must run as fast and far as he could, or this half-living, half-dead thing would get him, and, if it didn't, the coldness of the closing night would. He bellowed to the wolf-dog to follow him.

It was then that she opened her eyes. Just for a moment, the eyelids flickered up and she looked sideways to where it lay under the flapping red shawl. She stared at it, while Pavel stared at her, and then she let out a sound that came from deep in her stomach, as if down inside her was a big hole newly filled with all the sorrow of the world.

Pavel's heart was opening and closing like a gate banging in the wind. He didn't know who she was, or why she was, but he knew that sound as if it had come from his own gut.

He leaned towards her and rolled the back of his hand across her forehead. Her eyes moved then, away from the grief that was on the ground beside her, to look into his face. He knew that look. He had seen it before, in animals before slaughter, in the calf when it smelt the blood of its dead brother. He could read those eyes in a way he could not read lips, or sentences, or tongues. In this creature too weak for speech, he could feel his own need, to mouth out a single word that would make the cold line of the horizon a little warmer.

He was in a place, now, of instinct. He pulled the shawl from under her back and covered the tiny creature with it, touching its skin once, with his fingers, by mistake. It was dry and cold. He put the little bundle behind a rock so that, if she opened her eyes again, she would not see it.

Then he returned to her quickly, afraid that the chill in the wind would carry her off, too, to the land of the cold blue skin.

Wrapping her skirt around her legs tightly, like one of the woodpiles he carried home from the forest to kindle the fire, he hoisted her over his shoulder, her head and arms dangling down his back, an ungainly rag doll that made him stagger as he climbed up the steep sides of the rock bowl. The wolf-dog ran ahead of him, impatient at the slowness of the pace, then stopped to turn back, barking, urging Pavel onwards.

Panting, sweating, he carried his burden back down the mountain, all the way muttering and sliding under her weight, yet full, inside, because of what he had shared with those eyes.

When Paraschiva and Ioan Trifoi rounded the last curve in the road that led to the house on the hill, they saw Pavel and Luka waiting under the big wooden gate, as the first stars appeared through the spaces in the bat's wings.

Between them lay a bundle of cloth and skin and hair that Paraschiva thought might be alive, because of the way Pavel was stroking the eyelids, as if trying, against all the odds, to make them open and talk to him, and to the sky above them.

7

People aren't born on time, people don't die on time, and there's no good time for sick people to land on your doorstep. That much was sure, thought Paraschiva, as she spun around the kitchen, with fifteen tasks at once in between her old hands.

There was water to be boiled, lots of it, in a pot too heavy for her to lift. She barked orders at Ioan Trifoi, who obeyed like a schoolboy. There was firewood to be gathered: she shooed Pavel out of the kitchen to fetch it. There were poultices to be made, garlic and cinnamon and mustard, to spread all over the ragged girl who lay stretched out on the floor on a brown blanket that was the same colour as her skin.

"She must drink." Paraschiva thrust the wooden cup into Ioan's hands, while she held the girl's head. Her lips were lined with cracks, which the water seemed to hurt, for the girl winced and moaned, her head wobbling, and most of the water spilling down her chest and onto the floor. "Make her drink," Paraschiva insisted.

Ioan Trifoi was looking from the girl to the door. He knew the journey home would be cold, with the spring snows already in the air. Yet he longed to exchange this room, which would soon be hot with the fire and the boiling of brews, for the peace and solitude of the downward track, with his horse clopping out the distance home.

Paraschiva picked up his thoughts. "And don't you even think of leaving. I need two pairs of hands."

So their hands worked, unwrapping the remaining rags of clothes from her body.

"Holy God," said Ioan Trifoi, when she lay naked and stretched out in front of them.

Her feet and legs were ravaged by fissures that seeped yellow in suppuration. On the hands, the skin was white and flaking, criss-crossed with a mass of tiny white cracks. The body was emaciated, with the ribs sticking out, gaunt spikes from under the skin, which seemed too thin to hold the bag of bones together. But the swell of the belly showed that the dried blood that spread in a red-brown web over her thighs had been spilled in a birthing. Around her, the ground had come alive with the tiny grey-brown bodies of lice, forced to flee their host, and now disappearing into cracks in the earth floor. Paraschiva took a deep breath before going to fetch some lime to sprinkle around her.

Then she got down to business, moving quickly from shelf to table, cutting garlic and pounding it in a mortar, before laying it in thick crusts onto gauze bandages. The legs would have to be bound tight enough for the poultice to enter the wounds, but loose enough to let the skin breathe. And the quicker the better, before more serious infection set in.

"Put some vinegar in the pot," she barked the orders now at Ioan, for there was no time to lose. "And wash her."

Ioan Trifoi shook his head, then rolled up his sleeves. If Father Diaconu or one of the village women could see him now, he would have to do a month's penance. Another taboo broken, he thought, still unable to believe in a god who would send you to hell for wiping the mess off a sick woman's thighs, and send you to heaven for letting her die. The thoughts went through his head in rhythm with the movements of the cloth, up and down the length of her legs.

He sponged away the grey layer of grime that had tinged her skin the colour of ash, and there where the surface had not been exposed to wind, or brambles, or parasites, it was smooth and dark, the colour of pine-bark.

They treated each part of her body in turn, mechanically, working fast, with precision. Paraschiva bathed her feet and legs in brine, then bandaged each of the oozing cracks. The hands and fingers she anointed with olive oil, to moisten the flaking skin. When they had finished, the girl looked like the shiny, painted victim of some ancient sacrificial rite, but for the hair that hung in matted clumps around her head.

Paraschiva took down a pair of scissors from a hook on the wall. Her knees cracked as she lowered herself onto the floor, steadying herself with one hand on Ioan's shoulder. "Hold her head," she said, and her own voice was weak with fatigue. He held its weight in his hands, spreading his fingers through the undergrowth of her hair. The fire threw leaping shadows over the girl's face, strangely serene as the scissors clipped away, and her hair fell in tangled masses onto his lap.

When it was done, he gathered them up and threw them on the fire, which hissed up and flared in a sudden white blaze, illuminating for a moment the shorn skull of the girl.

"If people are going to die, this is the time of night when they do it," Paraschiva thought, slumped now in a chair by the fire, opposite Ioan Trifoi. Both were exhausted. They had bathed her scalp and face, had propped her up between them and spooned a broth of camomile and ox-tongue down her throat, they had covered her in a gauze sheet and a woollen blanket, and then collapsed, each one into their own welcome land of sleep.

Ioan Trifoi dreamed that he was holding his daughter to his chest and stroking the swathe of her fair hair, when a man with a bullet head and black eyes burst into the room with a pair of shears and shouted: "Your life for hers!" In the dilemma of his dream, he woke up. The room was almost dark, at that hollow time of night before the first light of dawn, but he saw from the glow of the dying fire that the girl had her head turned towards him. She was watching him, and beneath half-closed eyelids, her eyes shone like hot chestnuts.

The last stars were fading as Ioan Trifoi made his way back to the sleeping village. Thoughts flitted across his mind, small restless bats. Then he was aware of a physical sensation – a lurch in the abdomen, a tightening of the muscles, an overwhelming feeling that he could not give a name to, but that lay somewhere between elation and dread.

He wanted to halt the night right there and then, to take time to collect himself, to savour the moment before dawn, with the last of the stars shining dimly above the rooftops, the clop of the horse's hooves on the road, and the windows of the houses all shuttered down, wooden eyelids shut tight in sleep. But already he could see his house at the end of the dust road, with a light shining from a downstairs window.

Lifting the latch of the front door, he pushed his weight against it gently, so as not to wake the household. But the door swung open as if of its own accord. His wife stood in the doorway, her round eyes red-rimmed from lack of sleep.

"Where have you been? I've been up these last two hours." Her words were reproachful but her voice was kind.

He took her head in his hands to embrace her. As he found her lips, he felt her mouth purse and then open, drawing his into a kiss. He felt suddenly tired, and more in need of a glass of hot black tea than the touch of his wife. He pulled his mouth away and stroked her face, brushing a strand of hair from her cheek. Her full white face looked up at him, luminous in the first light of day. In her eyes, he detected, first, a shadow of hurt, and then a look of relief. Better to get down to business, the look said. Which Magda did as well as any wife in town.

She bustled into the kitchen and was soon skimming the cream off the milk while Ioan held his face over a steaming glass of tea, warming the end of his nose with its vapour. He told Magda of the night's events in a quiet voice, so as not to wake his daughter, asleep in the next room. He spoke of the journey up the hill with Paraschiva, and of what they had found at the end of it.

"Paraschiva's a good soul," Magda said, crossing herself, "and she'll go straight to heaven, in spite of what some people say."

"She will," Ioan nodded. "It'll be the idle-tongued ones that won't be there to meet her." He knew that a faction in the village would have had her driven out as a witch long since if they'd had half the chance. But they hadn't and wouldn't. She was too loved, and by too many, and that was that.

Magda plied her husband with questions as she kneaded the dough for the day's bread. Would the girl live? Yes, he thought she would, in Paraschiva's care. Where had she come from? From the other side of the mountains probably, for she had been wandering in the cold for weeks, by the look of her. What could she be doing there alone, and why would a girl risk the crossing of the peaks with the winter still in the air?

Magda slapped the dough from one palm to another to flatten it. Slap, slap, slap. Ioan felt his eyelids drooping shut to the rhythm of the sound. He wanted an end to the questions. Above all, he did not want to talk about the swell of the girl's belly. His wife had a good heart, but she also had a lively tongue. The girl, if she were to survive, could do without rumours rustling from house to house.

"Enough, Magda," he said wearily, with a coldness in his voice that made her eyes narrow. She squashed the flattened-out dough back into a ball, and punched a hole in the middle.

The dawn was spilling into the kitchen now, throwing pools of grey light onto the flagstone floor. Soon their daughter would be up and wanting hot milk and bread; in the shed the cow was already making its first restless stompings. If he were lucky, he could get an hour's sleep before the bustle of the day began.

Magda saw the weariness of him, the slowness in his legs as he moved to the kitchen door. She hesitated, then pulled out a dirty, tightly-folded piece of paper she had tucked into the cuff of her nightdress.

"This is for you. It was left on the gatepost. I didn't see who left it, but it's from one of Surdu's men."

She pressed the paper into her husband's hand, as though relieved to be rid of it. He hung his head.

"Later, Magda."

"I think you should read it now. They're having a meeting this morning. I think it's important."

Ioan Trifoi sighed. Another meeting. Ever since he was a child, he had never been able to fathom why some people could not be satisfied with the sight of the stars, or the flash of a fish in a spring brook, or the new-born making its first cry to the world. But then he had always been accused of being a dreamer, even by his own wife. No one else sang to their horse. Or spent half the night trying to recall a song his father had hummed to him as a boy.

He opened the paper, tearing it slightly as he did so.

"In view of the notable lapses of behaviour on the part of the town clergyman, the third in a series of meetings will be held to discuss a positive course of action. It is desirable that the head of each household attend. In the event of the head of a household being unable to attend, that household's vote will be counted as affirmative of the motion that Father Diaconu be removed from office, to be replaced by request to His Holiness the Bishop of Birtiza."

The rest of the scrawl gave details of the time and place of the meeting. Ioan had torn the paper where the signature would have been. He sighed. It didn't matter who had signed it. It could be any one of half a dozen of Surdu's henchmen. The tactics were the same. Give written notice of a meeting to villagers, many of whom could not read. Ensure that only a select group would attend.

He crumpled up the paper and put it in his pocket, aware that his every movement was closely watched by his wife.

"You will go?" Magda's voice was urgent.

"I have the pigs to feed, and the fence at the top pasture has a hole nearly big enough for a calf to walk through. Do you think I have to take up the good fight for Father Diaconu? Let the old drunk get a good warning. Maybe for once he'll listen, and I won't have to take to the pulpit in his stead."

Magda frowned. It was rare to see her husband so tetchy.

"Ioan," she pressed her hand over his. "You must go, Ioan. I have spoken to Irena. Her husband was at the meeting last night. Surdu wants Diaconu away. Gone, for good."

"He always wants him gone for good."

"This time he means business."

"He always means business. He's a dog with teeth, but nothing to bite. This village will never expel its priest."

Ioan's voice was rising. He longed to be away from the heat of the kitchen, to be stretched out on the mattress before his daughter Doinitsa woke up and plied him for every detail of the night's business.

"You will go, Ioan, please. You will go for me and our daughter. Radu Surdu is a dog who can't bite for one reason, and one reason alone. It's *you* who have muzzled him."

Her face was flushed and her eyes flashed as she spoke. She was right, he knew. Surdu was harmless only because Ioan and a few others had forced themselves to attend the meetings, had been able to deflect the rising voices and cut short the long babble of discourse with a few well-placed words of common sense, or a joke that brought laughter to break Surdu's spell. More than anyone, Ioan had been able to make Surdu and his supporters look like fools.

"I will go, Magda." He folded his wife in his arms and felt the gentle heaving of her back, as if she were trying to fight back tears. So, it was that important to her, and should have been to him. She was right. It was more important than sleep.

From the next room came the sound of shuffling and yawning, then the humming that told them that Doinitsa was awake.

Ioan went into the yard and hoisted a pail from the well, cupped his hands and splashed the cold water over his head. He could hear the sound of shutters banging open all down the street, and the creak of the first carts setting off on their slow journeys down the road.

Radu Surdu's house was made of grey brick, with round windows in the roof that stared out like vacant eyes. Ioan Trifoi stopped in front of it. His head was hammering with a hundred small nails. He looked towards the road, winding along the river, past where the trees thickened, and on up to the hills, where the mud would soon be drying and the buds bursting into blossom on the trees. He longed to follow the road. He would rather be anywhere than at Surdu's front door. Better not hesitate. Wait another instant, and with a tug on the reins he would turn the horse's head towards freedom, and the mountains.

He could hear the swell of voices as he walked into the dark of the hall. His eyes felt swollen and heavy, his jaw seemed to be drooping of its own accord, his head tired and prickly after the length of the night.

The room was thick with the men from the village. Squashed elbow to elbow on benches, like winter birds huddled together on a branch. He was suddenly alert, the weight of the night gone. He had been prepared for the usual smattering of Surdu's followers, the tight-lipped villagers who had walked away from the funeral the day before. Not for this expectant crowd.

The Illitch menfolk were there, taking up the front bench. Vasile and Toader Illitch, twin brothers who looked as alike as a blackbird and a goldfinch, twisted their heads around to the door and caught Ioan Trifoi's eye. He raised his hat in greeting. As neighbours, they often helped each other to repair broken fences or with the birthing of calves. Now they looked away from him, turning their eyes to the floor. Ioan Trifoi understood and cussed under his breath. It was Diaconu's fault, he thought. By not officiating at Alina's funeral, he had taken that drunken step that left him teetering over the abyss. Toader Illitch's eldest daughter was soon to make a good marriage to a farmer's son from the next village. Ioan understood the Illitchs' apprehension. What if Diaconu failed again in his duty, this time with the future of the entire family at stake? There were seven children in Toader Illitch's family, five of them daughters and none of them yet married. The fiasco of a wedding without a priest could mean ruin. The Illitch family had friends across the village and into the next one. If Surdu could count on their support, Ioan thought grimly, he would indeed have new and powerful friends.

Ioan Trifoi looked around the room. Usually there was a bareness to it, with its yellowing walls and grey stone floor on which benches were laid out in neat rows for a gathering that never filled them. Now Trifoi could count only four empty seats. He looked around for Barbu Temeru. He would need support if he were to sway the crowd in favour of giving Diaconu one last chance. And why, indeed, did the old man deserve it? Only that Diaconu burned with but a pale heat, and Ioan feared the flame that might replace him.

The room hushed with the sound of approaching footsteps from an anteroom at the back of the hall, and the murmur of the crowd was silenced by the opening of a large dark wood door.

Radu Surdu walked down the aisle in between the rows of benches, flanked on one side by the thin, concave figure of Pavel Micu, and on the other by Miron Corvan, his big pale head perched on his neck like a balloon.

Surdu's step was firm but unhurried. When he reached the table at the front of the assembly, he carefully prised some documents from their brown wrapping. Lingering over each piece of paper with precise movements of his hands, he allowed his audience to finish with their shuffling and scraping of chairs. Only when there was absolute silence did Radu Surdu raise his head. Still he did not speak. His eyes moved along the gathering row by row, taking in each man present. He did not smile, but Ioan saw a momentary gleam in his eyes as he acknowledged the size of the group. From where Trifoi was standing, he looked like an anvil – the small, flat bald head perched on top of the jutting, square shoulders, with no neck at all in between.

Ioan Trifoi leaned the back of his head against the wall, hoping that its coolness would relieve the persistent pain in his head. He closed his eyes, took a deep breath, and prepared himself to listen to what Radu Surdu had to say. Whether it was the ache in his head, or the airlessness of the room, Ioan could not concentrate on Surdu's convoluted sentences of introduction, but only on the sound of his voice.

It was thin, reedy, and in no way exceptional except for its cadences. For Radu Surdu had learned what many speakers never understood in a lifetime of rhetoric: the power of silence. Surdu would speak half a sentence, leave it dangling in the air, and allow the pause to spread around the room for a fraction longer than expected. In that small, added measure of quiet, every wandering eye or thought in the audience would be brought back to the speaker. Why had he stopped? What would he do next? Would his eyes fall on them? Their attention was riveted, like that of their neighbour's, on the black eyes of the speaker. Only when the whole room had joined in the power of a collective hush, would he continue.

"Friends," the thin voice stretched across the room, "I thank you for attending in such numbers for a decision of the utmost importance, on which the health" – here a pause, the word suspended in mid air, for health was vital, without health one perished – "of our whole community" – here the arms outstretched, to embrace every member of the room, the face cracking into a smile – "depends."

The voice continued. "This is a matter of contention. The Bible speaks of the Judgement Day" – a long pause, all eyes gathered in fear of the final meeting with the Maker – "but, friends, here in this world of frailty where we are as dust, is not every day of our lives a Day of Judgement?" – another pause; no one wanted to meet their judgement today – "And if we are found lacking – as a husband, as a father, as a son, as a member of the community – is it not right that we too be judged, and that we accept our judgements as Men of God, and praise those who judge us for showing us the error of our ways?

"I tell you, friends, that the one amongst us who should be whitest in the eyes of the Lord, he who would sanctify our lives, has been found lacking. Lacking, friends, in his knowledge of the ways of the Lord. Lacking, friends, in his love of God. We who love God, we who have met here so that we tread in the paths of righteousness, it behoves us to act as the mouthpiece of God, so that we look into our hearts and find there the courage to cast out him, who, in our midst, is the instrument of the Devil."

Here the voice found a new resonance, so that the walls echoed it back to the speaker. From the secure shelter of the room, each mind now conjured up the dark wings of Satan, flapping up sulphurous fire, in which they, too, could be consumed.

"Friends, be not afraid. Trust in the Lord who will never fail. Do not falter. Our priest has failed us. Failed us by his lack of wisdom, failed us by the abuse of the word of the Lord, failed, most lamentably, Alina Metrovna, she who had all her life been most respectful of the ways of the Lord. Her soul is, at this moment, wandering, lost, in the land of wailing."

A long pause. Breath inheld in the room. An electric fear in which each man saw his own wraith of a soul, left to float, friendless and abandoned, on a river of eternal solitude.

In the pause, a sound gusted in from the street outside. Possibly the rising of the March wind in the branches, or the eddy of air around a rooftop. Surdu heard it and his eyes closed in satisfaction. With his head tilted back and upwards, palms of his hands open, who, among the assembly, could doubt that the presence of God was with him, and that his words were Good?

Ioan Trifoi's thoughts were racing. He was not a man of rhetoric. At smaller gatherings, a jibe or a joke had been enough to deflate Surdu's power. What words, what arguments could he now find to break the spell that had already been cast over the gathering? Though he would admit it to no one, Ioan Trifoi did not believe in the God of the church, and certainly not in the God of Radu Surdu. He felt no great fear of the Lord or the Devil. The moments of holiness he had found were the passing of a finger over the head of his newborn child, or the stars' last gleaming just before dawn. Nevertheless, he now prayed to some deity of his own making to lend him inspiration.

None came.

"Friends," the voice started up again. Now Surdu picked up the documents from the table and fingered them gently. "I am not a vengeful man. I stand here in front of you in humility, as leader of our village council, elected by yourselves." An attempt at a smile that cut his face in two. "Now I would put to you that our Father in Heaven, who looks after our every need, wills that we rid ourselves of Father Petru Diaconu, who has brought shame on our heads, and will not cease to do so. That he be relieved of his priestly duties as of this day, that a written document which I have in front of me, drafted by our elected village council, be sent without delay to the Bishop of Birtiza. With our trust in the Lord, we can be sure that another shepherd will be sent to lead his sheep. We place ourselves in the mighty hands of the Lord God, our creator, who sees into all our hearts and is watching us at every moment in preparation for the day when we shall stand before Him and await His final judgement."

The voice rose and fell with the power of a breaking wave. It was the voice of complete confidence. Surdu's hour had come.

"Friends, I would ask you to act without delay. For those innocent, unborn babes who must soon be brought to our church for baptism," – a pause, for everyone to give thought to the two young women of the village whose time was at hand – "for those who are soon to pass from this world to the next," – a longer silence, as one man thought of his ageing, infirm mother, another of his sick father – "for those who are about to offer up their sons and daughters into the Holy State of Matrimony," – here Surdu looked straight at the front row, at Toader Illitch, as protector of his eldest daughter – "I implore you to take courage. Our village is a good village. Let our village be known as a place of Honour, Virtue and Purity, and let us cast out the Evil that has come amongst us."

A murmur of approval spread from row to row.

"Friends, show me your faith. Let all those in favour of Father Diaconu's dismissal now raise your hands."

Ioan Trifoi's heart was pumping in his chest. He knew the room to be carried away by the tide of Surdu's rhetoric. But he would yet try for a moment's grace. He stood up, scraping his chair on the floor, with not an idea in his head of what he was going to say, and wishing he was a true Believer, and that the

God whom everyone else was so sure existed, would be on his side.

"I beg the right of speech."

Rows of heads turned around. Starched collars creaked as shoulders and necks craned to see the speaker. Then the silence of expectation. And the only sound in Ioan Trifoi's head was the beat of his own blood.

"I wish to speak on behalf of our priest."

From somewhere in the hall came a snort of scorn, followed by a rumble of disapproval. Ioan Trifoi knew he must seize the moment, before others seized it from him.

"Father Diaconu has been found failing, especially in recent months. Our priest has fallen prey to bad habits."

The rumble rose, the crowd contesting the leniency of the words. If he left a pause, even for a second, the rumble would become a roar. He took a quick breath, and continued.

"But who amongst us here has not been found lacking?" He looked into the terrible blank that his mind had become. From out of it, there arose a blur of words, parables, phrases half-remembered. He snatched at one of them.

"Did not the Lord teach us of forgiveness? Who amongst you would cast the first stone?" He looked around the room in supplication. Above the rows of listeners, he could see the bald anvil head, with the small beetle eyes staring at him, implacable.

Ioan Trifoi faltered. He had no more speech. He raised his hands.

"I am not a man of words..."

"Then why don't you keep them to yourself?" an angry voice barked out from the centre of the assembly. In the second of silence that followed the interruption, Ioan looked at the floor, registered the dull sheen of the stone, and prayed again to some god of his own making.

This time, his prayer was answered. There was the scraping of wood, and the large oak door at the back of the hall swung wide to reveal the newcomers: Barbu Temeru, burly and bearded, guiding, with one thick muscled arm, the elbow of the bloated old priest.

With head bent low, his body crumpled like a piece of damp parchment, Father Diaconu walked slowly, step by step, up the aisle, supported all the way by the huge figure of Barbu, who had quite shaken off the effects of yesterday's tuica, and now, with his shaggy black hair and wild beard, took on the appearance of an avenging angel. If anyone had dared to speak out against the wavering old Diaconu, they were not about to do so in the presence of the dark giant at his side.

Barbu led the priest to the front of the assembly, stopping only when he had ensured that the old man faced the centre of the crowd. Almost. He himself took that spot, precisely at the place where the bulk of his frame completely obscured that of Radu Surdu.

At the back of the hall, Ioan Trifoi suppressed the urge to laugh out loud. Only Barbu could have placed himself so stubbornly and perfectly in a position where he instantly turned Surdu into a shadow. And Surdu, hemmed in by his two henchmen, could do nothing. Any shuffling to the right or left would be unseemly. So he stood, immobile, his only view the well-worn brown leather grain of the back of Barbu's jacket.

Barbu's voice boomed across the room with all the force of great bellows that would blow a spark into a bonfire.

"Fellow villagers, my family and friends," Barbu glowered at the front row of Illitches, with whom he had an ancestral battle over rights to use the lower, richer pasture land in summer, "Father Diaconu has come to plead his case."

The priest looked around the hall with an air of contrition. The old man's shoulders were hunched, his beard was ragged, his hands were trembling. His eyes, a pale blue, were ringed with the white of old age. Not a noble man, nor a holy one, but a man so clearly devoid of power that no one could associate him with the black breath of Satan.

"I have come here today," quavered the voice, almost as high as a girl's, "to ask your forgiveness. I have been a sinner among you. I have not fulfilled my duties as a priest, nor even," and here the old man's chins began to tremble beneath his beard, "as a human being."

Ioan Trifoi held his breath. Whatever strength Diaconu had, he was using it wisely, for it lay in his weakness.

"I have come here among you today, not to excuse my failings as a priest – for they are without excuse – I come here only that you understand my actions as a man."

Heads shifted from the middle of benches to get a better view. In church, no one had fought to see the priest's face, contenting themselves with the drone of his prayers. Now, each neck craned with the ghoulish desire to witness a human at his most vulnerable.

The priest's head wobbled on his neck as he looked out across the hall of his judges. He began his speech.

He had been called to the ministry by death, he said, by the passing of his beloved mother when he was yet a young man. Only God could accompany him in his grieving, and, in thanks to the Lord who had held his hand through the valley of despair, he had decided to devote his life to his Maker, and take up the priesthood, leave his hometown, friends and family, to administer to the needs of the flock of this village. And for long years he had been a good priest.

He looked into the crowd for approval. It was true. Many could remember him in his better days, many had themselves been held in his arms as he touched their foreheads with holy water.

His voice trembled now, his head bowed in confession. In recent times he had been weakest among the weak. He had strayed from the ways of the

Lord, but not through wickedness, not through Evil. It was another death (and here the voice became barely audible, so that a crowd of heads leaned forward to catch the old man's speech).

Two years ago, he said, he had lost the one person in this living world who, after his mother, had most mattered to him, his adored sister Petra. She who had so resembled his mother as to have sometimes effaced his grief altogether. And now she was gone and, in her going, had brought a double pain. The loss of a dearly loved sibling, the only surviving member of his family, and a reminder of the agony of grief for a dear mother.

The first death had pushed him towards God, and the second (here the old man's lips pursed in an attempt to stop up the tears that now demanded to flow), the second had pushed him to take refuge in excess, to seek out a slow and cowardly path toward oblivion. All knew of his shame (here the old man began to crumple and had to gather himself in order to continue) but none felt it as he himself. Of sinners, he was the worst, and deserved whatever punishment was deemed fitting, only, only, he begged for one last chance, for the love he bore for the village, for the love of the church, for the love of the babies he had baptised, the faithful couples he had joined together in matrimony, and most of all, for the Love of God.

Tears welled up in the pale old eyes. Ioan Trifoi felt his own eyes stinging. If Father Diaconu preached half as well in church as he was doing in the room of judgement, thought Ioan, he would not be here in the first place.

The moan of the rising wind, accompanied by the drumming of heavy raindrops on the windows. A long pause while the priest, his hands clasped on his chest, looked straight out over the rows of heads, beseeching the assembly for one last chance to redeem himself.

The crowd was silent, its earlier angry resolution fading, as the priest's plea cast ripples of silent sympathy around the room.

With a voice like a bell, Barbu intervened quickly, calling for the raising of hands, but never moving his body, so that the eclipse of Radu Surdu remained total. "Any person here gathered who is against the principle of forgiveness as taught to us by the Lord Jesus Christ, anyone here in favour of Father Diaconu's dismissal, raise their right hand." The patter of rain, louder now, beating out a heavy rhythm on the roof. "And quickly, before our cows all sink up to their knees in mud."

Sidelong looks were exchanged from row to row. There was a shuffling of knees and a scratching of necks. Truth to tell, most of the menfolk's minds were already turning to the pastures, to bringing down the herds before fields turned to liquid.

Of the fifty or so gathered, Barbu could count no more than ten raised arms, which fell as quickly as they were raised, not wishing to linger in defeat.

The old priest's body sagged with relief. Barbu's face relaxed into a smile that showed an uneven line of teeth. With a grand sweep, he stepped aside to give the assembly a clear view of Radu Surdu, small and clenched, mouth tightened so that his lips disappeared altogether, leaving his chin a featureless surface of stretched skin.

In the relieved murmur that followed the vote, Surdu gathered up his papers, folding each one in perfect symmetry before walking to the back of the hall at the same measured pace with which he had entered. As he passed Ioan Trifoi, he paused, but Ioan had his eyes fixed on the floor, which he deemed to have been his friend throughout the entire meeting.

The assembly dispersed quickly, each man walking down the road and going his separate way, anxious to be rid of the confusion of Right and Wrong, of Punishment and Forgiveness, eager to return to the simplicity of combating the havoc of a spring storm.

The last to leave, Barbu Temeru walked with the priest to his home, went inside the old man's house, lit a fire, then emptied each and every bottle of tuica into the puddles of the back yard, so that the chickens, when they drank from them, would have the most memorable and wobbly day of their short lives. Nor did Barbu Temeru pause in his task, not even when the priest admitted, in a blubber of confession, that he had never had a sister, that his mother had died long before he could remember, while he was still a babe in arms, and that, consequently, he had never shed a single tear for either of them.

8

Water. Water hurled down from the sky, the gods emptying huge buckets over the valley. Water spooned down the girl's throat. Ladles and ladles of it, so that Paraschiva's arms ached from the raising of the girl's head and the refilling of the heavy wooden vat.

No amount of water, poured onto the girl or into her, reduced the fever. She had the body of a starved fawn, and the heavy breathing of a sick calf. Her skin was burning up, and the body inside with it. The eyes, round and without expression, seemed to have already journeyed to some world beyond. The soul was leaking out of them.

Paraschiva knew when to battle for the breath of life, and when to stop. She stood by the window that looked across the valley, now barely visible under a sheet of white rain, and stared beyond, towards the edge of the forest, a band of dark green, the trees now tossing wild heads to the sky. She knew what she must do.

Putting the ladle in Pavel's hand, she showed him how to hold the girl's head at an angle so that the water would not spill over her chest. She made him soak a rag and pass it over the girl's head and neck, over and over again, in a soothing movement. Pavel, eager and concentrated, learned his lessons quickly. He had hardly taken his eyes off the girl for seven days, not since he had borne her down the mountain. Nor had he left her side. Satisfied that the girl's body was in safe hands, Paraschiva wrapped herself in a woollen shawl, and stepped out into the storm to seek help for the girl's spirit.

Grey hailstones splashed onto puddles, now as big as small ponds. "Pah!" Paraschiva let out her own sound to the sky, which replied by drenching her to the skin even before she had reached the wooden portal.

The base of the gate was stuck in the mud, and she had to haul it free. She was surprised at her own strength, as if the deluge was washing away her years, stirring tired tendons and loosening stiff muscles, so that she walked swiftly, in spite of the rain, to the edge of the wood, where the trees were waiting for her.

The forest creaked and heaved in the wind. Paraschiva slithered on paths slippery with mud, through puddles awash with dead leaves and slugs. At times the path disappeared altogether, and she had to push aside wet brambles and hoist herself over fallen branches. Twice she heard the cracking sound, loud as a whiplash, as a branch broke away from a trunk and crashed onto the forest floor.

She came to a place where the ground rose into a shallow mound. The spikes of broken branches jutted up, black and gleaming in the rain.

A peel of thunder rolled around the forest, faded away, then rumbled again with a bigger voice. Paraschiva climbed to the top of the mound, sometimes slipping backwards down the slope, catching hold of a branch or a rock to steady herself. She found her spot at the top. Here, in spite of the gusts of wind that blew leaves into eddies all around, a single black crow's feather remained lodged in a crack in the broken trunk of a pine tree.

She sat on the stump, feeling the cold cushion of wet moss beneath her. Letting her thoughts fall with her shawl to the ground, she closed her eyes, and waited.

Sometimes she would sit for hours before the spirits came. Once she had waited for days. Today, they came immediately, as if they had been expecting her. She knew they were there by the sudden pressure in the centre of her chest, her heart no longer her own, greater than the confines of her body.

Her mind went to a place of darkness, a black well buried in stone, where the body sank and slowly drowned, trusting in its drowning. She recognised the surge of her earthly self, longing to return to its daily twittering – little dawn birds anxious for daylight – and she paid no attention to its sounds.

Instead, she chose to seep into the hidden corners of the mind, knowing that, when she and the spirits were ready, a veil would lift, revealing that half-lit terrain between this world and another.

In her journeying, she saw a procession of faces, some known, most unfamiliar: twisted faces, heads with the tops of their skulls open and gaping, filling up with rain. She saw heavy animals, not of this earth, lumbering, their flesh in shreds, their mouths open, patient for blood. She saw the owl's eye at night, and went into its speckled amber, and knew it to be the sun. Then, with a lurch, she was the mouse frozen by the great yellow terror of the stare in the middle of the night, in the moment before the monstrous bright eye, and all the rest of the world, disappeared as talons pierced through fur and skin. She journeyed past haunted trees, waving their twigs towards the sky, fingers reaching for nothing but cloud and vapour.

Then she arrived.

A place of nothing. Of complete quiet, without light or dark, hope or dread. A place where the soul drank and was drunk.

Here, she asked the spirits for help. By the sighing in the branches, she knew she was heard.

In the middle of the day, Pavel, who had fallen asleep by the girl's bedside, was awoken by a sound he first took to be thunder, then recognised as a growl coming from the corner of the room. He cried out, certain that something had come to kill him and the girl, whom he now wanted near him for the rest of his life. He sprang to his feet. Then he let out a whoop of relief when he saw that it was Luka, whose stake had come uprooted in the mud. The wolf-dog, for once set free by non-human hand and terrified by the storm, had found his way through the wooden door and into the house.

Pavel stroked the animal's wet fur and smoothed back his ears, squatting down with his back to the girl, so he did not see the way her chest suddenly rose and fell with unnatural speed, or how her eyelids flickered, the whites underneath gleaming too brightly, and then, with a shudder of her whole body, the eyes closed altogether, and her weight sank back onto the mattress.

It was dark when Paraschiva arrived, with ice in her veins and a ravenous hunger. The storm had abated. The house was quiet. She opened the door and listened to the room for its changes. She heard a harmony of breathing, then saw their shadows interlocked in the lamplight – Pavel, with one sleeping arm around the dog, whose paws twitched in a dream world, and the other arm stretched out beside the girl, who breathed now with a deep and quiet breath.

Paraschiva saw that she was in the sleep of a healing, and knelt in front of the fire to mutter a chant of gratitude, to no one but herself and those who lived behind the veil. It rose above the sound of the rain, which beat quietly but persistently on the roof of the house.

God must be very busy, reflected Ioan Trifoi, for everyone in the village was talking to Him night and day since the heavens had opened. The river had swollen and broken its banks in two places, forcing families out of their houses and into their neighbours', an arrangement that could last comfortably for but a few days before both families began calling on the

Almighty. On the mountainside, fences were torn out and flattened, and farmers who would prefer not to speak to each other were forced into discussion.

Radu Surdu's followers met and prayed for the deliverance of the village from the evil of their priest, and those who had defended him. Declaring that the storm was a sign of Divine Retribution, they begged God for more signs, that, fortunately for the village, were not forthcoming.

The main street, which ran for two miles along the river, was awash with mud, which did not stop folk from crossing and re-crossing the street to avoid talking to one another. Ioan Trifoi never knew when the doffing of his hat and a smile would be met with a greeting and the reassuring exchange of woes, or with a back turned and a shoulder hunched against him. He attributed such behaviour to human folly, and waited for it to pass, with the rains.

At least, he thought, the floods had brought with them one blessing: no one had the mind or the time for the new arrival up on the mountain. Every morning, when he awoke, his eyes followed the road that led up to Paraschiva's, now a river of mud. It would be at least a week, if not longer, before the road was passable. He did his own small talking to the Divine, asking for protection for the old woman, her simple son, and a sick girl.

Meanwhile, he busied himself with the catching, killing and collecting of rats, which had overrun the village when the river had spilled out across the streets. No one had ever seen such rats. As big as cats, they scurried into houses in the middle of the day. Others lay dead, half-buried in the mud, their beady eyes staring out, glazed, as if in a pretend half-sleep.

There were rats in the stable, rats that made new homes in the hay, rats rustling behind walls at night. Magda and Ioan had moved their bed, and their daughter's, into the kitchen, for fear of being bitten during the night.

Besieged, the family sat around the fire and listened to the rain. Ioan looked at his daughter Doinitsa, with her face which was not beautiful, nor even pretty, but which glowed, pink and white, exuding the girl's good nature.

Magda sat close to the fire, sewing red and green flowers onto her daughter's white blouse. She had removed her shawl and loosened the neck of her dress. Ioan observed the fullness of Magda's graceful arms and shoulders, the glow on her skin, made ruddy by the heat of the fire. He admired her hair, the way the flames shone flickering lights through its blondness. He looked from wife to daughter and back again, marvelling at their likeness, at the miracle of procreation. Then he felt the familiar sadness that they had only been granted one child. The birth had been a difficult one, in which mother and child had nearly lost their lives. It had left Magda barren. Prayers, and all of Paraschiva's potions, had proved to no avail, and through the long years of silent grieving, the couple had learned to celebrate the blessing of their only child rather than mourn their unborn. As the wind moaned down the chimney, Ioan turned his mind away from the shadow of loss.

He saw the years stretching ahead, saw his Doinitsa grow tall and slender as her mother had once been, then saw her married and portly, with her own offspring, around her own hearth. He felt his own life winding around him, and with it, the quiet walking of an old man's step.

A log dislodged itself and spat sparks across the hearth. For a moment, they glowed fierce and orange, before quickly fading into black husks, later to be trampled into the ground. Ioan Trifoi fell asleep to the sound of the wind and the fire, and dreamed that he lived in a house full of holes and empty beds, where every hole was suddenly stuffed with fresh spring grass, and every bed was filled with flames.

Father Diaconu sat on his bed and prayed, in a fervour of sincerity, for the strength not to walk the twenty paces to the outhouse, where ten bottles of tuica, hidden under log piles, lay waiting for consumption.

It was dusk, the time of day when he felt temptation at its greatest. He listened to the rain, relentless drops beating against the window panes, little entities demanding entry. His thoughts were as insistent as their patter: he had lied, blatantly, and in public, about his past. There were a host of witnesses to his deception. And one of them knew the truth. He prayed that Barbu Temeru would hold his silence, as he had promised, and not tell anyone (and least of all his wife Tunde, who had a twittering, nervous tongue) about his sorry lie. In times gone by, he thought, the village would have forgiven him. But now, with so many voices rising against him, he could hope for little mercy. He repeated his prayer again and again, until a roll of thunder brought him out of his trance, and he remembered that he should also be praying for forgiveness.

"Dear Father in heaven, forgive me for my false words. Dear Father, forgive me. And let me not cross the yard to the outhouse. Let me not cross the yard. Let me not cross the yard."

The more he repeated the words, the clearer the image formed in his mind. He could see himself opening the back door. He could see his feet walking across the mud. He could see himself in the outhouse. He could see the bottles stacked, gleaming, behind logs.

He must not. He could not. Not now. Now his hand was on the doorknob. Now the door was open, the rain on his face. Now he was in the yard, his shoes clogged with mud. Twenty paces to the outhouse. Still he had time to turn back.

He prayed again, but it was as if his words were dissolving in the rain, which fell from his hair down over his forehead and into his eyes, blurring his vision.

It was then that he glimpsed it. Out of the corner of his eye, a movement in the yard, to one side of him.

He turned to see what it was. Nothing. Just the dark bulk of a barrow, its outline barely discernible in the failing light.

He walked on. Two paces. This time, he heard it. Something creeping alongside him, keeping pace with him. He stopped again. The noise stopped.

The rain was falling more heavily now. A rising wind blew drops against his face.

Then he saw it. It was on the ground, the same colour as the mud. It was a rat, large, brown, and its black eyes stared at him. It stayed still, as he stayed still, neither of them knowing which way to go.

Father Diaconu was breathing fast, his immobility caving in. It was as if the rat knew it. It was quick. In a second, before he had time to move, it had streaked past him, out of the yard, under the gate, and into the village beyond.

Still the priest had time to notice, in a split second, something about the rat's belly that was big and swollen and slithered under it as it moved across the ground.

The priest returned to the house. He closed the door, sat on his bed, and stared out at space.

Paraschiva knew better than to curse the rains that followed the storm. Now that her road was a brown river, the only way to get to the village would have been to float there and arrive drowned. She allowed the mountains to wrap her in, and protect her from the prying eyes and nosy faces of the villagers, who, she knew, would otherwise have come trekking up the path to inspect the thin brown rag of a woman.

There was not much to see. The girl lay inert, speechless, and without a name.

Paraschiva gathered pine needles, crushed them, and mixed them with milk and water, boiled the mixture over the fire, and had Pavel spoon it faithfully down the young woman's throat twelve times a day. For the first three days she lay still, eyes half-closed, but on the fourth day she spat it directly at Pavel's nose. Paraschiva marvelled at his patience as he carried on spooning, and also at the accuracy of the girl's aim, for one who had not yet fully returned to the land of the living.

On the fifth day Paraschiva spoke to the spirits in the yard while she was feeding the hens, and asked them for guidance. They said one word: "Dumplings".

Paraschiva proceeded to make a thick soup of bacon, cabbage, beans and pork fat, with fluffy pale dumplings floating on its surface. Trusting in the world beyond, she was not surprised when the girl sat up in bed, roused by the rich smells that had pervaded the room, and slurped down the whole bowl quicker than Luka could eat the bone of a freshly slaughtered pig, before staring Paraschiva straight in the face with eyes the colour of autumn.

The rains stopped as suddenly as they had begun. The wind dropped. Without the constant buffeting of the elements, a new calm descended on the village. The river shrank back to a manageable size, and the trees began to shoot pale new leaves.

Two young girls sat under a poplar in the early morning sun, arranging stones on the ground as if they were treasures. Doinitsa held up a red stone.

"This is my most secret wish in the world."

Her best friend, Gabriela, hid a black stone and a white stone behind her back in clenched fists.

"This is my most secret wish and my biggest fear."

"Tell."

Gabriela looked at the ground. What could she tell? That she did not have wishes like other girls. That her wish was for a father who came home, for once, not smelling of tuica, for a mother who didn't wake up pale and sick, crying at the sound of her husband staggering through the door. That her wish was to have been born into another family and to have had a father like Ioan Trifoi.

"Tell," Doinitsa insisted.

Gabriela shook her head and laughed – a high, nervous laugh.

"Tell me yours," she said, and moved close to her friend, so that her chestnut curls brushed against Doinitsa's blonde hair.

Then both girls wagged their heads in pretend gossip like the women of the village, before Doinitsa confessed that her secret wish was to marry Mihai, who was fifteen and the blacksmith's son.

"Doinitsa! Gabriela!" Magda called out to the

girls from the door of the kitchen. "Come! I have something special."

The kitchen smelled of sweet buns cooking on the griddle. Magda sat the two girls opposite each other, put a finger to her lips, and disappeared into the hall. Both girls held their breath in unison in an old game: whoever breathed out first would break the spell.

The girls were red in the face by the time Magda reappeared, cradling in her arms a white bouquet of cloth as carefully as if it were a child.

Breath was let out in a balloon of laughter, as the girls rushed to unfold the surprise ruffles of Doinitsa's spring festival dress, and two white blouses embroidered with green and red flowers, one for each girl, for their Sunday best. With the rustle of cloth, the girls' giggles, the spring air prancing into the kitchen, Magda felt a warmth rise from her chest up into her throat, some overflowing gratitude at the fullness of her life, crystallized in this one moment, which, if she could, she would have frozen forever.

"Let's show Papa, come." Doinitsa danced on the spot with excitement.

Ioan Trifoi was cutting up one of the silver birches felled by the storm when Doinitsa stood in front of him, slowly twirling, a little porcelain doll in her white dress, her arms outstretched, inviting his admiration.

"Is she not beautiful?" Magda pressed her head against Ioan's shoulder, allowing the weight of her body to lean against him, full with the presence that was neither his nor hers, but all that they had created together.

Ioan Trifoi beamed at his child, and, feeling his wife's warmth beside him, patted her hand.

In the detached lightness of her husband's touch, she felt a loss, like a feast day without food. For Magda, the spring day stumbled and lost its stride. Though her mind tried to reason its way back to happiness, the moment had passed.

She pulled away from him. "I must get back to the baking. The meal will soon be on the table."

"I will eat later. I must prepare the horse – I should visit Paraschiva, take her provisions."

He moved towards her and kissed the top of her head, smoothing her hair with his hands, as if to make everything the way it should be, and rarely was, except in moments that vanished like the pitter of rain.

9

Strange words breezed into Paraschiva's head with all the suddenness of a spring wind. The old woman didn't like it. She knew the house to be newly bewitched, and she knew who was the cause. She persistently asked the spirits for guidance, but all they said was "omelettes", "bacon" and "pork fat". She obeyed them, and made dish after dish, which the girl ate voraciously, hardly pausing to look up from her plate.

Paraschiva, too wise to try to unwind the ways of the other world, decided to treat the girl as if she were a sick animal: feed her, watch over her from time to time, and otherwise leave her be.

But out of the corner of the old woman's eye, she observed that the girl was as strange and as changeable as the March sky. Sometimes she would follow Paraschiva around all morning, never letting the old woman out of her sight, so close as to be able to touch her skirt. At other times the girl was distant, walking on stiff, weak legs around the yard, sitting huddled up close to the well, draped in a blanket. She would stare out, ignoring all attentions, unaware even when the rain trickled through onto her skin. Or she would curl up in front of the fire with Pavel next to her, and allow him to touch the stubble on her head, which Pavel found a constant source of fascination. Then she would shoo him away with a low whistle that he immediately took as a warning. This was the only sound she made. Paraschiva tried talking to her in the dialect of the village, then in her own language from her homeland on the plain beyond the mountains, then in Pavel's language of signs and guttural splutters, but the girl's eyes never flickered or betrayed any sign of recognition.

It was as if her mind and heart belonged to the crack in the mountains, cold and vacant, while her body craved the world of hearth and soup and fire, touch and sustenance. To Paraschiva, it seemed as if there were two girls wedged within the same skin, and the dislocation in her soul made the old woman afraid, for it was a place of danger where bad spirits could come to lodge.

She felt them around and inside the house. The old woman had difficulty inhaling, as if the air were too heavy for breath. Her thoughts came and went in sudden flurries, and she could make no sense of them. Odd words and phrases jumped into her mind at all times of the day or night, where they shifted around in order and disorder to make meaningless sentences. It was as if she was under some spell of the air. She cursed more than ever, and took to shouting at Pavel and the girl in turn, and to kicking Luka, who found a way to be constantly underfoot.

She had let him remain free ever since the day of the storm when he had come into the house, for she noticed that whenever the wolf-dog came near, the girl softened, the two disjointed parts of her seeming to come together. Luka would flatten his ears and his body would writhe and wriggle in joy at the sight of the girl, while her eyes would momentarily lose their vacant look, and would light up with the hint of a smile.

After two weeks, the flesh was already returning to the girl's bones, and her sores were healing with a speed that even Paraschiva found astonishing, revealing a skin that had an almost unnatural sheen, as if beaded with gold. In the evening lamplight, Paraschiva found herself compelled to stroke the girl's arm. Then the girl would hold the old woman's hand and press it against her cheek, and sit staring into the coals. Once the old woman felt the trickle of tears on the back of her hand. And thus the two women began to know each other, without a single word passing between them.

Yet in the middle of the night the tenderness would seem as a dream, and the house rocked with harsh noises, so that Luka fled outside and returned to his shed. Paraschiva had given the girl her own bed near the hearth in the kitchen, while she herself slept under a pile of covers in the ante-room, from where she could hear the knocking of cupboard doors. Once she lit a candle and, by its dim light, she caught sight of the girl stuffing pieces of dry bread into her mouth so that her cheeks bulged.

The old woman tried to take the girl's hand to calm her, telling her that here she was safe and that no mountain animal was coming to eat her or her food, but, at Paraschiva's touch, the girl let out a cry that woke Pavel, who, frightened by the wild look in her eyes, ran out to sleep alongside Luka in the kennel in the yard.

If the girl was bewitched, thought Paraschiva, all she could do now was to pray. Yet when the old woman came to mouth her invocation, she found herself asking, not for the salvation of the girl's spirit, but for a visit from Ioan Trifoi.

He arrived two days later, on the same day as the girl disappeared. Paraschiva searched for her everywhere, in the outhouses and up the path that led to the mountains, but she was nowhere to be found. Maybe she was gone for good, thought the old woman, and was surprised at the twinge in her heart.

10

Ioan Trifoi wore an old felt hat shaped like a bell pulled down low over his face so that his eyes were barely visible, and his nose stuck out from under the brim. The hat always made Paraschiva laugh.

"And pray God that you don't wear that hat in bed, or your wife will never touch you," she chuckled as she hugged him to her.

She pulled down the bottle of tuica and filled two small glasses to the brim. When they had been downed, she poured another two. The warmth of the alcohol, and the light in Ioan Trifoi's eyes, always ready for laughter, soothed her spirit. Later, she would ask him for a song. For the moment, she wished, more than usual, for some trivial village gossip with which to occupy her mind.

Ioan Trifoi recounted the tribulations the villagers had suffered: the invasion of the rats, the rift that had split the community, the threats of Radu Surdu. His voice was quiet.

"You had best be looking to your own safety, if he ever had his way." He looked at the old woman, noting how she looked ever more tired on each of his visits. Now he noticed small blue veins on her cheeks and the deepened lines on her brow. But her good eye still twinkled turquoise.

"Pah! A tin soldier who thinks he can command armies. I could arm you with charms that would make his power as a snowflake, if you should require it."

"No, no, but thank you." Ioan Trifoi held no more truck with the world of spells and incantations than he did with the fear of the Devil.

"And the girl?" he asked, lowering his eyes. He still bore the memory of the breaking of taboos, of the long nakedness of the girl's legs against the movement of his hands.

"Vanished. During the night or early this morning."

"She'll return to you."

"As if I would miss her."

"And would you not?"

"Do I require another mute to exchange stories with?" Paraschiva laughed out loud at the irony of her fate. Then her face clouded over and she sipped from the tuica glass as if for sustenance.

"Her body heals faster than I can say my prayers. She would eat the cow whole, and its shed. Soon she will be fat like a sow before the slaughter. Yet her spirit ails both herself, and this house. Can you not feel it?"

"I feel nothing but the warmth of your welcome." Ioan Trifoi leaned over and put his hand on hers.

"You have noticed nothing because your eyes are only ever fixed on goodness. Also, the girl is gone. Also, the other world enters the house with the night.

Pavel now sleeps in the dog shed, in spite of the season."

"Shall I not look for her now?"

"You may try, but you won't find her. Even if she is still here, she is full of fear and is hiding in some dark corner. Should you find her, she would be silent as a shadow. Best leave her to her own ways. But of you, Ioan Trifoi, I would ask one thing, a large service to render..."

Ioan Trifoi looked up over his tuica glass. Paraschiva had never had to ask a favour of him in this tone, so sure was she of his good will in advance.

"This is no place for a woman of her age. Her spirit is broken in two, so that the shadow ones are drawn to the dark gap in her. Should she stay here, and I am no more..."

Here the old woman paused and took another sip. Ioan Trifoi pressed her hand more tightly, adding his warmth to the skin of her palm.

"What do you want of me? Speak your mind, for you know there is nothing I would refuse you."

"I would ask of you then, Ioan Trifoi, just as you promised to take Pavel into your household when I die, that you should take in the girl. But now, not after my death, that she should heal in the company of women and children. I fear that if she stays here she will know no one and nothing but the winter crows and the sad sick fold that come up the mountain, and have no talk but with the growling dog and the squawking hen. That is no life, and I suspect she has a rare beauty of spirit, should she find her soul whole once more."

Ioan Trifoi picked up the poker and frowned as he prodded the shards of wood. "You know I would do anything for you..."

He poked at the fire until the flames licked up the side of the log like leaping hounds.

"You need say no more. I know that you are thinking of your wife and child."

"It is so. Already my name is strange on some tongues. This is a thin time for kindness."

"Let us speak no more of it."

The old woman got up and went to the stove, ladled out three healthy portions of chicken and lentils, bawled at Pavel to come in out of the cold of the late spring afternoon, and together they sat down to eat, drink and exchange some songs, for there was nothing Ioan Trifoi liked better than to hear the old woman, fired by tuica, sing airs that stirred with passion for the country of her childhood. And there was nothing the old woman liked more than the sparkle of Ioan Trifoi's eyes to accompany her song.

Pavel sat close to him, moving his head from side to side in time to the tune.

Ioan slapped his hat down on the chair and started a dance step to make the floorboards shake.

From her hiding place in the cowshed, where she had slid herself in between two bales of straw, the girl heard the sound. She eased herself out and pressed her face against a crack in the wood of the wall.

Through the kitchen window, she could make out the figure of Ioan Trifoi, his eyes fired with tuica and song, his head tilted up to the ceiling as if he were opening himself to a call from the sky.

She moved away and squatted down between the bales that now seemed to close in on her. She pressed straw up against her ears and eyes and tried to cover her head to block out all sound. But still the strains of laughter and the stamping of the dance reached her, until an ache in her chest spread up to her throat and she felt a lump that could only be dislodged by tears. She started to cry silently, feeling the salt tears on her tongue in the dark. Soon she was sobbing and shaking, and a sound like a low wail came out of her that would have reached the kitchen, had its occupants not been so loud in their song.

It was Pavel's favourite. He jumped up and down, trying to break a hole in the floor, and Ioan Trifoi took hold of his hand to steady him, so they swirled around together, hand in hand, stamping and stumbling, imperfect in the dance, careless of their imperfection, until they collapsed, roaring with laughter and thirsty for water from the jug.

Ioan Trifoi poured another tuica for himself and Paraschiva. And thus they celebrated the night, so that neither of them noticed that the moon had already risen and that stars were peeping through the spring clouds.

When Ioan Trifoi stood up, he was surprised to find that the floor rose to meet him. Paraschiva shook her head. She herself could drink innumerable tuicas and, in her younger days, had still been able to stand on one leg. She had long since suspected that in her veins flowed something other than blood, and whatever it was gave the tuica a warm welcome. She roused Ioan Trifoi enough to guide him to the cowshed.

In the middle of the night, he awoke with a banging in his head, the comforting thick smell of cow in his nostrils, and a mind empty of memory of where he was or how he'd come to be there. He lay half-asleep, staring at the open window that framed a perfect square of stars with a half-moon frozen in their midst. The shed was bathed in light and shadow, so that the white of the cow's hide shone like silver.

A shuffling sound from a corner of the stable caused him to sit up, suddenly sober, fearing one of the giant rats that had besieged the village.

Alert, now, he shifted onto an elbow and stared into the corner, there where the moonlight gave way to darkness. He could just make out a pile of ragged clothes. If he strained his ears, he thought he could detect the rhythm of breathing.

He rose and went slowly towards the sound, his movements hindered by the sudden loss of light as the moon passed behind a cloud. When he came close to the corner, he paused, not wishing to stumble, preferring to wait for more moonlight. It came quickly, and in its shaft he saw her. She lay as if she had tumbled and fallen asleep where she fell, unconcerned, with her bare arms spread out on the hay. A black scarf was wound around her head, and its long drape coiled over her chest like a dark question mark.

Paraschiva awoke the next day heart-warmed from the night's dancing and singing, and gave thanks again for her capacity to absorb firewater. She noticed only that her balance was mildly affected as she stumbled against a tin bucket placed on the kitchen floor to catch the raindrops that dripped through a large hole in the roof, where the wooden slats had been ripped away by the storm. She must tell Ioan of them, that he repair them before the roof become one big hole to let the sky in, and what if they had snows and cold winds in April, as they had had the year before, and she sitting by a dead fire blown out by the gale, and shivering with the snow melting before her eyes on the kitchen floor?

She opened the door of the cowshed and looked at the imprint his body had made in the hay, and the wool blanket she had left him neatly folded beside it. Then she went to the outer stable and saw that his horse and cart had gone, and their owner with it. She spat then, angry at herself for not having risen earlier to catch him. Now she would have to drag her old bones down into the village to enlist his help, while she had had him in front of her late into the night, and she knew there was little he would refuse her. Only the taking in of the girl. Perhaps it would be as well if she never returned.

The sound of the clinking of the well chain distracted her from her thoughts. She went back into the yard. Her hands dropped to her sides in surprise. There stood the girl, winching up the chain with the weighty bucket at the end of it. Paraschiva knew instantly that the crack in her spirit had healed by the calm of her stance, and the way that she turned to smile over her shoulder as soon as she felt the old woman's presence.

The girl offered no greeting but carried the water into the kitchen, poured it into a pan, and put it on the stove to heat. She laid the table with three wooden bowls, thick chunks of bread, and slices of red sausage. Then she took Paraschiva by the hand, led her to the table, and filled the bowl in front of her with steaming water, honey, and mint leaves. The old woman smiled. Wherever the girl had disappeared to, or whatever strange healing she had found for herself, it had closed the chasm within her, and the whole house felt the lighter for it.

Later, the women sat opposite each other on either side of the fire, Paraschiva with her leg stretched out in front of her on a stool, while the young woman worked her knee with pork lard, as the old woman directed, to relieve her aches and pains. Pavel sat in the corner of the room, then stole closer to try to touch the girl's forearm. Paraschiva slapped him away, but the girl took his hand and placed her palm, slippery with fat, against his.

"Pav – el." She spoke so quietly as to be almost

inaudible, but both the old woman and her son heard the sound.

"Para-schiv-a!" The old woman pointed to her chest and said her name louder and louder, until the girl repeated it, faltering as if her tongue was stuck to the top of her mouth, but nonetheless finding her way around the syllables.

"Mariuca." The girl looked down at the floor as she gave her own name, as if bad luck, or shame, came with it.

"Mariuca." The old woman spoke the name aloud four times, to the four walls, so that they would bid its bearer welcome and keep her safe within their stone.

Nevertheless, the old woman reflected, when she took the girl down to the village on the day of the spring festival, she would call her Maria, which was more formal. She would also cover her from head to foot, so that not a hint of the gold-brown skin of her body would draw prying eyes to her, or call to unwelcome hands.

Radu Surdu retreated into a place of poison, and the whole house felt it. Anca, the woman who cooked and cleaned for him, walked around the house like a quiet ghost, anxious not to attract attention, waiting for nightfall when, with relief, she closed the front door behind her and walked down the steps that took her to the main street, and all the way home to a friendlier household.

Surdu sat at a desk in a bare-walled room at the

back of the house. In front of him were neat stacks of papers. He could attend to none of them. He stared at the wall, where the flickering shadows cast by the light of an oil lamp were a source of irritation. He turned the wick down so that the room was in a half-light. In the penumbra, his anger cooled, and with its cooling, his mind cleared, seeking a way out of the impotence that had festered inside him ever since the day of his humiliation.

That he should be eclipsed by the rhetoric of rough peasants and the excuses of a drunken priest… the memory snapped him back into its trap of rage.

A noise from outside the house distracted him. It came from the woodshed: a clatter, and the banging of an open door in the wind. He threw the pen onto the desk. He found the intrusion into his thoughts an outrage. Taking the oil lamp, he advanced down the corridor that led to the door at the back of the house. His feet echoed on the stone floor. Even the sound of his own footsteps were an annoyance. The lamp shed light fleetingly on portraits on the walls – Katya, his wife, who had died in childbirth, taking their baby boy with her; his father, who had carried his mad cruelty to the grave so many years before, and the mother he could scarcely recall. He walked on, faster now, not caring for ill-lit faces from a past too painful to remember.

Outside, the wind was stirring the leaves of the poplar trees. Their rustle was abhorrent to him, as was the sound of rushing water from the stream, there where it ran over the stepping-stones of rocks. Then he heard the noise again, from the outhouse, of some intruder, come to disturb. The ugliness of the world invaded him, with its hollow prattle.

He would find a way to still it.

He opened the door of the shed quietly. The oil lamp lit up a pile of chopped logs, an axe on top of them, some cobwebs, the shadows of some rusted tools, a few hams hanging in a row – the remains of a winter's provisions – and the boxes of old papers that he had discarded, now ready for the fire. Everything was solid and inanimate. Nothing moved. Yet he could feel a presence.

He walked slowly towards the woodpile and picked up the axe. Still nothing stirred. Then he caught sight of the red glare of eyes gleaming from behind the logs. He stayed quite still, looking at the glint of the eyes that watched him from their hiding place. Their light must be extinguished. He raised the axe and brought it down with a thud, right at the place where the eyes had glittered. There was a yelp and a scuffle, and whatever had crept in for shelter flashed across the floor, and disappeared into the darkness.

Radu Surdu stood holding the axe that dangled limply at his side. His mouth was pursed. The woodshed and its contents were a place of ugliness that required some remedy. With a sharp breath, he raised the axe again, and brought it down on a box of old documents, so that papers were chopped with a lethal cut.

He stood in the middle of the debris he had created

looking at the letters, now sprayed across the floor. All of them bore the official stamps of the Council of Birtiza, witnesses of years of his correspondence, his attempt to stop a straggling village from descent into disorder. Now they lay on the earth floor of the woodshed like so much litter, the waste of his past. His mind retracted into a funnel of fury.

He raised the axe a third time, now ready to release his rage on the harder substance of the woodpile. But it remained poised in mid-air, and did so until the tightness of Surdu's face suddenly relaxed, and he lowered it slowly. He let out his breath. The idea had come.

He returned to the house, seated himself at his desk, turned the oil lamp up high, took out pen and paper and began to draft a letter, choosing each word with care. He wrote with complete concentration, broken only occasionally by the scurry of the wind around the roof, which he now found nothing more than a harmless distraction.

11

Habits. Paraschiva didn't much care whether they were good habits or bad, but when she saw that the girl was forming them, she knew that the cracks in her soul were healing, at the same rhythm as the growth of the stubble on her head, and the mending of her skin.

Not that some of the habits weren't strange. The sway-slide-and-say-hello-to-the-sky one, as Paraschiva called it. She first witnessed it on a morning when a cold wind had blown away the clouds and brought a breath of ice. The girl was in the yard, standing by the well, preparing herself to hoist up the heavy bucket. She paused, called by a change in the air, perhaps, or the cry of a bird, or the play of light. She began to sway, her black skirt moving like a slow river, and her body some deep current running in it, then she slid to one side, her feet soft and assured, as if they knew that the ground was in love with them, and raised her arms like soft snakes reaching up to stroke the sky.

"Where did you learn that?" Paraschiva shouted across the yard, when she realized the water from the well might be a long time coming.

The girl said nothing. Nor had Paraschiva expected an answer. She talked to the girl as she spoke to Pavel and Luka, more to make conversation to herself, to remind herself that she still had a tongue. For in three weeks of healing, the girl had opened her mouth to eat, drink, laugh, and cry, but had never uttered one word besides her name, and theirs.

So be it, thought Paraschiva, if the girl wanted to speak with her arms instead of her mouth. What did it matter, up here on the hill, if people spoke in a language of limbs, so long as they could understand each other?

Which they did. Pavel and the girl would stand talking in the yard, with not a sound passing between them. It was Paraschiva who felt like the slow learner. "Tree", she knew, was a round snake traced in the air. "Luka" was a ripple of hands close to the heart. Different foods involved an intricate series of gestures: hands opening, closing, waving. "Fire" was their favourite: arms tracing whirls of flame in the air, followed by a shimmying of the hands that made Paraschiva's head spin. But she enjoyed the spinning, for this swirling language was accompanied by balloons of laughter. So what did it matter what was said? To Paraschiva's mind, the language was lovely, for even when it proved lacking, and neither speaker could understand the other, it ended in joy, for every error was repaired in friendship.

The language, reflected the old woman, was a kind of home in which they could live. It was safer than a roof or walls, or even a town, which could always be burned down. It was a place of security, where anger and fear could come to rest, and then be soothed into the air with a gesture.

So, after a few futile attempts to get the girl to speak with her mouth, Paraschiva accepted her arms instead. Maybe the girl was a simple child whose family had driven her out – one less mouth to feed and why not the one without the mind? But no, there was a measured grace in her movements, an intelligence in the body and eyes, that spoke to Paraschiva more than a mountain of new words. Perhaps the girl had chosen silence, thought the old woman, and perhaps it was better that way, for the day when they went down the hill and into the world of people, and words, with all the danger they carried.

The other habit, for which the girl displayed a natural gift, was the art of vanishing. One moment she would be behind Paraschiva, so close it was as if she longed to attach herself to the old woman's back, the next minute the old woman would turn around and find the room filled with nothing but the leftover sound of disappearing footsteps. Which meant that the girl would be nowhere all day, and would return in the evening, silent as ever but with her clothes and hair shouting out their story of dirt and brambles, one that matched Pavel's and Luka's, and Paraschiva would know that they had been wandering up the mountain paths, no doubt with limbs gesticulating to the peaks, in some discussion with the sky.

Thus it was that the girl was nowhere to be found to help Paraschiva sort through the old trunk in the corner of the kitchen. The old woman cussed. She hated sifting through pieces of her past: books crumbling with age, reminding her of her father, with his love all turned to dust; old bits of clothing she no longer wore: headscarves with flowers faded out of recognition, skirts stained with age. She would have liked the girl's youth beside her, young fingers pulling out stale fragments, helping to find an old costume to put on her young body, one seemly for the eyes of the village.

Paraschiva fretted over the task, but at last found what she was looking for: a white blouse with a high neck and cuffs at the wrist, embroidered on the shoulders and sleeves with delicate yellow flowers, a long white skirt, a hessian black-and-red striped overskirt, thick cotton socks, a brown woollen belt, and a pair of leather shoes now creaking with age, their criss-cross black ribbons like stiff braids of hair. And a heavy black wool waistcoat to hide any trace of a womanly shape. She laid the garments on the table, glaring at each one as if it were an insult, which it was. For every one reminded her of the frustration she had felt as a young girl, having her waist belted and her neck frilled about with the trussings of tradition.

And she felt anger for doing to the girl what she had refused to do to herself. But her hand moved of its own accord to touch the place where her eye had once been, with its memory of the price to be paid for the silent world of self-exile on the mountain.

"Mariuca!" Paraschiva went to the door and roared out the girl's name to the yard. If the girl were dumb, she was not deaf, of that the old woman was certain. If she had chosen to disappear for the tenth time that day, the power of Paraschiva's voice could reel her back in like a river fish.

It did. A few minutes later, the girl stood under the portal, with its spaces in the bat's wings, in a pose as demure as the spring day, a face on her that said everything was as it should be. Only it wasn't. For the girl had changed colour. From light brown to black. Or rather, like a skewbald horse, brown and black in patches.

The girl was covered in mud. And behind her, like members of a lost clan, stood Pavel and Luka – fur, skin and hair matted with a mixture of soil and water.

"You look like the valley end of a goat heading for the mountains," shouted Paraschiva. The girl broke out in soft laughter, like the ripples of a lake, which made everything liquid, so Pavel joined in, as Paraschiva would have but that a doubt was buzzing in her mind, making too much noise, crowding out the space where her own laughter lived, some question as to why the girl had laughed at a joke in a language she could not understand.

She grabbed the girl's hand and marched her down to the stream that flowed past the far end of the yard.

"Wash. Wash and then come inside. We're going to dress you so you look like you were raised in a church pulpit."

The girl stood, shivering now in the crispness of the afternoon, then bent down, obedient, to take off her shoes, heavy with mud. Paraschiva walked away, leaving her to her privacy, turning around only once to see her perched on a slippery stone, putting one toe into the water and withdrawing it as quickly, shocked by the coldness of the water that was like a pain.

The old woman looked from her to the road that led down to the valley, and the village.

"However slowly I ease you in, however strongly I hold onto your arms as I lower you into the water," her mind spoke to itself, "it will never feel like anything but ice."

Then she went into the house and laid logs on the fire, so that the hearth would be there to call out to all of them with its welcome of warmth.

12

Lazarica, Lazarica,
In the centre of the world
Turns Lazarica
Her father fell from the broken branch
Her husband fell from the broken tree
Lazarica, Lazarica,
Dance in the centre of the spinning world
Till your father stands upright
Till your husband's blood is as sap
Till the seasons circle in harmony
Lazarica, Lazarica,
Mend the broken tree
In the centre of the world
Turn, turn, Lazarica.

Under a bright green vault of oak and poplars, on the banks of the river, six little girls held hands in a circle, and practised their song.

Their sound carried beyond the rushing of water to the road that led into the village, reminding any passer-by that spring had burst over the valley with all the force of a green tide.

It was the third Saturday in April, the festival

of Lazarica, a celebration of food and flowers, the day when the dead prised open the gates of heaven, waved greetings to the living, and showered them with blessings.

The sky, stripped of clouds, was a clean blue. Every house in the village was loud with colour: fences, ledges of windows, edges of gates noisy with yellow, purple and white, the bright petals of primrose, violet and crocus. From kitchen doorways, smells prowled into the street and up people's noses, tempting them with the feast to come – buns glazed with honey, corn bread plaited into golden braids, linking the living with the dead.

"Come, girls, come. Help your father with the horse!" Magda's voice broke the circle of sound, which dissolved into a whirl of giggles, as the girls raced up the path to the stables, to find Ioan Trifoi brushing his horse's coat so that it shone amber in the sunlight. Its ears and tail were bedecked with garlands of flowers.

"Oh!" The girls surged forward in a wave of delight.

"One at a time. One at a time," Ioan chided, as he tried to protect his horse from being smothered by the attention of so many small hands.

"Gently, gently," he insisted, yet he too felt the rising excitement of the morning. Was that all that was needed, he thought – a little girls' song and the rush of spring – to salve a person's soul?

The sound of a steady drumbeat reached them from the village square.

"Come, Papa, come. The procession is starting!"

There was agitation now, and a flurry of impatience as horse was harnessed to cart, and Ioan Trifoi hoisted six little girls into the back of it, a precious cargo of white cotton dresses, shining hair and laughter.

Magda waved them off from the kitchen doorway.

"Mama, won't you come with us? Come!" Doinitsa pleaded, calling down to her mother from her place of honour next to her father.

"Later. I'll join you later. Let me finish the baking."

Doinitsa succumbed without further protest. Truth to tell, she was already enjoying her seat in the cart, which her mother would otherwise have occupied, because of its satisfying view of the floral arrangement that had turned the horse's tail into a spring bouquet.

Lazarica, Lazarica,
Dance in the centre of the spinning world
Till your father's soul stands straight
Till your husband's blood runs strong

From the back of the cart, the girls' song kept time to the turning of the wheels. Ioan Trifoi was silent. He looked up the road to the mountain, knowing that Paraschiva would be making her way down on foot, as she did every year, her homage to Lazarica, whom she honoured as a healer of souls. This time he knew she would not come alone, and found himself saying a quick prayer to Lazarica, that the stranger would find herself among friends.

Then he joined in the song, his voice like slow-burning wood on the fire of the little girls' chant.

Lazarica, Lazarica,
Mend the broken tree
In the centre of the world
Turn, turn, Lazarica.

Doinitsa turned to her father, bewildered. This was a woman's song. He looked at his daughter's eyes, round with surprise, and, when he saw the light of laughter in them, he gave her a smile, and winked.

They walked in unplanned symmetry – Paraschiva ahead, Pavel and Mariuca ten steps behind, side by side, so close they could have held hands.

In spite of the crispness of the air, the girl felt her legs itchy and hot under the thick cotton skirt. Her toes hurt where the hard leather pinched them. Pavel dragged his feet, unhappy to leave behind the farm, and Luka. Paraschiva was lost in her own thoughts: how quickly a journey passed when you dreaded arrival. She fixed her eyes on the ground, careful not to stumble on a rut in the road. She had placed the girl's wellbeing in the hands of the spirits, with prayers and incantations. But her old legs and feet, she reasoned, were her own responsibility.

So they advanced down the mountain, until they came to a small, unpainted wooden cross by the side of the road. Paraschiva drew Pavel to her side, and, putting her hand on his arm, she carefully lowered herself to her knees, then motioned Pavel and the girl to do the same.

Staring at the cross, she said: "This is my father's grave."

She was close enough to see the grain of the wood, eroded by snows, wind and time, but with the whorl still visible, like an old faded fingerprint.

Behind the cross, some young birch trees that grew as close together as sisters rustled their new leaves. Paraschiva reached out one hand to Pavel's, and the other to the girl's, and closed her eyes.

In her mind, the whorl of the wood began to spin, slowly at first, then faster, until its lines blurred, and it became a brown whirlpool where faces emerged, disappeared, then resurfaced in new shapes and forms. She saw a rainbow of flowers, and a torrent of ghosts, their hair full of petals and water, their faces filled with laughter and longing. She saw hands cupped, waiting for life to be poured back into them, and she saw arms waving goodbye, on their way to another world.

She saw her father's face, wrinkled with lines of restlessness, and, greeting his soul, she wished him peace on this day when the dead and the living joined hands. She waited for his blessing. His words came to her as though through water, muffled, as if drowning, so she could not understand them. They were whispers, not of benediction, but of warning.

In the chaos of the river of the dead, she could make out a group of people, their faces made ugly by shouting, possessed by a spirit that had lost its way in the darkness. The crowd moved out of the shadows in unison, while behind them the dark spirit folded and unfolded its silent wings.

Then her father, his words, the twisted souls and all the tumult of the dead sank to the riverbed, where a soft creature was weeping tears that made the river flow.

The cawing of a crow brought her back to the road, and the cross, and the day. The visions of her mind receded until they were patches of light fading behind her closed eyes. When she opened them, the wind had dropped, the sun was high in the sky, and on the ground were three people holding hands.

The horse shook his head in agitation, so that the little girls grew anxious for the garlands of flowers around his ears. Ioan Trifoi hummed and shushed, trying to calm him, but the heavy beat of the drum and the shrill cacophany of pipes drowned out his soothing noises.

"Sounds like a goose being strangled," he said. This set Doinitsa thinking.

"Where do they go?"

"Who?"

"The dead."

"I don't know. Some say to heaven. Some say to hell. Some say to somewhere in between."

"Where do you think they go?"

"I think they go into the earth."

Doinitsa frowned. On Lazarica's Day, the dead were supposed to sit on the rooftops, and stand at gateways.

"Have you ever seen them?"

"No."

"Then how do we know they are there?"

Ioan Trifoi sighed. He was never at ease with questions of the afterlife, deeming that there were enough difficulties in this one to keep a mind occupied.

"We don't know for sure."

"Then why do we bake bread for them?"

"In case."

"In case of what?"

"In case they're there."

"Mama says they're there."

"Some people believe in them. And some people don't know for sure. There's room for the thinking of everyone."

"I wonder what they look like, the spirits."

"Ask Paraschiva."

They found the old woman near the cemetery, under the blossoming white shade of a hawthorn tree, and, behind her, almost invisible between the dark of the tree trunk and the old woman's back, Pavel and Mariuca, as close together as to form a single shadow.

The little girls jumped down from the cart and ran to the old woman, encircling her and pushing posies of blue and white campanula into her hands.

"Paraschiva! Paraschiva!" They jostled for priority of place near the old woman, who, they knew, would treat them to stories of ghosts and spirits, of trees that came to life and animals that turned into people, and back again.

Paraschiva dug into her pocket to produce a poppyseed cake for each child, and good-luck bunches of clover blessed with water from the well.

"May you have protection from the cold wind," she took in each child with her smile. "And may you one day find a husband who laughs at himself, and never at you."

She stepped back to include Pavel and Mariuca into the circle.

The little girls, overcome with shyness and finding nothing to say, stared at the young woman, with her dark golden skin and the clothes that hung on her in a strange way, as if her body was not made to be in them.

Paraschiva broke the silence. "She doesn't speak our language, but soon she will learn. You must be kind to her."

Ioan Trifoi arrived behind the little girls. Paraschiva noticed there was something troubling him, by the way he kept glancing at the ground. The moment passed, and he was soon smiling his usual welcome.

Gabriela moved forward to take the girl's hand. "We are the bridesmaids of Lazarica," she said proudly, "and you will be the bridesmaids' best friend."

Paraschiva watched Mariuca's face relax, lighting up with a smile as the little girls offered her their warmth.

Thus they all bundled up together in the cart, like pieces of straw in a bale – the little girls vying for the newcomer's attention, oblivious to her silence, giving her a long and detailed description of the day's forthcoming events, so that their voices rose in an enthusiastic battle against each other and the earth-beat of the drum. Paraschiva breathed a sigh of relief, thinking that, in spite of the dark spirit she had seen on the mountain, the day might after all open itself up like the flowers that it celebrated.

The procession arrived, a great multi-coloured snake, at a clearing on the outskirts of the village. A bird flying high overhead would have seen groups of people joining, breaking up and re-mingling like pieces of confetti in the wind. Old alliances were renewed, and old hostilities waived in favour of the festival.

Barbu Temeru went from family to family, greeting friends with the grip of his huge handshake until everyone's hands hurt except his own. Father Diaconu hovered on the edge of groups like a fat white moth, and, to the relief of all, stayed well away from the flagons of red wine and bottles of tuica that were being emptied at a galloping rate, as the menfolk dutifully anointed the outbreak of spring. There was a jollity that was like a breath exhaled, and not a few remarked that the lightness was due to an absence, that some thickness had gone from the air: Radu Surdu had stayed behind the closed doors of his house. Indeed, he had rarely been seen for weeks, not since his humiliation in front of the village assembly.

"May he grow into the walls of his room, and may the stones of his house be his only friends," Barbu mumbled to Ioan Trifoi, his mouth full of rabbit stew.

"There are stones that stay still, and stones that stir." With a movement of his eyes, Ioan Trifoi indicated a group that had gathered near them, under a willow tree. He had felt their gaze following him, while their bodies remained still, like dark birds, watching.

"Pah! Let them go back to the graves where they belong." Barbu washed down his last mouthful of rabbit with a generous gulp of red wine, before turning a black-eyed glare on the group, who immediately looked away in collective confusion.

Paraschiva sat on a chair carved out of an oak trunk, and felt herself surrounded by sun. There was the sun in the sky, and the sun of the people around her: Pavel on one side, Mariuca on the other, Ioan and Barbu close by, and the little girls flitting to the tables and back, as if their prime mission was to fatten the young woman. At one point, as they tried to give her yet another titbit, Mariuca broke out in laughter and placed her hands on her stomach to show that it was close to bursting.

"Enough! Leave her alone," Paraschiva chided them good-naturedly. "Go and prepare your song." As they ran off, she called after them, "And make it a strong one."

So, thought Paraschiva, it seemed that the spirits had been wrong in their warning: with all the noise and bustle, the girl's entry into the village had passed with the lightness of a spring shower.

"Here, these are for you," Ioan Trifoi stood in front of them, blocking out the sun for a moment, before he squatted down. In his hands, he held two bunches of purple flowers. He gave one to Paraschiva and held out the other to the young woman.

"It is good that you are among us."

The girl watched him. He handed her his gift and felt a tightness in his throat as he did so.

"Welcome, welcome to the village."

Paraschiva looked at him quickly when she heard the tone of his voice. The girl took the flowers and smiled, but kept her eyes on the ground. Paraschiva shuffled on her chair, sucked in her breath, and was relieved when the strident sound of pipes announced the beginning of the festivities.

There was the horse dance, with the boys and young men dressed in woollen manes and tails, stamping the ground, enjoying the laughter of the crowd. There was the serving of wormwood wine, for protection and purification, which had many mouths curling in a grimace as they sipped the bitter liquid. There was the late arrival of the women who had stayed behind to bake loaves in the shape of a figure of eight, for the spirits who would visit the clearing in the night.

And so the day passed, with its spring brew of dance, gossip, and wine, until the sky was streaked with the last rays of the sun.

The slow beat of the drum announced the beginning of the bridal dance. The light of seven flaming torches, carried by village boys, flickered through the birch trees. Behind them walked the six little girls, in single file, dressed in white, each carrying a young green willow branch.

"Lazarica, Lazarica,
Mend the broken tree,
In the centre of the world
Turn, turn, Lazarica."

The villagers parted to let them through to the middle of the clearing, where they formed a circle, with the boys around them.

"Lazarica, Lazarica,
Dance in the centre of the spinning world
Till your father stands upright
Till your husband's blood is as sap
Till the seasons circle in harmony."

The girls' feet moved in light steps to the left and the right, then stamped heavily, anchoring the sound to the ground, while raising their arms to the sky, as if to cast their song free to vanish into the air.

Barbu Temeru struck up a chord on his ailing violin, marking the rustic rhythm of the dance.

The boys started up a cry, holding their torches above them, moving around the girls' circle.

"Lazarica! Lazarica!" The little girls shouted back, at the tops of their voices, kicking up their feet, as if in a loud rivalry to win the rites of spring.

Three sharp beats of the drum brought them to a sudden halt, each girl opposite a youth, but for one young man left alone, in the place of honour and vulnerability.

It was time to choose the bride.

The little girls stood still, facing the young men, and, beyond them, the crowd of villagers, and beyond them, the birch trees that were turning into shadows in the failing light.

From where he stood at the edge of the group, Ioan Trifoi marvelled at the power that had transformed the young girls into small priestesses, solemn with the weight of the moment.

It was Gabriela who broke the circle, walking to the outer ring of villagers, never hesitating until she stood in front of Mariuca, whom she led back into the centre, into the empty space facing the young man.

There was silence in the clearing, and the eyes of the village were on the couple.

Paraschiva's hand tightened on that of the woman beside her. Part of her mind was racing, yet part of her was calm, watching the scene as if it were unfolding like a pageant, in which the young woman, the little girls' dance, the flames, the trees, the sun that had now gone to light another piece of the world, and she herself, were all just a fragment.

The violin struck a chord that hung suspended in the air, before it faded into silence. Not an empty silence, but one that was filled with the note that had come before, and the one that was to follow. It was the pause between sounds, between seasons, the crack in the night through which the dead slipped to speak to the living in their dreams, the inheld breath that contains all the unmanifest power of the wind.

The boy, a bashful young man, saw that his bride's shyness was greater than his own, and held out his hands to her. As the violin struck up the heavy beat of the dance, he guided and she followed. Three steps to the left, three to the right, a linking of arms around waist and shoulders, and two handclaps in the air, to wake up the spring. The girl moved in unison with the young man, her eyes fixed on his, trusting in her feet to follow his steps.

Paraschiva watched them, saw their faith in the dance, and noticed the villagers' faces warm with compassion for the girl in her vulnerability, willing the elected young couple to succeed in their celebration of the spring.

After the fourth twirl, their hand clapping was taken up by the little girls. The rough strains of the violin and the staccato beat of hands bounced off each other and around the trees, stirring the crowd to join in the dance.

A long human chain of villagers quite forgot the troubles of the winter, made a larger circle around the young couples and abandoned their bodies to the bright swirl of movement. The circles spun in opposite directions, so that each dancer saw a flashing procession of eyes, hands and feet, merging into a hypnotic blur of light and changing colour. Faster and faster they turned. Paraschiva felt her chest about to burst with the relentless twirling. Pavel found himself breathless with laughter.

In the spinning, each little girl in turn broke away from her circle to stand in the centre, raising her arms and stamping her feet, becoming, for a moment, a bride of the spring.

Mariuca felt the hand that held hers release her, and she too took her place in the centre. Her arms rose as if of their own accord, the headscarf that hung down her back swaying around her like a black snake, her hips undulating, so that her whole body rippled, as if moved by a current that came from somewhere in the centre of the earth. At that moment, an electricity passed, coming from her, and yet not of her. For though she, in her dance, had conjured it, she was still but a part of it.

The chords of the violin grew more strident, like an animal calling in the night. In the spaces between chords, Paraschiva felt a new presence caught in the centre of the circles, and the circles were caught by it. It passed from hand to hand, magnetic, causing the human wheels to spin with a momentum of their own, causing the little girls to start up a ululation, drowning out the familiar beat of the village dance.

In that moment, in the dancing, the doors that divided worlds flew open, and in place of each person's separate being, there was the dark space inside them that connected them to power, and magic.

Each villager would remember that moment – some in fear, some with longing – when they lost themselves to the dark, and found another lightness within it.

Paraschiva felt it in her chest: the pounding of her heart grew quicker until she knew that her body could no longer contain the spirit that had entered it, and her legs gave way beneath her, and she fell to the ground.

The dance stumbled to a halt. Whatever spirit had been invoked, vanished, leaving the villagers dazed, adrift in some limbo land that was neither the frenzy of the dance, nor the reality that now faced them. In place of the girls' wild cries, there was a confusion of shocked whispers.

"Quickly, give her water."

"Don't gather too close. Make space for her to breathe."

Ioan Trifoi pushed his way through the crowd. He knelt down beside her and touched her.

"Gently, gently," he soothed.

Paraschiva moaned and muttered something about faces on a river bed.

"Hush, now. Hush."

The old woman looked around her with wild eyes.

"Pavel… the girl…"

"Hush, now. We will look after you. You will come to my home."

The old woman nodded feebly, then turned her head away, mumbling words, in some indecipherable language, about the drowned, the angry, and the restless grey crowd of the dead.

13

Nothing was real, and everything was real. Nothing was illusion, and everything was illusion. Paraschiva knew this as she lay in the cot near Ioan Trifoi's hearth.

Lying in a delirium, her eyes fixed on the uneven white surface of the ceiling, Paraschiva knew that there was no safety, and no danger either, no life or death, but something no one had created a word for, something which lay in between. There were simply pieces of light and shade, forming and reforming, and voices making sounds then retreating into silence. They lasted a while and then slipped apart, in what seemed like death, but was simply a reshaping.

She saw beyond the room to the yard and the barn, above which she could make out the shape of a fire of blue and red flames. She was struck by the immense beauty and passion of whatever was in the process of creation. And around the luminous colours, she saw beings of shadow, intent on its destruction.

She cried out, and tried to raise herself from the bed. Magda leaned over her, stroking her forehead and rubbing her arms until the vision receded, and she lay back on the pillow, aware of nothing more than the whiteness of the ceiling.

Mariuca sat on the ground, her back against the slats of the wooden wall of the barn. From within, she could hear Pavel's gentle snoring. He had led her here, after they had both been pushed further and further away from Paraschiva's bedside by the flurry of Magda's healing hands. The distance from the house was comforting to the girl. She was glad to be away from the kitchen, with its heavy air and its pungent smell of milk poultice.

Putting her arms around her knees, she let her head drop forwards. She had no reason to look up: there were no stars, and a thick veil of cloud obscured the moon.

She prayed for the old woman, for Pavel, for herself.

"If, when I look up, I can see one star, all will be well."

Something in this superstitious bargain with the sky brought her some comfort. It was as if by pretending there was a benevolent force beyond her, she could conjure it into existence.

She raised her head, searching for the single point of light. An implacable dome of air, dark grey and opaque, looked down on her.

She closed her eyes again and listened to the sound of the river that flowed nearby. She heard the soft voice of the water and then another sound. The crackle of leaves. Footsteps. She craned forwards, trying to discern who could be coming to the barn in the middle of the night. She could make out the silhouette of a man, close now.

Ioan Trifoi stood in front of her, his face barely visible in the dark. He held a bundle under one arm.

She got up quickly, smoothing her skirt, her eyes on the ground, even though on a night with no light no one could see in which direction her eyes were looking.

His voice was gentle. "I brought these for you and Pavel, in case you were cold."

He handed her the blankets. She took them, holding them to her chest, pressing her face down into them, breathing in the odour of wood smoke. Its smell called her back to another world, to the wood smoke of her own hearth.

Burying her face in the blankets, she hugged them to her as if they were father, mother and lover in one, and abandoned herself to a silent flow of tears.

She felt his arms enfolding her. Her tears flowed, and all the while he held her, until her grief was done and she was still, her breath quiet, like an animal that has been calmed.

She raised her head to look at him. Still she could not see his face, but felt the touch of his lips on her forehead.

Then his body shuddered as he broke away from her, stumbling as he made his way back to the house, leaving her alone with the bundle of blankets in her arms, and above her, a sky that refused to reveal its stars.

"Look! The old donkey is back on her feet!" Paraschiva muttered to the morning air, as she limped out of the kitchen doorway. A sharp pain darted through her knee. She winced, staggering back to the support of the doorpost. At least the fever had left her, moving on like a whirlwind that leaves one rooftop to devastate another. The spirit that had burned her with its heat was neither good nor bad, she knew, but a messenger, come to her with a warning. She remembered her vision of the blue and red liquid light, and beyond it the creeping of shadows.

"Mariuca!" she called out.

The girl emerged from the barn. She stood for a moment, blinking in the early sunlight, then uttered a cry of surprise as she caught sight of the old woman, and streaked across the grass towards her.

Paraschiva watched her run: her blouse was unbuttoned at the neck, showing the brown of her skin underneath; her headscarf had slipped back, revealing the shadow of the regrowth of her dark hair. She ran with the stealthy grace of a fox.

The two women hugged. Mariuca held Paraschiva close to her. It was the old woman who broke away first.

"Look!"

She raised her skirt to show an ugly black and yellow swelling around the knee. Mariuca knelt on the ground, feeling the kneecap where it had twisted. She shook her head.

"I know, I know. Three weeks of healing, maybe a month." Paraschiva spat the words over her shoulder.

A month in the worrysome world of folk, with their little round of woes. She longed to be back on her hill, in the wider world that she shared with the spirits, Pavel, the girl, the animals. Luka! The wolf-dog had been forgotten in the surge of events.

"Mariuca, Pavel needs me and I need him. He will stay here. You must get back to the farm. The animals! And Luka! Luka!"

At the sound of the dog's name, the girl nodded, and mimed that she would soon be on her way. Then she touched her heart, to show that in her absence she would stay close to the old woman she loved.

Ioan Trifoi was bent over a bucket of water by the well, splashing his face, so he did not hear her come up behind him. When he turned around she was facing him, holding out a gourd in one hand. As they looked at one another, their faces lit up with the same light.

Ioan fetched a jug and filled it with water. The girl held the gourd steady while he poured, filling it to the brim. Then his hand trembled, and drops spilled over her skirt and shoes. Her own hands shook, so that more water splashed from the gourd, this time over Ioan's trousers. Nervous, they laughed out loud.

Ioan looked at her. The laughter had made her face relax. It was smooth with trust. He looked back towards the house. Magda would be preparing his breakfast. His daughter would be stirring. And in front of him stood this young woman whose face was beautiful and open, like a gift. His throat tightened so that his words sounded harsh.

"There. Now you can be on your way."

The light that had illuminated her face flickered for a moment, and went out. She nodded, turned away from him, and walked towards the house to make her farewells.

She made her way along the road that led through the village, with the river on one side and houses on the other. The houses had the look of faces, their blank façades staring out, expressionless. Above each portal, the stencilled forms of animals showed the outline of a deer, a bear or a wolf, their bodies filled with nothing but sky.

Three women walked past her, dressed alike in their black-and-red striped aprons, heavy black skirts, white blouses and floral kerchiefs. To her relief, they smiled at her and she returned their smile. But as she walked on, she could feel their eyes on her back.

Soon the houses became fewer, and gave way to poplar trees. She breathed more easily. Ahead of her lay a fork in the road, one path continuing along the river, the other leading up to the mountain. She quickened her pace. On the river side of the road was a hawthorn, a twisted riot of white petals and black thorns, and beyond it a cluster of alders, almost hidden from view. Something was moving inside the grove. Not a bird, not a small animal: something larger. She clutched her gourd, as if the inanimate object could bring her comfort.

They jumped out in unison. She gasped. Then her face broke into a broad smile of relief. Doinitsa and

Gabriela stood in front of her, full of mischief and blossom. Their hair was dishevelled, their identical white blouses covered in grass stains that matched the green of the embroidered flowers. Mariuca laughed. She guessed they must have taken a shortcut and scrambled through a path in the woods to intercept her. In their hands, each held a ragged bunch of flowers – dog roses and celandine and harebell. They laid them on the ground in front of her as though in honour of a queen.

She was about to bend down to pick them up when something in the girls' stance made her pause. It was as if this were some ceremony, and she must play her part in it. So she waited. Doinitsa stepped forward, then, suddenly shy, stepped back again. Gabriela took her place, her serious young face at odds with the tangle of twigs and leaves that had caught in her long chestnut hair. Mariuca felt a desire to laugh, but seeing the solemnity of the child, she stood still and watched.

Gabriela raised her arms to the branches of the alder trees. Doinitsa echoed her movement, in a faultless imitation of the young woman's dance in the circle of Lazarica.

The sun filtered down through the leaves, causing an effect of light, so that Mariuca was transfixed by the interlacing of the hypnotic white snakes of the girls' arms and the twisted dark branches of the trees. It was as if light and dark, animate and inanimate, were calling to one another, each affirming the other's necessity.

She started to sing a song which curled its way around half-notes, stopped in the middle of a phrase, hung suspended, then rose again out of silence, and all the while, her hips swayed and undulated around the coils of sound.

When she had finished, the girls' eyes gleamed with excitement.

"Please – teach us your songs." Gabriela's voice was earnest.

"And your dances." Doinitsa took up the plea.

The girl raised her arms as if to say: "If it be the Will of God." Then, seeing their faces staring up at her with such intent, she looked from one to another, and nodded.

They clapped their hands so loudly that Mariuca looked around her furtively. This morning the eyes of the village had been half-asleep. Now, with the sun rising in the sky, she was afraid. She kissed both girls quickly and gathered up her gourd. Slinging it over her shoulder, she stepped out of the grove towards the bright glare of the road that stretched ahead of her.

Luka's howls of delight echoed across the mountain and back, as he saw the girl's figure winding its way up the path to the house.

So boisterous was his welcome that she found herself knocked over and lying in the dust, covered by a wriggling mass of fur and joy. She released him from his chain and went inside the house. It smelt of damp wood. She flung open the windows and opened wide the doors at the front and back so that a clean breeze blew through the rooms. The wind called to her body: she tore at the buttons of her blouse and the waistband of her skirt. She wanted rid of the village, with its watchful eyes.

She ran to the stream and followed it to where it widened into a rock pool. There, she slid from the bank and waded in, feeling the water's icy hands moving up past her thighs to her waist and chest, and then she sank down up to her neck, and was cleansed in the liquid dark.

The box was square, about the size of a child's hand, and painted in delicate patterns of brown and green swirling leaves.

It contained a blue agate necklace, one that Radu Surdu had given his wife on their wedding night. He had closed the box seventeen years earlier, the day after she died. He slid it from its isolated corner on the desk towards him, fingered it for a moment, then pushed it back again across the shiny oak surface. It was a gesture he repeated many times a day, always with the same staccato movement – towards him, away from him – of a box that he would never reopen.

He was interrupted by the dull chime of the doorbell.

On the doorstep stood a man of some years, with a grey face made greyer by the grime of travel. He wore a broad-brimmed black hat pulled low over his forehead that announced him to be a member of the Council of Birtiza.

Radu Surdu extended his hand. "Come in, sir, and refresh yourself. Your visit has been long expected."

The man shook his hand. "I would have come sooner, but after the rains... the roads, you know..."

"Of course, of course. Come in and refresh yourself. Later, we will talk."

Radu Surdu completed his greeting with a smile that for once stretched all the way from his mouth to his eyes.

The woman who stood in front of Father Diaconu was tall, long-limbed, had a belly that looked like a tortoise shell, and a skin that was tinged with blue, as if she had just stepped out of her grave. She moved towards him in slow motion and, when he could feel her breath on his face, she opened her legs wide to encircle him, and he felt the coldness of her loins against him. "Petra, oh Petra." He called her name again and again, stroking her stomach that was as cold and dry as snakeskin.

Just as he was about to take her, he was awoken by a thunderous knocking. God, or the devil, was banging at his door. He would be taken up to heaven, or thrown down to hell, for his act of incest with the sister he never had.

"Open up!"

The priest floated back to the safety of wakefulness. Anything was better than the Divine Reckoning.

He released himself from the tangle of sheets and shuffled across the room to a corroded mirror.

"Wait, wait," he called out.

The face that looked back at him was puffy, sagging and ravaged beyond redemption.

Resigned to himself, he opened the door. Radu Surdu stood in front of him, blocking out the sunlight.

There was a silence while the priest stared at him, speechless, as if he had come from another world. After their last meeting, he was the visitor the priest least expected. But he collected himself.

"Come in, come in. May I offer you something? A tea, perhaps?"

"Thank you. I have had breakfast."

Surdu walked into the darkness of the priest's abode, taking in, with distaste, the dingy tapestries on the walls, the worn upholstery of the chairs, the unmade bed in the corner, with its imprint of the old man's body.

He stood in the centre of the room, avoiding physical contact with the priest's furnishings, as though he might contract some strange ailment from them.

"I will be brief," he said. "I considered a personal encounter to be appropriate given the nature of this..." he paused to remove an envelope from his pocket "...document."

He handed it to the priest. "Open it."

The yellow paper of the envelope shook between Diaconu's old fingers.

"It is already open," the priest's high voice trembled, matching the quiver of his hands.

"Why, so it is. It was addressed to me. But I would be most happy to share its contents with you."

The priest took out the letter and walked to the window to read it by the morning light. He tottered for a moment, then lurched against a chair as if about to fall.

"Perhaps you would care to sit down?"

The old man sank onto the chair, his face drained of colour, like a fish that had been out of water for a long time.

"I thought it would be of interest to you..."

The priest was breathing fast, as if trying to gulp in air or salvation. In his hands, he held his own true story, written in a careful script, by a councillor of Birtiza, the page bearing the official stamp. In his hands, he held the proof of the lies he had told about his past. Surdu leaned over and took the letter from him, carefully folding it and replacing it in its envelope.

The priest looked at him, the pupils in his pale eyes unnaturally dilated.

"Is it...? Are you...?"

"Is it the only copy? Am I going to do anything about it? Well now, that's why I'm here. I thought we might discuss it... together."

"Yes, yes." The priest's eyes were moving from side to side, as if uncertain of which way to focus.

"Good." Surdu paused, thoughtful for a moment. "I think, after all, I will take up your offer. A tea, perhaps?"

He settled into an armchair, his hands folded in his lap, with the envelope and its contents firmly between them.

A wind sweeping down from the mountain pass seemed to have found a home in the chimney. The girl huddled in front of the fire, her gaze fixed in the hypnotic blue and gold flames. Troubled, she got up and paced about the room, her feet silent on the earth floor. From his place in front of the fire, Luka watched her, half-asleep, his paws dangerously close to the coals.

For a week, he had been her only companion, following her around on her chores, walking with her up into the hills. She spoke to him, telling him stories of her life on the other side of the mountain. The half-wolf, half-dog seemed to listen better, she reflected, than the noisy mass of men. But then her words would fade away and she stared straight ahead, her mind returning to the people she loved. She thought of Paraschiva, lying with her swollen knee in the valley below, of Pavel, with the language that was in his limbs. She thought of Ioan Trifoi, and tried not to think of him, and thought of him again, and then decided to give up trying not to think of him.

On the eighth day, she walked out of the house and down the mountain.

14

Ioan Trifoi was restless. He sat in a corner of the kitchen, repairing a scythe whose blade had come dislodged, listening to Magda recounting village gossip to Paraschiva, who lay in her cot, counting the days to her healing. Diaconu and Surdu had been seen walking together in the main street, Magda said, by what mystery or magic no one knew. Barbu Temeru was to have a gathering the following week to celebrate his eldest daughter's forthcoming marriage to a farmer's son, Grigore Rusu, from the next village. Not much of a celebration, she said, for the farmers from Tirga were known to be rough and unmannered. But the match was his daughter's wish. There would be dancing. Dancing, yes. Magda paused in her stream of words. Little had been said about what had happened on the day of Lazarica, as if folk were afraid they might reinvoke the spirit of the circle that had spun them into some orbit that was beyond their control.

Ioan Trifoi looked up from his corner: "You come to Barbu's this time, Magda." There was an urgency in his voice. It was as if he were pleading for his wife's presence as protection.

"No, Ioan, I prefer to stay at home. Our patient needs company."

"Go, Magda, go." Paraschiva propped herself up in bed. "I have long been used to my own company." Truth to tell, she was growing tired of so much talk about the little affairs of men.

"No, truly, I would rather stay at home."

Ioan sighed. His wife had never liked celebrations.

"Well, I'd best be going. I have a roof to repair."

He took his hat from the table and kissed Magda on the head.

"God protect you," Paraschiva called out her blessing to him.

The village was quiet. Most of the men were out in the fields, the women at home at their chores. On the main street, Ioan passed Elena Barescu, walking as stiff as a bottle, with her long nose in the air. He doffed his hat to her from where he sat in the cart, but she walked past without acknowledging him. She had a heart as sharp as her nose, he reflected. Nor was she the only one. Half of the village was against him, ever since he had challenged Radu Surdu. The other half he thought of as his friends. And so it goes, he mused. You are lucky to have half the world on your side.

His thoughts were interrupted by the sound of laughter. Looking towards the river, he could see them: Doinitsa and Gabriela, and, alongside them, the young woman. Ioan Trifoi wondered why his horse had slowed to a halt, until he realized that he himself had pulled on the reins.

The girls were teaching her one of the village dances – a bouncy, fast-paced jig. At one point she stumbled, and landed on the grass, which caused the girls much glee, so that all three were soon on the ground in a bundle of skirts and merriment. He watched as she put her arms around them and made them sit up to listen as she sang one of her people's songs. Her voice was soft at first, barely audible to Ioan. The two girls sat motionless on either side of her, entranced by the strangeness of the tune, and her voice, which grew louder at the refrain, the notes rising in the air.

The song slid into Ioan's heart, and he was afraid. Giving the reins a shake, he moved on along the road. Still her voice remained with him, even when the sound died away in the distance.

The sun was high in the sky so there were no shadows. He saw it quite clearly from a distance. A dead horse by the side of the road. When he was close, he jumped down to look at it. No marks betrayed the cause of its death. It must have died very recently, for there were but a few flies buzzing around its glazed eyes. It was a handsome creature, he thought, with its sleek chestnut coat. Now it would be cut up in pieces, and its bones used for tallow, and its hide for shoes. He felt anger at the waste of mortality. Perhaps that was why he so loved the old woman, he reflected, because her spirit was turned towards another world. Perhaps that's why the girl called to his flesh, with her song that came from another place in some timeless hollow of the soul. It called to him now. It was the song of life. He turned away from the death that lay by the side of the road.

He got back into the cart and turned around, retracing his way to the village. He passed the place where she had been but there was no one there. He rode on until he came to the fork in the road, and paused. Then he pulled on the reins, and turned the horse's head away from the village, towards the path that led up the mountain.

He caught up with her near the cross that marked the grave of Paraschiva's father.

She had heard the clip-clop of horse's hooves on the path behind her, but had not turned around. When he was level with her, she answered his greeting with a smile, as if she had been expecting him. She took the hand that he held out to her, and climbed into the cart beside him.

They rode on in silence, past the cross, through the birch woods, until the village and the valley were out of sight. He reached his hand across and took hers. She noticed they were the same colour – his, rough and weathered brown by the sun; hers smooth, with its own natural sheen. Their eyes stared at the path in front of them, while their hands began a tentative dance of fingers and palms. She felt as if a flock of birds had come to nest inside her body.

He drove off the main path, down a rutted track that led deeper into the woods. The cart lurched, throwing them against each other, jolting their hands apart, so that he pulled on the reins to bring the horse to a halt. It snorted and shook its head, perturbed by the unfamiliar route. Ioan jumped down to quieten it, all the while his own hands shaking.

And then he was helping her down, and leading her through the undergrowth. They walked quickly, in an urgent silence. When a bramble caught on her skirt, she tore it away, not caring about the rip in the cloth. They came to a place where the ferns gave way to a bed of moss, under the overhang of a beech tree. Light filtered down through the radials of its branches, casting patterns of light and shade on the ground.

They looked at each other, suddenly awkward, caught by the stillness of the air, the intimacy of the moment.

She looked at the ground then back at his eyes, which were bright with the light that was inside him. Still she was afraid and turned away.

She felt his hand reach to her headscarf where it hung down her back and push it gently aside to kiss the hollow in the nape of her neck. Her skin shivered. The space around her seemed such a solitary place, and she alone in its landscape, that the need to be close beside him, touch against touch, cried out to her louder and stronger than any of her fears. When she turned to face him, she took his hand and placed it on her breast.

Ioan Trifoi felt as though he had been a sleepwalker and here was she in front of him, his awakening. He pulled her against him so that the length of her body was pressed against his, and there where their loins met, he felt the subtle undulating movement of her hips and her belly.

And so they lay down on the moss, in the glade, under the beech tree, and surrendered to the touch, the strength, the body's hurry to be rid of buttons and belts and cloth, to be close and supple in the brush of skin on skin.

She closed her eyes and felt his hands moving over her with a touch so light that her body shuddered, where a hundred sad dark places within her were suddenly called to life and a new radiance. Her mouth cried out words in her own tongue and her legs wrapped around him, and with the movement of her loins she called to him.

The sun had moved across the sky. They lay on their backs, side by side. She looked up at the beech tree, with its spinning pattern of leaves and branches. Why had she never seen that a tree was so like a dance? Why had she never noticed the spiral that linked them all – the tree, the dance, the skin, touch, life?

They breathed in unison. Then in unison they turned on their sides to face each other. He drew her to him and they lay, interwoven, the warm dampness of limb upon limb, the cooler moisture of the moss beneath them, the rich peat smell of the forest floor around them.

He traced a finger along her forehead, then along the dark arcs of her eyebrows. She closed her eyes and felt his touch on each of her eyelids in turn. When his hand moved up to stroke the stubble of her hair, she shook her head as if in shame. So he stroked her cheek instead, and then put his fingers on her lips, as if to coax them into speech.

"I wish you could talk to me," he said.

She took a deep breath, paused, then looked away from him, staring at the moss as if it held some secret spell. She frowned, pursing her lips, hesitant, teetering on the edge of some dive into the unknown. Then she plunged. She let out her breath.

"I can," she said.

She spoke with an accent. Her voice was deep and rich, like the colour of her skin.

Around him, the forest froze. He pulled away from her, watching her now as if she were one of Paraschiva's visions come to haunt him.

"I can speak your language," she said again. "I was born near your village."

There was a pause as both sought for words. He found them first. "Then why–?"

It was as if she had prepared her answer in advance. "Silence is safer."

He put his hand on hers, offering the reassurance of his touch.

"My family – what remained of them – 'left' your village just after I was born, but we still spoke the language."

He nodded, his mind racing, trying to fit together pieces of her past, feeling as if he knew the story she was about to tell even before she told it. He recalled once more his terror, as a child, on the night of the screams and the smoke, when they had driven out the folk who lived down by the river. He remembered, too, his fear of the shouting that followed, the slamming of doors in the village, as family turned against family, brother against brother, each taking a different side in the confused aftermath of guilt and blame.

Now she spoke in a flood of speech, as if months of silence were a dam that had suddenly burst.

"I never knew my parents. They never had a grave. My mother's sister took me to the other side of the mountains, to the village of Vitra. There was just her and myself, and a few of our kind. She married me off to one of them."

"Did you…?" Ioan Trifoi broke off, as if his words were intruders.

"Did I love him?" She smiled a matter-of-fact smile. "He was kind enough. I felt safe. That, at least. Safe."

"And then?"

She shook her head, as if unwilling to go on, and looked at the ground, fingering a leaf, before speaking. "History repeats itself."

Ioan wanted to reach out to her, but the pain of her story had surrounded her like a wall. The expression on her face told him that she was alone now, in that isolated place of grief. She spoke in a monotone, as if it were possible to speak about such things only if they were stripped of their sorrow.

"I was out of the village when they came. When I returned, there was nothing left." The leaf she was fingering was torn now into green shreds. She spoke quickly. There would be no detail. "I was the only survivor. I tried to cross the mountains. There were rumours that maybe some of our people still lived in villages around here, although I did not truly believe it. But it was my only hope. I had no one else. I thought I could survive the journey through the mountain pass. Then I found I was with child. I couldn't be seen in a village – a woman alone and with child. So I decided to stay in the mountains. I survived the winter living off anything I could find, but the snows, they wouldn't leave, and I had no more strength, and my child..."

Her face began to tighten, and she turned away from him, ashamed of her grief.

He had to stay calm now, for her, but his heart was raging with hatred for the killers – those who had come from the surrounding villages, yes, but also his own people. The blood shed on that night had touched both Ioan and Magda's families, for Ioan's father had led the call for justice against the perpetrators. It had earned him the enmity of many, including Magda's father. Though the years, and the birth of Doinitsa, had smoothed the rough edges of the ill will, there was still a sharpness that time had softened but not erased.

The glade was silent. Ioan Trifoi put his arms around her. They sat speechless, overcome by the unreality of the moment: the bright miracle of the afternoon, the strangeness of discovery of skin and touch; and beyond, the timeless shadow.

They walked without speaking. The silence was both a refuge and a trap. Neither could break out of it. When they came to the cart, they looked at each other, not knowing what to say.

It was she who collected herself first. She had found the courage to tell her story. She had felt the wild birds in her belly.

"Will we meet again?"

His answer came before she had time to breathe.

"Tomorrow, here, at the same time," he said.

She took both his hands in hers, then pushed back one of his shirt sleeves to where the brown of his arm met the white skin that had not been exposed to the sun. She looked at the strange frontier of colour, and bent her head to kiss it.

Then she was gone, leaving only the movement of ferns behind her, where her passing had disturbed them.

Magda pulled the green yarn taut before plunging the needle back into the cloth. She made a quick stitch and pulled again, too hard this time, for the tightness of the yarn made the cloth ruffle. She put her work down on the table and looked at it. It was to be a wedding gift for Barbu Temeru's eldest daughter: a square of white cloth. On it was a row of women, all of the same height, holding hands in the same way.

Only their colours differed: a brown girl, a pink girl, a green girl, a red girl, each as poised as a miniature doll, with hands held at shoulder height, linked with those of her neighbour: a line of women, continuous, unbroken, issuing a blessing of harmony and stability for the newly wedded couple.

A shutter banged open somewhere on the upper floor. Magda jumped. From her cot in the corner of the room, Paraschiva watched her as she picked up the cloth, smoothed out the ruffle, and returned to her stitching. The old woman knew that something in Magda's soul required soothing. She also knew better than to probe. Magda's was an open heart, and one that required protection. She was like a field without fences, and the villagers came to her often with their talk and their troubles.

There were rumours in the village, flying around like wispy black spirits, contaminating the late spring air, troubling the night sleep of many. Bad rumours about Barbu Temeru's future son-in-law. "A ruffian," said some. "A barbarian," said others. "And his friends! A bunch of brigands." Magda had doled out the gossip to Paraschiva, much as she did her medicines, with a dexterity and a regularity that Paraschiva found overwhelming.

But now, in the overheated room, Paraschiva longed for some chatter to relieve the tension of the silence.

"Do you think he's so bad, this rogue that's to marry Barbu Temeru's daughter?"

Magda looked up, drawn out of the web of her own thoughts. It took her a moment to reply.

"Oh, you know how it is. People talk. They say he will bring bad blood to the village."

The old woman sat up in bed. "Pah! And since when was the blood of this village so good? It has other blood on its hands that it once called bad, and the only badness was in the hands of those who shed it."

As soon as she had spoken, Paraschiva wished that she could spit out her tongue. Now was not the time to goad Magda with memories of the past, and her father's part in it. Magda kept her eyes lowered, intent on her embroidery. She sewed the last stitch onto the green woman's hand.

Both women looked with relief at the door as it swung open to let in the late afternoon sunlight, and two small dishevelled girls. They ran to Magda, in a clamour for embraces and tea.

"Go along with you," Magda chided, but she held Doinitsa close to her on one side, and Gabriela on the other.

"Now, what have you been up to?" She looked down at Doinitsa's blonde head, which was covered in grass, and Gabriela's chestnut tangle. "You look like you've been fighting with the scarecrows. Go now, quickly, and clean yourselves up."

Two little faces looked up at her. "Can't we play outside?" Doinitsa pleaded. "Please. Just until Papa comes home."

"All right then. But not for long. He'll be here at any moment."

The girls were gone as quickly as they'd arrived. Paraschiva sank back against her pillows, relieved by the fresh air and sunshine they'd left behind them, and by the noise of dishes, that announced that Magda was back to her bustling self.

In a pause in the kitchen clatter, Paraschiva heard it. Singing, coming from the field just outside the door. It was close, yet at the same time faraway, stretching back into the past. It was one of the songs of the people who had lived down by the river. Yet it was in the language of the village. Magda heard it too, for the saucepan she was holding remained suspended in mid-air, as she listened to the strangeness of the sound, halfway between a wail and a chant.

Barefoot, I take the road in front of me
Then shoes I make from soft leather
The soil speaks through their soles
Now all is well
I own good shoes
I can walk far
The spirit of the earth is beneath my feet
I fear no frontiers

Paraschiva craned her neck to see where the sound was coming from. The window framed the green grass of the field and there, in the middle, the two young girls were dancing as they sang. Not one of the village dances, with its fast hops and twirls, but a slow, rippling dance that uncoiled to the cadences of their song.

In the kitchen, the two women listened in silence, hypnotized by the sound, until the song was finished. Neither of them spoke, but Paraschiva saw the frown lines deepen on Magda's forehead, and wished only for Pavel to come in from the yard to tell her about his day with the movement of his hands, which he did, and they laughed until Pavel turned his head to the door and gazed at the road that led along the river and up the mountain.

"Not long, Pavel," Paraschiva stretched her leg and felt only the trace of a twinge of pain.

"Soon, Pavel, soon."

15

Ioan Trifoi dreamed he was walking along the path by the river. It was slippery with mud, so he had difficulty keeping his foothold. At one point, he lost his balance and began to slide towards the water. He grasped at a willow branch overhead but it was dead, and broke away in his hand. He slid faster, his fall unstoppable now, towards the rush of the river that was big and swollen with rain. He was afraid of the current, and afraid of his own fear. Then he abandoned himself to the slide, and he was under the water, which, to his surprise, was cool and healing. She was there, floating above the riverbed, as if she had been waiting for him, her black scarf trailing behind her in the reeds, like a winter eel. She wrapped it around his waist and they glided along, drawn by the flow, and he was surprised at the ease of his breathing.

He awoke to the pressure of Magda's body against his. The heat and darkness of the room were oppressive. Longing to return to the green beauty of that other, transparent world, he closed his eyes, and hoped for sleep.

It didn't come. Instead, Magda stirred beside him.

"Ioan, Ioan – are you awake?"

"Yes."

They both spoke in whispers, although their daughter's room was on the floor below, and there was no one else for their voices to awaken.

"You called out in your sleep."

Ioan felt his breath quicken.

"What did I say?"

"I don't know. I couldn't hear the words."

"It was just a dream."

"This is the third night, Ioan, that you have called out in your sleep."

Ioan reached out to take his wife's hand. He squeezed it, but felt her hand limp, without response.

"Magda, it was only a dream."

She withdrew her hand from his. There was the rustle of bedclothes and he could make out her form, sitting up, her nightdress striped with the light of the moon gleaming through the slats of the shutters. In the room, the night gaped with unspoken words.

They remained thus, in silence, until Magda turned to her husband.

"I need to talk to you, Ioan."

"Then speak. We have always spoken freely." He longed for his voice to have a lightness to it, but the sound came out as a rasp.

"It's the girls."

"The girls?"

Ioan's head relaxed into the pillows.

"What about the girls?"

"They are dancing."

If Magda could have seen her husband's face in the dark, she would have been struck by its look of infinite relief and tenderness.

"And what of it? Little girls dance, and these two dance well."

"They are strange dances. The dances of…"

Magda paused, and looked towards the window, as if she were studying some secret landscape of the night.

"They are dancing the dance of… of… Mariuca." It was as though Magda had difficulty in saying the young woman's name out loud.

"And what of it?" The tightness had come back into his voice.

"There is harm in it."

"No harm can come from little girls dancing."

"You know it can, Ioan."

There was silence again, but for their breathing.

"I say there can be no harm in little girls dancing."

Magda recognized the tone of her husband's voice. It came from the part of his soul that was inaccessible to her. This side of him was stubborn and hard as a field during a drought, and it frightened her. It was as though there were a fissure between them, a fault, which involved not just them, but their histories and their families, and made this a place of danger. Neither they, nor their words, could reach down into it.

"I say there is no harm in the dance. And I will not stop my daughter, or any other girl, from her dance, or her song."

"People will talk, Ioan."

"Then let them talk. If we go down the road of fear of the wagging of busy tongues, then I say that it is a road that leads to nowhere."

He would not speak of past blood, neither of the spilling of it all those years ago down by the river, nor of the bad blood between their families, but both he and she felt it in the room with them, between them on the bed, as real and thick as the space across which they could not reach out to take the other's hand.

"Now think no more of it, woman, and let us get some sleep."

She lay down beside him, stretched out on her back, eyes fixed on the darkness above her. He had never addressed her as "woman" before. Many of the men folk in the village addressed their wives thus, but Ioan had never shown her this disrespect.

And so they lay, each in the turmoil of their own thoughts, waiting for dawn, and the relief that the distractions of daylight would bring.

Paraschiva was awoken by the presence of an intruder in the kitchen. Through half-closed eyes, she scanned the room in the dawn half-light. Everything was neat and orderly as Magda always left it: the pots and pans hanging in a row on the wall in a corner, the milk in a churn on the table, ready for breakfast. There was nothing out of place. Yet Paraschiva knew she was not alone.

"Who are you?" she asked out loud, speaking only to the four walls, and the inanimate objects they contained. Silence, except for the song of the first bird, whistling in the sunrise. She closed her eyes, quietened her breathing, and listened. She could feel it now, close to her. If she opened her eyes, she knew it would disappear, so she kept her eyes shut, and waited to hear what it had to say, and whether it brought help or harm.

Its message was confused, appearing in a series of images, each one superimposed on the one before. First, she saw again the liquid blur of the blue and red lights she had seen in her delirium on the night of Lazarica's festival. They were astonishing in their beauty, as if clear water and bright plasma were dancing together, each separate, yet complementary. Then the blues and the reds faded, and in their place she saw a dark mob roaming the streets with clubs and hoe handles, battering the weak and diseased, leaving a trail of blood and broken bones. Then this too vanished, and gave way to a strong wind. It blew through the house, whistling through holes in the walls and in the roof, lodging in the chimney, blowing people away from each other, cooling the warmth in their hearts, extinguishing the candles of kindness.

A dish clattered on the table.

Paraschiva opened her eyes to see Ioan Trifoi pouring himself some milk from the churn.

"I'm sorry, I woke you."

His eyes were red-ringed from lack of sleep. His body seemed drained, the energy gone from it during the night.

"No, no. I was already awake. Just dozing."

Ioan opened the shutters. An eerie pink glow filled the kitchen. Ioan studied the sky, ruddy and crimson, with its streaks of angry light.

"I think we're in for a storm."

"Good. The air is too heavy."

"Yes, it is strange, this heat, so early in the season."

Ioan poured a bowl of milk, and handed it to the old woman.

They both drank in silence, as the sun rose behind thick ribbons of cloud. It was Paraschiva who spoke first.

"Ioan, I want you to take me home."

"But Magda says you are not yet healed."

"I can walk well enough, if I have to."

She smiled at him, the old smile he recognized, with her one turquoise eye glittering with warmth, but now he could detect something else in her face, something akin to fear.

"What is it, Paraschiva?" He put down his bowl and laid a hand on her shoulder. He tried to read the anxiety on her face, but all he could see was the frailty of old age.

"Ioan, be careful. Look to your house. Look to…"

The door opened. It was Magda, entering the kitchen, her hair tucked under a neatly tied kerchief, her face pale as the moon, but composed to meet the day.

Paraschiva was struck by how two backs were suddenly turned to each other, and to her, and she counted the days till she would find herself once more sitting under her own roof, sheltered from the winds that blew people apart, and together, and apart again.

They walked in single file deeper and deeper into the beech wood in search of the right shade, the right secret coolness, in the heat of the late afternoon. With every step, Ioan Trifoi felt his spirit lightening and the troubles of his mind dissolving in the stillness of the woods.

They walked without speaking. At a point where the path widened, Mariuca waited for him. She took his hand, and they continued side by side, hand in hand. From the firmness of her grip, Ioan Trifoi felt her trust, as simple as a green leaf. From the point where their palms touched, a force coursed through him, filling him with an ache, stopping him in his tracks, and her arms were around his neck as he lifted her off the ground, and her legs were around his waist, her head was tilted back, her eyes fluttering under half-closed lids, the sun shining through the leaves onto the dampness of her forehead so that her skin was beaded with gold.

Then the afternoon caved in around them, and they were on the ground, impatient with buttons and fastenings, and she was arched on her back on the earth. For her it was the green and yellow of light, pulsing behind her closed eyes, brighter and brighter, and, when she opened them, it was the sheen of leaves, the smooth grey of trunks, the soft encircling of trees. For him there was the softness of dark velvet drawing him in, deeper and further, opening to him, and an unstoppable brilliance was inside him, and a flood of light pouring from him to her, and a cry that was an arrow of sound, piercing through space.

Then he was lying on his side, his head on the earth, smelling the thick loam of the forest, and she lay on her back next to him, her eyes closed, her face flushed and shimmering, as if in another world.

When she opened her eyes, it was to stare up at a single leaf that was fluttering in a crazed dance of its own, while all around it the foliage was motionless in the afternoon air.

She spoke from a weary distance. Her words reached him as if from far away.

"Why is there always one leaf that dances?"

With a great effort, he turned onto his back and looked up into the lattice of green until he saw the leaf.

"It catches the wind. The wind likes it."

"But there is no wind."

"Then just a piece of air. The air likes it."

"Does the air choose it, or does it choose the air?"

"I don't know." He reached over and took her hand, prising open her fingers with his, until they were interlocking.

"Ask them."

She closed her eyes.

"They don't answer."

Then she rolled over and put her head in the hollow of his shoulder, curled up against him, and drifted into sleep. He looked at her face, marvelling at the black of her eyelashes against the bronze of her skin. He wanted her again then, but feeling her weariness as his own, he, too, closed his eyes.

They were awoken by a rumble of thunder coming down the mountain, a slow avalanche of sound.

She sat up, pulling her clothes around her. He watched her in his half-sleep, entranced by the brownness of her back against the green of the ferns.

Then the darkness came, a black cloud reaching down to the treetops and a clap of thunder, close this time, right on the edge of the forest. He heard the nervous whinny of the horse. He was wide awake now, looking up at the cloud that was heavy with rain.

She was fastening her blouse and wishing, on each button, that the heavens would open and the rains would render the road impassable once and for all. Failing that, she wished, now on the last button, that he could stay with her for just one night. If that was all the gods wanted to give her, then so be it. One night.

The horse was tossing his head, straining at the rope that held him fastened to a tree trunk. The glade, darkening in the storm, was suddenly blasted into brilliance by a sheet of lightning. The horse twisted in its harness. Ioan held its head, stroking its neck, whispering words of calm, then leading it at an even pace through the wood, which had come alive with the hard drumming of raindrops on leaves.

The girl followed, mesmerized by the intermittent flashes of lightning that transformed the movement of the cart, the horse and Ioan into staccato jerks that cut into the air's whiteness.

She should have been afraid. Instead, she wanted to freeze the moment forever. She touched the bottom button of her blouse. "One night. Just one night," she repeated the words to herself like a mantra, in time to the heavy beat of the rain.

When they reached the road, they stopped. One way led down to the village, the other up the mountain. The horse stamped his foot, anxious to be on his way, his head already turned to the valley.

Then the sky disgorged itself, drenching them in a deluge.

"I must go," he said, looking at the road that led down to the village, but pulling her towards him.

She nodded. Neither of them moved. Their bodies clung together through the wetness of their clothes.

They watched as a fork of lightning crackled down through the sky to strike the ridge of the mountain opposite. The girl shivered, but not out of fear.

"If I don't go now, the road will be awash," Ioan said. Still he did not move.

In the next flash of lightning, she saw it: on the road, running, a streak of fur, some animal darting down the road towards them.

"It's Luka!" she pointed to the wolf-dog, so that Ioan could see him.

"Luka!" she called out to him. "Luka!"

He was upon them in seconds, jumping up on Mariuca, his fur soaked, his tongue hanging out, quivering in his fear of the storm and joy at finding the girl.

Ioan saw her smile as she stroked the dog, soothing it with the softness of her voice. Something inside him lurched into a new place. He felt himself fall out of the solid world that he knew, and into another one, which was strange and molten. All this she had done to him. He could bear it no longer.

"I will be gone, then." He pulled himself away from her.

She nodded.

"You'll be safe getting back to the farm, if you stay away from the trees. It is just a short way."

She nodded again.

Their wet clothes steamed in the heat, drying in front of the fire.

She had found a spare shirt and trousers of Pavel's. The trouser legs were too long, so Ioan had rolled them up, but too far. His ankles peeped out, white and comical, at the end of them.

They faced each other, neither finding words, inhibited by the strangeness of finding themselves in Paraschiva's kitchen. Mariuca had yearned for this moment, but now that she was holding it in her hands, she grabbed at it too tightly, and it slipped through her fingers. Desiring him too much, it was as if she had become her desire. Instead of her body, all she could feel was a black and frightening void.

He stood with his arms by his sides, not knowing what to do with them or any other part of his body. He saw the blankness of her face, and felt suddenly adrift, lost in the unreality of it all: the familiarity of the kitchen, where he had sat so often late into the night with Paraschiva, now made strange by the presence of the girl. Questions hung in the air all around him. Where was his life? Where was his home? Where was the sound of his daughter coming in and out of the house he had built with his own hands? Where was Magda? And what was he going to tell her?

To escape the tangle of his thoughts, he took refuge in movement.

"I will see to the horse," Ioan threw a blanket around his shoulders and was gone.

She looked around the room. The corners of it seemed harsh. How strange, she thought, to have felt safe in the midst of lightning, and afraid now that there was nothing to harm her. She thought of Paraschiva, and her wisdom. What would the old woman do in her situation? The girl paused, then turned to the fire and spat. The incongruity of the gesture brought her back to herself, and she laughed. She put some onions on the table and began to peel them.

The horse munched from a bucket of oats, while Ioan stood beside him, looking out at the rain.

It came down in sheets, like a grey metallic wall, pounding on the yard and the barn. Occasionally a slash of water gleamed silver, shining out from the mass of liquid for a moment, before it went the way of all the rest, into puddles and mud.

He thought of her. There were too many feelings around this woman, and his head hurt. He wanted away. But there was nowhere to go. Whatever had sparked between them was palpable and alive, and there was no running from it. It was like being born, he thought. You're suddenly living, and your only way out of the whole muddle of blood and pain and joy is to die. And he wasn't ready for that, not yet.

When he came into the kitchen, she was bent over the table, her back to him. She was wearing one of Paraschiva's old muslin dresses, with the fabric worn thin in patches, so he could see the brown of her skin through the faded blue of the cloth.

He put his arms around her, feeling the curve of her back against him. She turned to him.

"You're wet through again," she said. "I'll have to find more clothes."

She unfastened the buttons of his shirt and slid her hands under the damp cotton, running them soft as feathers over his skin, making him shiver.

He untied the knot of her kerchief at the nape of her neck, and the black scarf fell onto the floor. Drawing her to him, he stroked the dark regrowth of her hair. When he touched it with his lips it was soft, like the fur of a small animal.

She lowered her head.

"I hate it," she whispered. "But it will grow."

He kissed the top of her head again and again, each time in a different place, as if he were moving around the shorn parts of her soul, healing each one in turn.

Then he raised her head towards him. She kept her eyes on the ground.

"Look at me," he said.

When she met his eyes, she saw they were shining. She felt as if until that instant she had never in all her life been seen in her wholeness. The sacredness of the moment overwhelmed her, and her soul withdrew in terror.

Then she surrendered herself to its gift.

16

Magda dug her hands into the soil to pull up an end-of-season beetroot. With the earth so clogged with water after the night of rain, wet clods clung to the purple of the beet skin. Her fingers were covered in mud, her fingernails black, a sore on her thumb now turned into something dark and crusty. She felt her hands to be ugly appendages at the end of ugly arms, that belonged to an ugly body, with a head full of ugly thoughts.

Those thoughts. It was as if she had been keeping them in a cupboard where they had all been shouting, but she had kept her ears blocked so as not to hear the noise. Now they had opened the door all by themselves, and they were too many and too strong for her to stuff back in.

Ioan had not come home. She had waited up half the night, fearful for his safety in the gale. Her mind had tossed around in time to the treetops in the wind. Perhaps he had stayed over at Barbu's. But no, it was the night before Barbu's daughter's party, and the house would be full of guests. And even if Ioan had called in, it was no great distance: surely he could have made it back home in the cart.

She went to bed in the early hours, but found no peace in sleep. They crowded out the room, those voices. Out of the cupboard, now. She knew where he was. There was only one road steep enough to have become a mudslide in such a storm. It was the road that led up the mountain.

And now here she knelt, left with nothing in her hands but some brown earth and a beetroot.

"Good morning. Terrible gale last night." Elena Barescu stood above her, straight as a tree trunk. She was the last person Magda wished to see, with her long nose always ready to pry.

"Yes, terrible." Magda kept her voice polite, while her hands dug deeper into the soil, ripping up the beet.

"I have just come from Irena's. She asked me to call by to have a word with Ioan."

"Ioan… Ioan is not here."

"Oh?" Elena looked beyond Magda to the house and the barn beside it, with its absence of horse and cart. It was strange for anyone to drive out until the sun had dried some of the mud off the road.

"Where is he?"

"He's… gone to the high field."

"Oh?" Elena had a nose that could smell trouble a mile away. Now that it was right in front of her nostrils, she sniffed at it with relish. It didn't make sense. No one would go to the high field when there was work to be done, putting the house in order after the shaking of the storm.

Magda stood up, rubbing her hands against her apron, aware of Elena's eyes on the brown and purple stains.

"Yes, I think he said... the high field, I think."

Magda was hardly thinking anything. The thought that had come out of the cupboard in the middle of the night was her only thinking. There was silence between the two women while Magda sought for some place inside herself in which to hide away. From the kitchen doorway, Paraschiva, overhearing the two women, knew that Magda needed a friendly body by her side. She moved her lame leg as fast as she could across the grass.

"Good morning, Elena Barescu." Paraschiva spoke the woman's name as if it belonged on the ground.

Paraschiva and Elena Barescu hated each other with an intensity that was almost a pleasure.

Something akin to a smile passed across Magda's face, with surprise at her patient's unexpected progress, and relief at the precision of her timing. "Paraschiva! You're walking so well!"

"Indeed I am. I believe I am fully repaired." Paraschiva turned her turquoise eye, a sharp piece of jade, on Elena Barescu. "Have you come to offer me your good wishes?"

"No... that is, yes." Elena was no match for Paraschiva, and she knew it. Truth to tell, her dislike was mingled with fear, which only served to increase her animosity. "In fact, I have a message for Ioan..."

"If you are looking for Ioan, he is in the high field. You see, I asked him to go up the mountain yesterday to make sure that my house is in order for my return home." Magda and Paraschiva exchanged glances. "Yes, he said he would stop off in the high field on his way back into the village. He must have got caught in the storm on the mountain, and is surely there now. Why don't you take a walk up and talk to him yourself?"

Everyone knew that in one corner of the high field was an underground spring that overflowed in heavy rain. The field would now be a bog. Paraschiva grinned at the thought of the hem of Elena's dress dragging her further and further down into wads of wet clay.

"If you go now, you will have time to clean yourself up before the party." Paraschiva gave Elena a broad smile, and Magda, in spite of herself, had to stifle a laugh.

"Or if you prefer, we can give Ioan your message."

"Perhaps that would be the better solution."

"As you please."

"Irena said that as she will not be going to Barbu's this evening, could Ioan collect Gabriela and take her to the party?"

"I am sure that will not be a problem. Good day, Elena Barescu."

Paraschiva dispatched Elena with the tone of her voice, so that Elena backed away and turned, losing her footing for a moment on the muddy path before stalking off down the road on her way to the village square.

The two women watched her disappear. Neither of them spoke. But Magda felt the touch of Paraschiva's hand on her shoulder. It told her that the old woman had also heard them during the night. All those angry voices.

"I will go home tomorrow. If this sun keeps up, with luck, the road will be passable by then. Ioan can drive Pavel and I."

"If he comes back by then."

By the gentle pressure of the old woman's hand, she knew that the old woman's heart was with her.

"He'll be back."

"I will miss you."

"I will miss you, too, but there are things up there that need fixing."

Magda looked at her and nodded, wondering if an old woman, even one who held such wisdom in her hands, could repair a house so rattled by the storm.

To Ioan Trifoi, making his way down the mountain, everything that morning seemed like a miracle. A miracle, the way the beech trees, poised as dancers, held out their branches; a miracle, the spread of the eagle's wings as it traced a slow circle in the sky high overhead. Small miracles, the rustles in the bushes, that spoke of a whole teeming world of tiny creatures, each one in its own universe. How strange this world, how extraordinary to be a part of this creation. His very breath, a miracle.

All this he felt as he walked slowly beside the horse, guiding it, steadying it when its hooves slipped on the path.

As he got closer to the village, his head became heavy, and the glory of the morning was lost to him. Looking down on the rooftops of the houses that straggled along the river, he thought of how each house contained a family with its history of conflict and joy.

This was life, he thought: a bundle of worries, a long march of troubles, a few beats of pleasure. At least he had had these, he thought, with Mariuca. When she came into his mind, his stomach churned as if he had swallowed a spinning top. Then he thought of Magda, and the spinning stopped.

What was he going to tell her? He was no good at deceit but, at this moment, he was no good at the truth either. Maybe he could choose the simple path: silence. As a man, he had no need to account for his absence. In the village, the menfolk could do as they pleased with their bodies, and some did, if they had the rare chance of putting their hands on a loose woman. Fidelity was the domain not of husbands, but of wives. Yet he had never thought to stray from Magda, or to lie to her. That was not the road they had set out on together. But had he had a choice? It seemed to him that he had no more chosen his path than a tree chooses to be struck by lightning. Still, the guilt weighed on him, as if he had swallowed a stone.

The whirling of his thoughts so engrossed him that he hardly noticed the journey home until he was on his own doorstep.

He was struck by an unnatural silence. No sound came from the kitchen, no Doinitsa ran out to greet him.

The horse whinnied, as if it too were puzzled by the hush.

"Is there anyone there?" he called out.

The kitchen door was open.

"Is there no one at home?" he called out again, louder, this time.

Paraschiva appeared at the door, and Ioan breathed more easily. Until he saw her face, with a scowl on it that told him he was not welcome.

She gave him no greeting. "They have gone, Ioan."

"Gone?" he felt as if the ground had shifted from under his feet. "Gone where?"

"To Irena's. She is not well, and Magda has gone to tend to her. She asks that you stop there on your way to Barbu's and pick up the girls to take them to the party."

Barbu's party! In his distraction, Ioan had forgotten all about it.

"I will. Of course I will."

Ioan looked at Paraschiva, searching her face for some familiar sign of warmth. He could detect a glimmer, but well hidden behind the glower of her anger.

"Magda also asked me to tell you that if you come back from Barbu's tonight..."

"Of course I will come back."

"...that if you come back from Barbu's tonight, you should sleep in the outhouse. She got little rest last night."

Ioan stroked his horse's neck as if to calm it, although it was himself that needed the calming.

"I'm sorry, I..." He could find no words.

Paraschiva looked at him. He seemed helpless, like a swimmer carried away by a current that was too strong for him. The old woman felt him slip back into a corner of her heart.

"I think I have made a way out for you, Ioan Trifoi. I told Magda that I asked you to go up the mountain to prepare my house for my return tomorrow. I doubt whether she believed me, but now we'll make it a truth. I told her to take Doinitsa over to Irena's. Otherwise these walls may have rattled with words that stay forever in the woodwork."

Ioan thought of the rooftops he had seen from the hillside, and all the heartbreak that was under them. He reached out to touch Paraschiva's hand, but she pulled away from him.

"So... you will drive me home tomorrow."

She was not asking him, she was telling him. He nodded.

"I will drive you home." He stood before her, dishevelled in body and soul, with spatters of mud on his clothes and turmoil on his face.

"Now go, Ioan Trifoi, and clean yourself up for the party. You look like you've been dragged along the river bed."

Standing by a barrel full of rainwater, his thoughts carried on with a life of their own. Paraschiva had opened up a safe passage along the rocky road he was treading. If Magda wanted to, she could choose the salve of silence. They could both pretend nothing had happened, and patch up the wound left by what had.

He thought of Paraschiva's return home, of the long drive back up the hill. But most of all he thought of Mariuca. If Paraschiva was offering him a safe passage, the question remained in his mind: did it lead to a place where he wanted to be? And did he have any choice but to take it? If he took another path, how would he walk it, with the burden of guilt so heavy upon him?

He splashed his face and chest with rainwater. The soft water soothed him, so that he felt better able to venture back into the world of men, each one neither like him nor unlike him, but with a kindred skin that held together all this rushing of blood, this conflict of love and choice.

17

Barbu Temeru lived on the outskirts of the village, in a dwelling that looked as shaggy as its owner, with a fringe of unruly wooden slats that refused to stay in place on the roof. It was a place that usually called to Ioan Trifoi's heart, with all the memories it held of nights by the fire, singing and drinking tuica until the early hours. Tonight, as he walked across the broad veranda and in through the front door, he was unable to put a smile on his face to suit the occasion.

Later, he would think back on the events of that night and his mind would go down the futile path of how it might all have happened otherwise: if he had been less distracted, he would have noticed the heaviness in the air as soon as he walked into the house. If he had listened to his daughter who, sensing some threat, immediately said: "Papa, do we have to stay?" And if, instead of replying: "Just a little while, Doinitsa, not for long," he had turned on his heels and walked out through the door with her and Gabriela. If the girls, troubled by the shadow-words they could hear hidden behind the niceties, hadn't decided to leave the gathering and go out into the garden, in the dark, to the hayloft. If the guests had not moved out onto the veranda. If the veranda had been smaller so that fewer people had been watching. If…

There is a set of circumstances that have to occur in order for an accident to happen.

"Ioan! At last!" Barbu put his arm around Ioan's shoulder, leading him into a corner. Ioan knew immediately, by the furrow in his friend's brow, that all was not as it should be. He glanced around the room, focusing for the first time on his surroundings.

What he saw looked well enough – a table groaning under the weight of pre-nuptial dishes: breaded brains, stuffed peppers, whole giant carps staring up with discs of red paprika where once were their eyes, succulent pieces of lamb from an animal specially slaughtered for the occasion, and each platter surrounded by a garland of yellow and white pansies, symbolizing fertility, health and the joy of a good union.

Then his eyes strayed to the guests, and he knew immediately what was amiss. They had divided clearly into two groups, with the backs of one group turned on the other.

Ioan looked at the two circles. One, close to the table of food, was made up of Barbu's old friends and relatives: the Temeru clan, talking to the Brumarus, but with their natural good humour stifled by the heavy air that hung over the room. In the far corner was another group – Grigore Rusu, the bridegroom-to-be, and three or four of his friends. They were turned away from Ioan, so he could make out none of their features. Their stance and the squareness of their shoulders suggested something as unyielding as a rock face. They reminded Ioan of someone, but for the moment he was at a loss to remember who. He did not have to think for long. As he watched, the circle widened to include another guest, who fitted into it with the ease that occurs when like meets like. It was Radu Surdu who seemed, by the way he held each man's arm as he shook his hand, to have finally found himself among friends.

On the edge of this circle stood the Illitches, exchanging tales of woe about the trail of damage left by the storm with Elena Barescu and Father Diaconu. Ioan was struck by some subtle change in the old priest: his beard, although still long, no longer straggled down his chest, but ended in a well-groomed wedge of white hair. His back, which before was bent under the strain of holding up his weight, was straighter now, as if he had found some inner assurance that he was, indeed, the upright leader of his flock. When Elena Barescu caught Ioan's eyes on her, she whispered something to the priest, and they both turned to look at him.

He felt the room closing in on him, the air filled with the spite of small minds. He looked around for Doinitsa and Gabriela, in search of some lightness. They were not there. He saw Tunde, Barbu's wife, a diminutive, nervous woman with fine features and wispy hair, flitting like a small bird, carrying plates and serving wine, as if a surfeit of food and drink could compensate for the tension in the air. He saw Valentina, Barbu's eldest daughter and the bride-to-be, a voluptuous girl with bright eyes and a generous smile, moving from group to group, trying to create some communion. Her every movement was followed by a small white dog, her pet; between them they offered a precious gift of warmth to the gathering. But no one, it seemed, was aware of it, so involved was each guest in their own circle. Ioan watched as Valentina's well-meaning smile turned into a desperate grin. His heart went out to her. He had an idea.

"Why don't we all go out onto the veranda?" he spoke to the room. "Barbu, get your violin." Barbu nodded gratefully.

Ioan led the way out into the night air. The guests followed, eager to escape the confines of a space that was pressing together folk who would rather be apart.

The veranda gave onto a field with a wood behind it. An evening mist had fallen, so that the trees at the edge of the field were barely visible. Just a stone's throw from the house stood a summer hayloft, a wooden structure with four posts supporting the roof and the loft under it, with the ground floor open to the air. It had been decorated for the occasion: from the roof hung long willow branches, intertwined with garlands of flowers, giving it the appearance of a rustic altar, the setting for some spring ritual.

In front of it was a sight so strange that the crowd's murmur of conversation immediately dissolved into silence.

Two pubescent girls were dancing, their arms tracing snakes in the air. With the light from the house filtering through the mist, their limbs were barely distinguishable from the willow branches and the garlands so that it was as if the whole wooden structure had suddenly come to life.

The girls, deep in their trance, unaware of the eyes watching them, began to sway their hips, while irregular breaths of wind gusted the willow branches into movement. To the crowd watching from the veranda, it was as if the human and the plant world had come together in some supernatural union.

Ioan looked around him at the faces transfixed by the spectacle that was unfolding in front of them. If he could have found words or gesture, he would have intervened to stop the dance, to protect the private world of the dancers, but he, like all the others present, had become part of the trance.

The girls were moving side by side, facing out to the darkness. In front of them, for a moment, the mist cleared, so that it was as if they were partnered by a piece of the night. They danced in total abandon, yielding themselves to the emptiness.

And in the dark space in front of them, a wraith-like figure emerged from the earth, moving in time to the coiling and uncoiling of the girls' arms, and to the swaying of the willow branches. It was glowing, and insubstantial as the air.

The crowd gasped. A wave of fear broke over the group. Mothers pressed their children's faces against their skirts, wives clung to their husbands' arms.

A hiatus, as dark called out to dark, and then the phosphorescent glow increased, a shimmering spiral of light.

"It's a spirit!" Radu Surdu's voice cut into the air. "There is evil here among us. May God protect us."

The crowd echoed his words: "May God protect us."

At a nod from Surdu, Father Diaconu's voice rose above the murmur:

"In the name of the Father, Son and Holy Ghost, may the spirit of evil depart from this place and return to the darkness wherein it was born."

"And may the Lord protect us," the crowd murmured in unison.

Recalling it later, Ioan would play the sequence of events over and over in his mind, in slow motion: the girls' arms suddenly hanging limp by their sides; their faces, pale, turned in terror to the crowd; the mist falling again, filling the space where the figure had appeared, and then the sound of his own voice trying to drown out the crowd's chant.

"In the name of God, it was nothing more than a trick of the light, and a will-o'-the-wisp. Have you never seen a will-o'-the-wisp before?"

For a moment the chant faltered. Everyone had seen will-o'-the-wisps, glimmering ghost-like spirals, on the edge of a field or on a riverbank, suddenly appearing out of nowhere in the twilight.

"It was a will-o'-the wisp!" Ioan called out.

"And May the Lord seal the door where evil dwells." The quiver had quite vanished from the priest's voice as he intervened to heal any cracks in the wall of sound. Surdu joined in, his voice thin as a reed, but with a relentless energy that was soon picked up by the crowd.

"And may the Lord seal the door where evil dwells." The voices' echo grew stronger.

Looking around him at the faces, Ioan knew that he had lost the war of sound. He felt himself as helpless as when he heard the screams of a woman in childbirth, only what was now being born before his eyes was not a bright new life, but some dark creature come from the shadows.

He felt a hand on his shoulder and turned to see Barbu's face, filled with a fear that mirrored his own.

"I must get the girls out of here," Ioan shouted in his friend's ear, trying to make his voice heard. Barbu nodded.

Ioan walked swiftly across the grass to where Doinitsa and Gabriela stood, paralyzed, terrified by the rising chant. He took each girl by the hand, and led them from the hayloft towards the cart. But their way went past the veranda, where sound had suddenly given way to silence.

He saw the rows of faces: the villagers, their eyes lit up with a new fire and, behind them, Radu Surdu, the bridegroom and his friends, with no heat in their eyes, but a cold and ruthless stare that rooted Ioan Trifoi to the spot where he stood.

Then he felt the trembling of his child's hand in his own, and he was filled with a rush of anger.

"There is evil here," he spoke to the crowd. "And it is not the evil of the dance. It is the evil that lies in your own hearts."

There was a beat, and he saw rows of eyes gleaming.

"You accuse us of evil?" Radu Surdu's voice was taunting, sure of itself, as sure as a hunter levelling his gun at a certain prey.

Ioan felt the whole crowd, its breath suspended, waiting for him to say the irreparable. On the edge of the group, Barbu shook his head in a warning. Ioan Trifoi paused before speaking.

"I say there was no evil in the dance. I say that no spirit was conjured. I say that what has been witnessed was a trick of the light, and a will-o'-the-wisp. And now, if you will excuse me, I have two frightened children to take home."

As Ioan Trifoi helped the girls into the cart, he could feel the eyes of the group still watching him, in a silence broken only by the bride-to-be, quietly weeping.

18

The sun shone on the surface of the water in the bucket. If Mariuca screwed up her eyes, the light refracted into hundreds of tiny silver stars. She picked up a mirror and propped it onto the stone wall of the well, then hunkered down to look at her own reflection, and smiled. The eyes that stared back at her were chestnut, flecked with gold in the morning sunlight, and radiant.

She took off her thin blue dress and stood naked, revelling in the air on her body. Then she splashed the water over herself, stroking her skin as she did so, imagining that her hands were his, and counting the hours that separated her from his touch.

When she had finished washing, she went to the gate and stood under the empty spaces of the bat's wings and looked down the road to the valley. There where the dark band of the pine trees gave way to the sharper green of the beeches and oaks, the road was hidden in cloud, and the valley below had disappeared into a bowl of mist. She thought of him down there, imagining his every movement, as if by picturing him in her mind she could conjure him into reality. In her mind, she saw him at the door of his house. She called him away from it. He was hesitating, about to walk down the path, away from his home. Then she saw the door of the house open. She could see Magda moving around in the kitchen, laying a table for him and his daughter. Later, they would sit down for a meal together, safe between the walls of their home. But there were cracks in the walls of the house that were of her own making. She shivered. She would not destroy the home he had made. She would fold away her feelings, tuck them away like useless clothes in a drawer. This, she would do.

She shook back her shoulders and returned to the yard and the well. She took down the mirror and looked in it again, as if to see some change inscribed in her face. But the eyes that gazed back at her were as bright as before, and as radiant.

Magda slammed down the saucepan with such force that drops of hot milk spattered onto the table, onto the floor and over Ioan's shoes. Her face, so rarely contorted in anger, was transformed: her lips were pinched, her eyes changed colour as the pupils dilated. Ioan felt he stood face to face with another woman, not Magda, his wife of twelve years.

He had told her of what had happened at Barbu Temeru's. He had not made light of the fear that was in his own heart. Yet still he would not condemn the dance.

Now the air was sliced by Magda's words. He was a dreamer, she said, not seeing the world around him as it was, but only as he wanted it to be. And now his folly had put their only child in danger. She wished she had married another man, one who would have put his family's interests before his own dreams, dreams that were as insubstantial as clouds. She wished she had married someone, anyone, rather than… she was pale with a white anger. She spat the words across the room at him.

"An adulterer!"

And then a silence too thick to be broken by words.

Ioan sank down onto a stool and put his head in his hands. He felt despair at the truth, spoken out loud. Adulterer. The word sounded foul on Magda's tongue. His guilt weighed heavy, like something rotting inside him. Yet the sin he had committed had also been his greatest act of love.

He looked up at the sound of the door opening. In the doorway stood Paraschiva, holding a small cloth bag into which she had packed her few belongings.

"I am ready, Ioan." The old woman spoke quietly. "Pavel is ready. We want to go home."

Ioan nodded, got up slowly and walked towards the door. As he passed Magda, he stretched out to touch her arm, but she turned away, and spoke to him, over her shoulder.

"I will take Doinitsa to church today, Ioan. I will not have her hide away in shame."

Ioan felt his own anger rising.

"It is not a good idea, Magda. Let things settle."

Magda turned to face him. Her eyes flashed.

"I will not have my daughter shamed."

"She is our daughter, Magda. And there was no shame in the dance. The girls held out a natural hand to a will-o'-the-wisp. I told you. It was the silly-minded who grasped that hand with the folly of their superstitions."

"I will take her to church. I will have her confess."

"She will confess to nothing. She has done no wrong."

"Ioan…" Paraschiva's voice was calm and steady. "Perhaps Magda is right. If the girls show their faces, it will be surely a sign of their innocence. If they stay away, those hands you spoke of may weave more malice."

Ioan thought for a moment. Perhaps Paraschiva was right. The girls' presence may indeed be their greatest protection.

"But no confession." He looked Magda in the eyes. "Promise me, no confession."

Magda stared back at him, unflinching.

"Why should I promise anything to a man who breaks his promises?"

"Come, Ioan," said Paraschiva, "let us be on our way." The old woman took his arm and led him towards the door.

Magda had turned to face the wall, so Ioan spoke his words to her back:

"Woman, I am your husband."

Even though she muttered her reply to the wall, Ioan could hear her words:

"You are not my husband."

In her room, Doinitsa lay on her bed, and trembled. The night before, her father had held her in his arms, talking to her, reassuring her, over and over again, that she had done nothing wrong, that everything would be all right. Her father never lied. But hearing the angry voices of her parents, she knew that everything was not all right. Looking around at her room, that had once seemed so solid and safe, she felt as if the very walls were changing angles, and she wanted to cry out. But she knew there was no one to hear her, not with her parents' voices so suddenly loud.

Their way was shrouded in mist. They rode in silence, Pavel huddled in the back of the cart, Ioan and Paraschiva side by side, enfolded in tension and fog.

The road had not dried from the rains, so the cart moved sluggishly through the mud, the horse struggling to pull the old wooden contraption up the hill. At one point, the wheels stuck, and Ioan had to get down and strain with the horse to pull the cart free. From then on, he walked beside the animal, holding the reins by its head, urging it on.

When they came to Paraschiva's father's grave, he stopped and helped her down, and they stood side by side in front of the wooden cross, as was their custom.

It was a month to the day since Paraschiva had last knelt here and seen the dark spirit folding and unfolding its wings. Looking at the whorl in the wood, she knew that the dead were anywhere but in the ground. She could feel their breath around her now, whispers coming out of the mist, calling her to a dim place where she could see dark red shapes: they floated in blackness like blood clots deep inside a vein. She swayed, dizzy at the entry to another world. Ioan caught her by the elbow. Leaning against him, she was pushed by an invisible current. In the darkness of her vision, she saw the river, and the strangeness of it, and she cried out.

"The colour of the water!"

The horse snorted in alarm. The sound broke Paraschiva's trance: she came back to the air, and the hour, and the day, but her eyes were far away, in the world of shadows.

He held onto her arm, knowing that he was the only reason she remained upright.

"The colour of the water, Ioan..."

He shook his head. He had had time enough for Paraschiva's visions before his world had been turned on its head. But now, with the villagers seeing spirits rise out of the earth like charmed snakes, he wanted only a clear head and the feel of his own feet on the ground.

"It is a memory, Paraschiva."

She remembered only too well that other time when the river had run red. Perhaps he was right. In trance, time twisted and turned, and a traveller could get lost in its labyrinth. But no, those veins containing the lethal clots. The body doomed. Of a person? Or a people? Or a land? She could not tell. All she could see was the unnatural liquid, the river water engorged with the effluence of some slaughter.

"There is danger, Ioan."

"It will settle."

"You must not see her again."

He said nothing, but fixed his eyes on the cross.

"It is dangerous, Ioan. For you. Even more for her."

He would not look her in the eyes.

"You are a man, you have the protection of friends, family. She has nothing. We don't even know where she comes from."

"Her people came from this village."

Paraschiva stared at him. A gate flew open in her mind.

"So, she has got a tongue…"

Ioan sucked in his breath, as if in a futile attempt to retrieve his words and render the spoken unspoken.

"Please, I should not have said it. I have broken her trust."

"Not a bad choice, to choose silence. If only her body had stayed as quiet as her mouth."

"Don't take her silence from her."

"If she can speak, then I must talk to her. There is danger, Ioan, too much danger."

From the cart, Pavel gestured to them. Bored and forgotten, impatient to see Mariuca, he was anxious for them to be on their way.

"You must not see her, Ioan. Promise me this. When we get to the last bend before the house, you will leave us there. The rest of the way we will go on foot."

Ioan would have protested, but for the fear in his heart of whatever fire was being kindled down in the valley. His place today, of all days, was by his daughter's side. So he offered no resistance.

But he had made no promise either. Not to Paraschiva, not to the village, not even to himself.

Mariuca tried to keep her mind on the task in hand, carrying buckets of water from the yard into the kitchen. They were heavy, and after a while the muscles in her arms and along the back of her neck began to quiver. Then the trembling took on a life of its own that had nothing to do with physical exertion. It began in her stomach. A wave that went through her body telling her that she was fully alive. Alive. Waiting.

She went to the gate and looked out at the road that led down to the village. The valley was still shrouded, the white froth of the clouds curling up to the hilltops. The mist blurred the landscape, making silhouettes uncertain, smudging the harsh line of the mountain ridge.

It was like her life, she thought, the uncertainty. Her past existed only in the blur of memory, with nothing to connect it to the present. Her future was as unpredictable as the mountain fog, which could descend in seconds, obliterating all safe paths. The only landmark in her life was the certainty that he loved her.

Luka, who sat patiently beside her, cocked his ears. Then he began a barking so crazed that the cocks joined in with their crowing, and the yard was filled with a cacophony of sound.

The dog streaked down the path and vanished into the cloud. Barks gave way to yelps of delight.

Mariuca strained to see the shape of a horse and cart emerging out of the haze. Instead, she saw the silhouettes of two people, one bent, walking slowly, leaning on the arm of the other, who carried a small bag by his side.

"Paraschiva! Pavel!"

Mariuca ran with her arms open, ready to wrap the old woman in her welcome.

But as she got close, she noticed the set of Paraschiva's shoulders. There was something stiff and decided about them. Mariuca's arms dropped to her sides.

Still she smiled at Paraschiva and, unable to stop herself, looked beyond her, scanning the mist for the horse and cart, and its driver.

Paraschiva watched her watching.

"Ioan has gone back to the home where he belongs."

The girl looked at her, expressionless.

"And you can play as mute as you like, but you will listen to me. I know you can talk. So let's go into the house, and talk."

Paraschiva walked past her, brushing away her offer of a helping arm. Pavel and Luka followed, the dog quietened now by the harshness of the old woman's voice.

Mariuca paused, then she too turned and walked through the gate, under the bat's wings, which were filled with nothing but the milky air.

19

The mist from the valley rose up the mountain, enshrouded the farm, and a breath of it followed the two women into the house.

They sat on either side of the hearth, a wreath of mountain vapour and a thick silence between them. The only sound was a shuffling in the yard, where Pavel and Luka, sensing the heaviness in the air, were exchanging subdued greetings.

Mariuca kept a stubborn silence, her eyes on the ground. Paraschiva stared at her as if she would transfix her to the spot. Finally she spoke:

"If you won't open your mouth," she said, "at least you can't close your ears. So listen. He's not coming."

Mariuca looked at her, then out of the window, whether in search of rescue, escape, or the silhouette of Ioan Trifoi, the old woman was not sure.

"Do you hear me? It's finished."

The girl shook her head slowly and breathed heavily, as if she were battling with something sharp that had lodged in her chest. And then there was the scrape of the old woman's chair on the stone floor as she lunged forward, raised her hand and brought it down sideways on the girl's cheek.

Mariuca felt the sting of pain, and the smarting of her eyes with tears that came of their own accord. Still she didn't move, not even when another blow came, harder this time, hitting the same place on her cheek which already burned.

"A month! I leave you for a month and you spread your legs wide and bring ruin to us all. Pah! Whore!"

Mariuca shook her head and took in her breath in a sharp gasp of disbelief. Many times, over and over again, during her days in lonely exile, she had played and replayed in her mind the conversation she would have with Paraschiva – telling her of her love for Ioan, listening to Paraschiva's stories of her own adventures, for according to what Ioan had told her, there had been many. She had anticipated the old woman's return with excitement. Yesterday she had cleaned the house from top to bottom, she had wrung the neck of the biggest chicken in the yard, had plucked it and cut it up and cooked it in a stew with broad beans and carrots and the huge bitter onions that turned sweet when simmered long and slow. She had also longed for the moment when, with pride, she would show Paraschiva how she had tended the farm in her absence: planting marrows and potatoes; weeding among the rows of cabbages and beans; raking the fields behind the house with manure and ashes from the fireplace, so that the earth would be rich and kindly; even mending the hole in the roof over their heads, which had been done with extreme difficulty, for it had involved perching on a ladder she had improvised by stacking three sacks of beans precariously one on top of the other on the table, balancing herself, hammer and nails in a workable position for the good part of an hour. All of this and more she wanted to share with the woman who now sat opposite her with a look like a cut stone.

Mariuca prepared herself for another blow. But none came. Instead, she was surprised by her own voice, speaking words that came out slow and calm, belying the torrent that was inside her.

"I see no ruin in it."

Paraschiva sank back into her chair. For all that she had been prepared to beat the girl for the troubles she had brought with her, the sound of her voice was as strange as having a new person in the room.

"Fetch me some tuica. And two glasses. You can talk? So you and I will talk."

Mariuca fetched the heavy earthenware bottle and two glasses and filled each one with a measure that both women downed simultaneously. Unaccustomed to the alcohol, Mariuca felt it burning her throat and stomach, and releasing her tongue.

"I never thought to hurt anyone. Some things happen unplanned," she said. "I never thought to hurt you."

"And Magda?"

"Neither."

"And Doinitsa and Gabriela?"

"The girls? What have they to do with this?"

"There is scandal prowling around the village like a flame about to meet bracken. The girls struck the match, that's all."

Maruica shook her head, bewildered by the old woman's language.

"Speak to me plain."

"They were seen dancing at the Temeru girl's party. Not one of the village dances. One of your dances."

"And is it a sin to dance?"

"They say a spirit got caught in the dance."

"A spirit?"

Again the girl shook her head, uncomprehending. Left alone up the mountain with only her own mind for company, she had filled long days with the weaving of her own imagination. Try to stop it as she would, she had woven a tapestry of her future life with Ioan: how she would stay up the mountain and look after Pavel and Luka, and Paraschiva in her frailest years, and Ioan would visit her as often as he could. She would not have had the whole of him to herself – that much she accepted. For she would rather have half of Ioan than any other man in his entirety, of that she was certain. And now the beautiful thing she had embroidered in her mind was suddenly unravelling, with Paraschiva's talk of dancing and bewitchment.

"I showed the girls how to move their arms and legs, not to speak with spirits. I have no talk with them. That is your domain."

Paraschiva looked at her, and was surprised by the fierce glare of her eyes, and by the anger in her voice.

"Do you believe it?" the girl said.

"What?"

"That they caught a spirit?"

Paraschiva's mind returned to the clearing on the day of Lazarica, to the current that had passed from hand to hand, to the pressure in her own chest that had made her topple to the ground.

"Who knows? It is possible. All things are possible. What matters is that people thought they saw it. And they are afraid. And when they are afraid, they turn vicious. And they were once afraid of me, but I found my way around their fear. Now they are afraid of you, and of your dances, and of your strangeness. These are new times, and bad times for a web such as this one."

"What will happen to the girls?"

"Probably a warning, and in a month or two everything will die down... if you stay away from the village."

A shaft of sunlight, breaking through the mist, shone into the kitchen. Mariuca turned towards the window, as if with longing for the road that led down the mountain.

"I will stay away from the village – of course I will."

Paraschiva nodded, knowing that this was the easy part of the bargain. She reached out for the tuica, filled both their glasses to the brim, and drank before she spoke.

"You must not see him any more, Mariuca. It is too much of a coil."

The girl kept her face turned towards the light. When she finally looked at Paraschiva, the old woman was faced with a pair of brown eyes whose sole intent seemed to be to burn a hole in her old heart.

"But I love him." She spoke the words softly, yet they had all the weight of a prayer. "You, of all people, you must know how it feels."

"Pah! This is how it feels!" Paraschiva raised a hand to the wrinkled skin that covered the empty socket where her eye had once been. The young woman said nothing, but reached out and took her hand.

Paraschiva looked down at her lap, reluctant to revisit the pain of the past. But then she felt the pressure of Mariuca's touch and knew that she had to tell her story, for, with all its anguish, it might hold a lesson for the young woman, one that, if learned, may lead to her salvation. So she held on to the girl's hand, took a deep breath, and began her story.

"It was many years ago – long before you were born, before they drove your people out of the village. I was in my middle years, and had left behind my wild ways. I had Pavel. He was my company. I was accepted – in a half and half way – shunned by those who were afraid of my difference, welcomed by the same ones when they needed my healing. Then one day there was a bad case of fever in one of the houses down by the river. It was a man, thin as a twig and nearly on his last breath. His wife and children gathered around and there was a lot of crying. I nursed him – I nursed him for three months… and when he was back in a half-life, I fell in love with him."

Watching the old woman's face, Mariuca marvelled at the transformation that was taking place in front of her eyes: it was as if Paraschiva had fallen out of time and was transported back to a hovel where, in spite of death and dirt and disease, she had lived out the moment that illuminated her life down through the years.

"His name was Hîntu. Hîntu." She drew out the syllables, as if to hang on to all that was left of him. "I fell in love with the soul of a dark man who was nothing but skin and bone. And when the flesh came back on his bones, I fell in love with his body."

Here she stopped, as if wishing this were the end of her tale. Her mouth pursed in resistance to the story she knew she had to finish, for the girl's sake.

"And then, nine months later, I had his son."

She reached out and filled herself another glass of tuica, but left it untouched on the table.

"A boy, with skin the colour of yours, and eyes the colour of mine. Such beauty." Her voice caught in her throat.

"What happened?" The girl's voice was barely audible.

"They came after me."

"Who, they?"

"The men."

"From the village?"

"No, they wouldn't have harmed me. But word had spread. They came from other villages."

The sun shone brighter now through the window, the afternoon light belying the dark sequence of events that Paraschiva now told in a flat monotone, as if to dull the memory.

"They came up the mountain. They took the baby. They said they would throw him in the river, a half-caste, and drive out Hîntu and his family if I tried to see either father or child again. I begged them to leave the child with his father, and in exchange I agreed to their terms."

"They took him back to his father?"

"Yes, they took him back to his father."

"Did you see them again – your son, and Hîntu?"

"No. I didn't see anyone for a long while. Not until the place where my eye had been had healed over."

Mariuca felt a sickness in her stomach.

"They said it was a warning. They said they would take the other one out, too, if ever I looked on him or my boy again."

The girl shook her head, as if to make the story disappear.

"I never saw them again. I never said goodbye."

The women fell quiet, finding themselves in a place too deep for words, where the absence of loved ones hung in the air.

"What was his name?"

"His name was Ioan."

The girl looked at Paraschiva questioningly.

"Your Ioan was born a few months later. His father was kind – so good to me. I think perhaps, in his goodness, he named his son after mine, that I might feel his absence a little less sharply. He would bring him up the mountain, knowing how I keened for my own boy. And he would bring me news of my own child, for he was one of the few who liked the river people. I swear Ioan Trifoi sat on my lap as much as he sat on his own mother's. That child was as my son."

Mariuca nodded. She had seen it already, time and time again, in the way Ioan looked at Paraschiva, and she at him. She knew that Paraschiva would let nothing come between her and Ioan, not even Mariuca herself. And yet she, too, was a part of their history. She thought of the delicate threads that linked them all together – her people, Paraschiva, Ioan – their destinies all interwoven like some fabric, threaded in blood.

"My parents surely knew your son and his father."

"Surely."

"Did you never see my people again?"

"Never. It was years before I returned to the village and when I did so, they had gone."

The bitter twist returned to her mouth, as she recalled the brutal stories that reached her ears of the night the river people had been driven out.

"Did you ever find out what happened to your son and his father?"

"Dead, or fled. It was better not to think on them. That way lies madness."

The girl leaned forwards, took Paraschiva's hands in her own, and kissed them. The kiss said that she, too, knew about the damming up of the dark river of memory that would otherwise drown the mind and the heart. But the price to pay was a harsh one, for it was at the cost of part of the soul.

"Is that why you took me in? Did I remind you of…?"

"Pah! You looked like a bundle of wood sticks that the fire forgot to burn. But with such beautiful eyes. Beautiful eyes. Try to keep both of them."

Mariuca closed her eyes, experiencing for a moment the darkness of the blind, refusing, in some part of her being, to accept a world where a woman would be mutilated for her loving. When she opened them, she raised her hand to touch the old woman's arm.

Paraschiva brushed her hand away. She was done with the pain of memory.

"I have one good eye, and one good son, even if he has no tongue in his head, and now I have a girl with speech but a silly heart. Come, enough of this. Show me how you have kept the house these last four weeks."

She raised herself from the chair, swayed for a moment as her bad knee threatened to give way under her, and then walked to the door to let in the afternoon sunshine, and Pavel and Luka, who all the while had been waiting patiently in the yard.

20

When Ioan Trifoi opened the door to his home, he was met by the sound of sobbing. Magda sat alone at the kitchen table, her head in her hands, staring down at the liquid dregs of a cup of black tea. When she raised her face to look at him, he saw that her cheeks were blotched red and white from crying.

"Magda, Magda, what is it?"

She held onto the cup as if it were her sole source of comfort. Her sobbing continued, and it was only with difficulty that Ioan could make out his wife's words.

"The girls… the girls have been…"

Her voice trailed off and she studied the teacup as if she were reading among the tealeaves, desperate for some good sign, some augur.

"Magda! If anything has happened to the girls… Tell me!"

"They have been… banned, Ioan."

For a moment, Ioan heard the word as if it belonged to a foreign language. There was no reality to it, and no sense in it either. Banned. Then the whole ugly force of the word came to him. It meant exclusion, no right to marry, to be a part of the community, to have a wedding, or to raise children, no right to a funeral, no right, even, to a grave. In his mind, he could see the bright faces of the two girls, and on them the stain of a word that robbed them of everything that made up a life.

"Tell me, Magda. Everything."

Magda stared down at the cup, fingering its surface, finding a chipped part on its lip that she rubbed in agitation, as if to smooth away its rough edges. Then she started to piece together her story. She had arrived at the church with Doinitsa and Gabriela. She saw them immediately: the group of new, unfamiliar men standing around in their heavy grey wool jackets. Among them she recognized Grigore Rusu, the Temeru girl's fiancé. They had seemed to be on good terms with Radu Surdu, for there was a fair amount of doffing of hats and murmurs of greetings before they finally went into the church. They had taken the two front rows of pews, with no respect at all for the regular occupants.

Magda sat at the back of the church with the other women and girls, separated from the men by a wooden barrier, each of its posts carved with figures ascending and descending from heaven to hell, according to their degree of sin or righteousness. She had settled herself down, holding Doinitsa by one hand and Gabriela by the other, for the girls clung to her like spring lambs huddling in the cold. She felt it straightaway: the change in the air, as though the church was full of something heavy and rotten. When she looked along the rows of women who were filling the pews, she recognized all the familiar faces of her friends and neighbours, but when she tried to catch their eyes to exchange a smile or a greeting, they looked away.

As Diaconu's voice incanted the words of the mass, and the congregation rose and sat and rose again in an age-old ritual, Magda felt her fears subside.

It was usual, after the chants, to hear Diaconu give a sermon from the pulpit. Based on the belief that some suffering was necessary for salvation, it was customary for the congregation to remain standing throughout. As Magda was a head smaller than the woman in the row in front of her, she could see nothing but the upper part of the wooden posts of the barrier that separated the menfolk from the women. The carved figures on them, being close to heaven, were clothed in fine drapes and wore on their faces the beatific smiles of the saved.

Diaconu wasted not a moment before coming to the point of the day's message. The quiver had gone from his voice.

"Last night we bore witness to the presence of evil among us," Diaconu's voice rang out around the church like a high-pitched bell. He is glad of this, thought Magda, staring at the carved oak figure of a young woman, her arms outstretched, drawn heavenwards by an angel. Of course if he can prove evil, he also proves good, and as he is on the side of goodness, or so he protests himself to be, then he becomes as indispensable as God. She felt the trembling of her daughter's hand in hers, and her own shortness of breath as a rage rose inside her. The anger quickly gave way to fear, as she tried to follow Diaconu's words.

The evil had come from without, he was saying, still in his high voice of triumph. Without, beyond. It had come down from the mountain, when Satan had crossed the mountain ridge and had lodged himself in the body of a woman, had possessed her limbs and captured her tongue, had given her the power to bring floods and plagues of rats upon the village, for had not the rains started and the river swollen and burst its banks and the pests overrun the streets and even slept in their homes at precisely the time the girl had come to dwell among them? And had she not been seen walking on the mountain road with a wolf, and was the wolf not also the devil's messenger, for who had ever heard of a tame wolf that would walk alongside a woman, close enough to lick the hem of her skirt? And had not the woman corrupted two young girls, on the edge of their womanhood, with the dances of the devil, dances the village had already seen before, the dances of a people who came from the dirt and went into the darkness, and was it therefore any wonder that the spirit of evil had joined them to revel in the gestures of swarthy souls? And it was for this reason that he called on each man present to raise his hand if he wished that Satan be expelled from their midst, and the woman driven back beyond the mountain ridge, and the wolf slaughtered, and the young girls banned until the shadow of the devil had been chased out of the village, and they could live in the clear light of the Lord once more.

There was a long pause. Magda stared all the while at the same blissful wooden woman, her place in heaven assured, her arms reaching out for the safety of paradise. As for her own hands, they were full, for each one held a piece of fear: in her right hand, she could feel her daughter's, that had kept up its trembling throughout the sermon, and her left hand held Gabriela's; it was cold and still, as if the girl was in shock, and badly in need of a mother, with her own at home and still sick in bed.

By the sound of the shuffling of feet and the creaking of collars, Magda deduced that the menfolk were raising their hands in plenty, especially as the two front rows were filled with Barbu Temeru's future son-in-law's friends, and with acquaintances like those, even the devil himself, she thought, would make himself mighty fleet of foot, and vault out of the valley at high speed.

She knew which way the vote had gone by the looks of the women around her. It was their eyes that spread the message, from woman to woman, so that those in the front who had a clear view through the wooden posts communicated it back along the rows. The eyes that before the service had not ventured to look at her now dared sidelong glances. Some were looks of satisfaction, but many were of sympathy. Only once, in most of their lifetimes, had anyone been banned from the village, and that was an old mad woman who had set fire to the Mayor's house three times, and, it was felt, would never learn her lesson unless she spent a few months deprived of the company of humans. She died out there, on the mountain ridge, in the middle of winter. If that happened to the young woman, so be it. She had seemed agreeable enough when she had first set foot among them, but no one had had the time or the inclination to get to know her well, so her disappearance or death was of no great consequence. But the girls… the girls were of the village, and many a woman who stood alongside Magda said a silent prayer of sympathy.

At the end of the pew, Elena Barescu leaned forward and stared past the other women to get a good view of Magda and the girls in their moment of shame. Magda met her eyes. They were lit with such a glint of malicious satisfaction that before she had time to plan her exit, Magda found herself pushing her daughter in front of her, pulling Gabriela behind her, and squeezing past the bulk of the women in their heavy wool skirts and aprons, until the three of them were outside the church, breathing in the spring air. It brought little comfort, for the mist still clung to the ground, rendering the day itself as cloudy as the words and minds of men.

Magda finished her story and stared down at the table.

In the silence that followed, Ioan looked at the walls of the kitchen. Everything was familiar. Yet nothing was safe. He felt like someone who wakes from a bad dream only to find the space around him has bred its own brood of nightmares. His daughter and Gabriela banned. He brought his fist down on the table so that the cup jumped up in the air.

"Hogwash! This ban is hogwash! There is no devil but the trumped-up demon of some twisted minds. I'll go to Diaconu and squeeze some sense into the old man's brain."

"No, Ioan, you don't understand. He has Surdu beside him. And Surdu wishes you nothing but ill. Diaconu is not alone now."

"But why? Why? There is no sense in it. If anyone has saved the old goat's hide from Surdu all these years, it has been me."

"No one can make sense out of it, Ioan. Maybe there is no sense. Many things have happened of late that make no sense..."

He knew she was thinking of Mariuca, but he had no reply. He felt like one who has followed a track in the mountains, all along knowing that it led to a precipice, but who has followed it nonetheless, because of some weakness in the brain.

"Where are the girls?" he asked.

"In Doinitsa's room. Both of them. Irena is still sick, so I brought Gabriela home. Besides, they would not be separated. I told them to lie down and rest, for neither had a moment's sleep all night."

"Then I will not disturb them."

Truth to tell, if Ioan had opened the door of his daughter's room, which adjoined the kitchen, he would have seen the girls, both in their identical embroidered Sunday blouses, kneeling side by side, ears pressed to the door. They were desperate to hear the adults put words to events that neither of them could understand. They heard the sound of footsteps on the floor, and then Magda's voice, shrill as a frightened bird.

"Where are you going?"

"To Barbu's. I cannot make sense of this alone."

"Barbu can do nothing, Ioan. You don't understand. The village is turned upside down."

"Then it is time it was turned back the right way up. The ban must be lifted, and the girl must be warned. An end must be brought to all this nonsense."

"Yes, bring an end to the nonsense, Ioan. I have been waiting for you to bring an end to the nonsense..."

Magda's voice trailed off. She stared at the table, then slowly righted the cup on its saucer. When she took up her sentence again, her voice was controlled and low, with a lethal strength to it.

"If you go up the mountain to see her again, Ioan, you can come back, but it will be to an empty house."

From her hiding place behind the door, Doinitsa shivered, as if some dark wind was blowing through the house from a cold and lonely land. Fear rose in her throat and stuck there like a jagged stone, so that when she tried to breathe, a sound came out of her that was strange and unearthly, somewhere between a cough and a scream.

It cut through the air, releasing husband and wife from their impasse of threats and ultimatums. Ioan was the first to the door. He flung it open and saw in front of him his daughter, seized by an unnatural gasping, still clutching the hand of her best friend as if her life depended on its grip.

In that moment, husband and wife forgot their differences, as each took a young girl into their arms. "Hush, now, hush," Ioan whispered, as he stroked his daughter's hair. "It is all the folly of foolish folk who know no better."

His daughter pressed her face against his chest, so her voice was tight and muffled: "Are we evil, Papa?"

"No, you are not evil."

"Is Mariuca evil?"

"Neither."

"And Luka, is he the devil in disguise?"

"Luka is a stray dog with some wolf blood that Paraschiva took in from the kindness of her heart."

"So he's not a creature of the devil, causing bad spirits to rise from their graves?"

"Now since when has the blood line of stray animals caused the bad spirits to rise from their graves? People are scared of what they don't understand, that's all. Now you take some rest, and I will find some sense in it all."

His daughter's rapid breathing now subsiding, he passed her into his wife's arms, and went to the front door.

"Keep them safe, Magda."

"Where are you going?"

"To Barbu's."

"You will not go up the mountain."

"I am going to Barbu's."

And then he had gone, and Magda was left alone with her arms filled with two frightened girls, and a coldness that was reaching down to her fingertips.

21

The flames leapt into the afternoon sky as if they were trying to lick the sun. Pavel ran around the yard with Luka chasing the bad hen, all three creating a caterwauling of barking, shouting and clucking. Only Mariuca was quiet as a priestess, carrying out Paraschiva's orders with all the solemnity of a ritual. She heaped on sticks and twigs, dried leaves and branches, until Paraschiva's fire burned bigger and brighter than even the autumn bonfire she made every October after the pig-killing, to smoke the hams for the winter in its embers.

"More wood," was all the old woman said, and Mariuca enlisted Pavel to join her running back and forth to the woodshed, until their arms ached with the cradling of sticks and the lifting of logs.

Just when it seemed that the fire had reached its full height, with smoke swirling around the yard and even as far as the stables, so that the sow took up an eerie squealing, Paraschiva stood in front of it and clapped her hands.

Luka skulked off to his kennel, finding the smoke made him cough and sneeze; the bad hen stalked off to peck at fallen sour cherries in the orchard behind the house, and Pavel and Mariuca stood on either side of the blazing woodpile, uncertain of what Paraschiva wanted of them or the flames but watchful, knowing, by the old woman's stance and the distant look in her eye, that the fire was part of an invocation, some call to another world.

Mariuca raised her arms and rippled her hands, mirroring the movement of the flames. Pavel echoed the gesture. Together they traced the word "fire" in their unspoken language, as if it were a sacred sign to be inscribed in the air.

"Now, fetch me a barrel of tuica, and some rags."

Mariuca was puzzled, but she smiled, thinking to herself that perhaps Paraschiva's love for the liquid was fast turning into something of a passion, but Pavel was already moving towards the woodshed to fetch the alcohol. Mariuca followed him. There, in among the sacks of lentils and potatoes and dried fruits, sat four plump oak barrels. Pavel dislodged one and shunted it across the floor using feet, hands and knees to shift its bulk. When he pushed it out into the yard, he squatted down and used the weight of his own body to topple it onto its side and roll it across the ground towards the fire, while the girl gathered some rags from a dusty pile in the corner of the shed.

A wind gusted down from the mountains. Paraschiva raised her eyes to the sharp ridge that cut across the sky and saw a cloud rolling down from the heights. She issued her orders in a calm voice that seemed to come from somewhere far away.

"Roll the rags together," she said, and watched as Mariuca wound up the first cloth, and then the others around it, so that on the ground lay a loose and dirty bundle full of the dust and stains from a winter of lying in the woodshed.

"Now douse it with tuica. Douse it well."

Pavel tilted the barrel so that its tap overhung the wad of cloth. Bending down, raising her skirts above her knees, Mariuca opened the tap and watched as the liquid, clear as water, soaked into the cloth, softening it, spreading stains of big dark flowers. The sweet sickly smell of the alcohol pervaded the yard.

"More." Mariuca obeyed Paraschiva, and carried on pouring.

When the cloth bundle was sodden, lying in its own pool on the ground, Paraschiva raised her arms to the sky and, in an echo of the unspoken language, she too traced the word "fire" in the air above her head.

And then she spoke in her own tongue. Neither Pavel nor Mariuca knew what she was saying, but from the guttural low sounds they gathered she was uttering something between a prayer and a song. Mariuca looked at her as she stood there, her one good eye half-closed, and she sensed that this was part of some ritual of protection and purification for Pavel, for the house, for Ioan, but mostly for herself, Mariuca. She shivered, for in her belly she felt a quivering, where some unknown muscle had decided to dance out its own movements of dread and desire.

For if she wished for protection for her body, she wanted no purification, none at all, from the touch of Ioan Trifoi.

At the same time as Paraschiva threw the soaked bundle onto the woodpile, the cloud rolled in from the mountain. Pavel gasped as the flames leapt higher and higher into the air, as smoke and mist mingled. Now they saw each other only as dark shapes across a sea of vapour, which swirled around the yard in a crazed yet graceful dance of its own.

Paraschiva, isolated in the opaque air, looked up into the flames and surrendered herself to the trance of the continuum of the birth, life, and death of each flame. In the ceaseless brilliance of the fire's motion, she saw again the blue and red liquid lights that surrounded the girl, but now, in the midst of the iridescence, she saw the intertwined roots of a beech tree that grew exposed above the waterline on the river bank, and she saw a mingling of blood, like the juice of two cherries crushed together. Then she watched as the red faded, all colour withdrawn. She saw a pile of grey dust and knew it to be ashes; her nostrils were filled with the odour of charred wood, and at the heart of the flames she could see something black and flapping in the wind, something that had always been there, linking past and future, joy and anguish, that wound itself around all of their lives.

They stood, the three of them, motionless, until the mist thickened around them, dampening the woodpile and quelling its blaze until it dwindled to the slow and constant crackle of a fire such as any villager could build to burn the leaves that piled up in his yard on an autumn day.

Paraschiva came back to herself, to the yard, to Pavel and Mariuca, who were still gazing at the flames, as if hypnotized.

When Paraschiva spoke, her voice was matter of fact. She said simply: "You can see him one last time."

Mariuca wanted to shout out some word of protest, but something – the dampness of the day, or the dying fire – stopped her speech, and all she felt was the quivering in her belly.

Then the old woman reached out to take her hand. "It is a terrible thing, not to say goodbye," she said.

22

A cricket had found its way into the house, and filled the room with the loud and irregular rasping of its hind legs. To the two girls who sat side by side on the bed, it remained invisible. On another day, they would have taken pleasure in finding the little creature, cupping it in their hands, and carrying it out with care to the field behind the house, or taking it down to the river and finding it a new and splendid home on top of a spreading fern leaf.

But on this day they remained where they sat, immobilized by fear and a crowd of thoughts. They had done something evil, of that there seemed little doubt. The condemnation of the village told them they had transgressed, crossed some invisible boundary into a new and fearful world.

"If a ban can be placed, it can be lifted." Doinitsa repeated the words she had heard her father say, searching for some comfort.

"If anyone can fix it, your father can." Gabriela added her own words of reassurance.

Then the girls lapsed back into silence, punctuated only by the cricket, which carried on its relentless call.

Banned. Doinitsa mused on the word. Truth to tell, she did not fully understand what it meant, and did not dare to ask. In her mind, it was something akin to dying. She had never seen a banned person, or a dead one, and in her imagination they wandered around the village, floating ghosts come from a hinterland of shadows. There was terror in such a place, and an even greater terror of finding herself alone there, with no house to return to. For had not her mother said that if Ioan went to warn Mariuca of the danger, there would be an empty home? Then her father must not go. But if he didn't warn her, then Mariuca would be in danger. Neither possibility held anything but cold comfort. She began to rock back and forth on the bed.

Gabriela interrupted her thoughts. "Did you see a spirit?"

"I saw something. Like steam. Did you?"

"Like smoke. It didn't scare me, though."

"Me neither."

In their minds, both girls replayed the scene in the summer loft, saw again the tendrils reaching into the night mist.

"Your father said there was no spirit. He said that the only bad spirit was in people's heads."

Doinitsa nodded. If her father was right (and, to her mind, he was right more often than anyone else she could bring to mind) and if her mother was right when she said that the God who was out there was good and kind – then between God and her Papa there would surely be some just intervention, which would bring them all back to a place of safety.

"Then it is not we who conjured the bad spirit, but they," she said.

In this, they found a certain relief, and the air in the room felt lighter. Even the cricket was silent, and in the new quiet the girls turned their minds to other thoughts.

"What about Mariuca?" Doinitsa voiced the question that hung in both of their minds.

They could picture her, up on the mountain, unaware of any impending danger.

"She must be warned," said Gabriela. Her brown eyes, normally so ready to open wide in laughter or surprise, were now focused and solemn. Doinitsa felt as if her friend were suddenly lost to her, and had entered into an adult world where there was no place for her, with her clamour of fears.

Gabriela stood up and went to the window. Drawing back the muslin curtain, she stared across the field to the wooden fence that ran along the road. At that moment the cricket emerged from its hiding place to spring, in a leap quite incommensurate with its size, onto the windowsill. Gabriela bent down, caught it in her hands and opened her thumbs just wide enough to peer at the little brown insect, now silent in the unfamiliar dark dome of her palms.

Doinitsa was soon beside her, her head close to her friend's, both of them staring down at Gabriela's hands, that looked as though they were clasped in prayer.

Then Gabriela half-spoke, half-whispered her plan to Doinitsa, who nodded, feeling herself suddenly transformed, as her friend had been a few moments before, into an adult woman of the village.

They both moved to the window. Doinitsa opened it far enough for Gabriela to release the cricket onto the windowsill where it sat for a moment, dazed by the sunlight, before leaping high into the air and disappearing into the grass.

There were two routes to Barbu's house: the shorter was along the main street to the outskirts of the village, the longer an overgrown towpath by the river. Ioan took the latter, preferring the vegetal world to that of humans, for the snags of bushes and brambles seemed to him far friendlier than the darts of people's prying eyes.

The river was swollen from the rainstorm. Where usually it ran in clear eddies, its white water breaking over moss-covered rocks, now it flowed brown and opaque and carried the bits and pieces it had picked up on its way down the mountain: twisted branches, the torn-away sole of a boot, a dirty sack that billowed above the waterline like a bloated corpse, before the current pushed it towards the riverbank where it bobbed, trapped against the rocks.

Try as he might, Ioan could put no order to his mind. His thoughts were as random as the flotsam that floated downriver. Too much had happened in too short a time, and he had slept little in the past two days. A fatigue came over him, so that his legs no longer felt his own, and he had difficulty lifting them over the fallen trunk of a silver birch that blocked the path. The upper part of the tree dangled in the water, its white branches outstretched like those of a drowning woman.

It brought back to him a memory: how once, as a small boy, he had stolen off in a small wooden boat with one seat in it and a paddle that had spent too long in the water so that the wood had rotted and split down the middle: with every pull, bits of it flaked off in the water. He had paddled downstream for two hours, going beyond the bend in the river that marked the boundary of land familiar to him, to where the river widened as it flowed through flatter ground, with fields stretched out on either side, and small farms dotting the landscape. Suddenly the speed of the current had picked up, and he realized that he was as insignificant to the river as a raindrop, and as feeble in its flow. He had felt fear then, and tried to steer the boat towards the bank, but the river would have none of it: his paddle was like a piece of straw caught in one of the winds that whistled down the valley in winter.

Fear gave way to panic that came with the knowledge that any action, however well devised, would be futile against such a force, and he abandoned himself and the boat to the current. The river gushed its way around a rock, and the eddy pushed him to the outer bend of a meander, and to the bank, where a willow's branches hung down to the water's edge.

He had caught one of the supple tendrils in his hand and gently, very gently, pulled himself to the bank, always with the fear that at any moment the branch would break away in his hand and the river carry him far downstream in its flow. Clumsily, he tied the boat's rope around the trunk of the willow before lying on the grass where he was found, face down and trembling, by some farmwomen. Later, back home in his village, he had taken a beating. Since that day, he had never ventured back onto the waters, preferring instead the safety of dry land. Now he felt as if he was in the river, which was neither a friend nor an enemy, but rather an indifferent great wet beast that carried him along, helpless as a child, in its relentless flow.

The sound of breaking twigs called him sharply away from his memories. Craning forward, he looked through the foliage, so lush after the spring rains that the track had turned into a green tunnel of leaves. There, cleaving a way through the undergrowth, was the burly figure of Barbu Temeru.

Ioan felt the strength suddenly return to his legs, and walked to meet his friend. The two men embraced, then stood for a moment in silence. From under bushy dark eyebrows, Barbu's black eyes stared out; under them were the smudges of fatigue that told of a night badly spent, and a household kept awake by its troubles. His face broke into a bitter smile.

"Things are in a sorry state when two grown men fear to walk along the streets of their own village. How are the girls?"

"Frightened."

"They are not alone. Our house rocks with fear. My daughter weeps. Tunde is beside herself."

Ioan stared at the ground. He felt for his friend, and for his own part in the trouble he had brought to his household. The dance, the girls' terror, Tunde's anxiety, Valentina's tears – all merged into a dark mire of confusion.

Barbu looked over his shoulder, then motioned Ioan towards a rock well shielded from the view of any eavesdropper, although few people passed this way.

The two men sat. Out of the corner of his eye, Ioan could see the sack, still bobbing up and down, swollen with air, trapped against the rocks.

"Tell me what happened after I left last night," he said.

"There was much talk against you."

"I can believe it."

"Tell me everything."

Barbu tore at a piece of lichen, so that it came away from where it had been anchored in the hollow of the rock. He crumbled it into green tufts in his hand as he told of how most of the families had dispersed quickly to their homes, as if afraid that the spirit might have kith and kin. Those that were left – Diaconu, Surdu, and Grigore and his friends – stayed up late, talking into the night. Barbu, finding their company not to his liking, had retired to bed, as had the rest of the family. He had fallen into a fitful kind of sleep, somewhere between slumber and waking, where the mind gets nothing but the worst of both states – troubled thoughts and scrambled dreams. Then he was fully awoken by the sound of a weeping coming through the walls of his eldest daughter's bedroom.

When he went to comfort her, he found her curled into a ball of grieving, so that it had taken him a while to unravel the knot of her sadness. She had told her story all piecemeal – words and tears and breath fighting each other – still, he caught the main direction of her story. From the veranda, she had listened to the men's talk. It was Surdu who wasted no time in proposing the banning, Diaconu who acquiesced with no opposition at all, and Grigore who had volunteered that he and his friends give their support by their attendance in church the next day, where they would take pleasure in putting a few noses out of joint by taking their places in the more prominent pews. It was then, in the dark, that Valentina knew there would be no wedding for her, for she could not couple with a man so ready to bring down harm on two young girls. Her tears flowed as much from fear as from grief, for she knew in the morning she would have to find the courage to confront Grigore, and his family and friends, with her decision to cancel a union that had been planned these last two months.

"She need have had no fear on that score," Barbu said. "For the next day, I made it known to Grigore and his folk that none were hereafter welcome under my roof, and that they should take their hats and bags and find some other lodging."

Barbu threw the remains of the shredded moss on the ground.

"She is well out of it," Ioan said, by way of trying to find some small comfort for his friend.

"That is what I told her. We never knew why she accepted him in the first place, none of us did. Yet she seemed to have her mind set on it, and she has a will as strong as her heart."

Ioan nodded, feeling that, with so many threads to untangle, now was not the moment to be probing into the mysteries that attracted a woman to a man, and vice versa. Besides, Barbu's account had started a new set of questions stirring in his head.

"It is strange, is it not, how speedily Surdu and Diaconu have gone from hostility to friendship…"

Barbu looked at Ioan for a good length of time, long enough for Ioan to hear the sound of some small creature rustling down by the water, where the roots of trees met the river.

"I have something to tell you, and it brings me some shame to say it."

The creature rustled some more, and then there was silence, but for the lapping of the water.

"I think I have had some part to play in this strange alliance."

Ioan looked at his friend in disbelief. This day, like the one before, was bringing too many odd events his way, and none of them to his liking.

Barbu spread his big hands across his knees and took a deep breath.

"I have reason to believe that Diaconu is the victim of blackmail."

Ioan listened in silence as his friend told of how Diaconu had confessed to him that the story of his dear deceased mother and sister was nothing but a web of lies.

"I think Surdu found out about Diaconu's deceit, and is using it against him."

Ioan shook his head. With his daughter facing a ban and his wife threatening him with an empty home, he cared little about the dishonesty of an old priest. Yet he waited for Barbu to finish his story, feeling all the while that it might contain a link in the chain that was closing in around him.

"If the truth came out that Diaconu has lied, while swearing in the name of God that he speaks the truth, the village would be a sorry place for him to show his face."

"But how would Surdu have known?"

"His nose is always in everything. Anca, his housekeeper, said that he had a visit from a man who wore the clothes of a councillor. He came and went discreetly, but others saw him too. He must have asked for an enquiry into the affairs of Diaconu from the Council of Birtiza."

A breeze stirred in the branches overhead. Ioan's thoughts buffeted about in his head.

"Why did you not tell me?"

Barbu stared down at his hands.

"I am sorry, Ioan. I thought it of little importance at the time. Diaconu seemed too weak to carry any great threat in him. I feared your reaction if I told you, with half the village already speaking ill of your name."

Ioan averted his eyes and looked at the river, lapping up its froth against the roots of the beech trees, coating their roots with an unwholesome brown foam. Then he saw the head of a water rat peek out for a moment from its hiding place, and disappear as swiftly.

An idea came to him. It brought with it the slender promise of a solution.

"We must go to Birtiza and get proof of Diaconu's lies. With that in our hands, and if Anca will speak out, we can show Diaconu up for what he is, and Surdu with him. No one will support a priest who lies, nor the man who blackmails him."

Barbu nodded. In the long hours before dawn, he had turned the whole coil over and over in his mind, and had come up with the same plan, but with a difference.

"It is I who must go, Ioan. I have had a part to play in this, and besides, your place is now here in the village. The girls will have need of you."

Ioan hesitated and watched the river, its surface thick and shiny, coated in mucus. Barbu was right, he thought. The girls would want him by their side, and they were not the only ones in need of his protection. His mind was already wandering up the mountain.

They parted on the towpath, in agreement that Barbu should leave by early light the next day. It was a good day's ride to Birtiza, in fair weather. They reckoned that with luck he could be back within three days, with some proof in his hands that bore witness to Diaconu's lies and Surdu's threats, which may yet serve to close the widening crack that threatened to open up and swallow them.

On his way back along the towpath, Ioan thought of the village and its houses – some of them big and rambling, others no more than leaning shacks with whiskered roofs to keep out the wind. He wondered, as he had so often before, why Surdu, or anyone else, should have such a hunger for power over the tilted, askew heap that was humanity.

The sun was setting when Barbu rounded the bend in the road that led from the towpath to his home. The house, normally welcoming with its lights shining through windows, was now shuttered and had the appearance of being asleep, or closed down for a mourning.

In the half-light, he scanned the field and the summer loft for any sign of movement, but could see none. It was the time of day when the sky and the earth blended into a single greyness, veiling shapes and blurring outlines. Yet he could see something white lying on the ground by the portal. When he got closer, he could make out the shape of Valentina's dog, curled up on the grass. As he approached it, he clicked his tongue to wake it, but it did not stir.

Even when he was standing above it, it lay inert. He nudged it with his foot and it rolled over on its back. Then he saw that it was dead by the thin deep cut that oozed dark blood in a clean line from throat to bowel, where some hand had cleft it.

23

In the darkness of the room, Gabriela lay awake listening to the soft breathing of Doinitsa beside her in the bed. Images floated into her mind, unbidden. The more she tried to chase them away, the more vivid they became: forest paths with lurching forms half-hidden behind tree trunks, a branch reaching out to claw at her, moonlight on shadows that moved towards her, then shrank back into their own world.

She turned in the bed to face Doinitsa. The closeness of her friend brought her some comfort.

To bring some quiet to her thoughts, she went over the plan in her mind. It was simple enough. The next day Doinitsa would feign a pain in her belly. With Magda distracted, Gabriela would slip away and take the back paths up the mountain. When her absence was noticed, as it surely would be, Doinitsa would say that she had returned to her house, worried about the state of her mother's mind and health. If Gabriela made good progress, she would be back home in the afternoon, before her absence had caused any alarm, reassured that Mariuca was warned of the danger that faced her.

The plan had seemed good enough by the light of day. She had even put aside the provisions she would take with her: a thick chunk of salty white cheese, cherries, some bread, a gourd filled with water from the well. When Doinitsa asked her if she felt afraid, she had said no, and meant it. Many a time she had been up the mountain road to visit Paraschiva: the route held no fear for her, nor any surprises. She had looked out from her place in the cart, wedged between her brothers, and seen the little tracks that led off into the woods, and found them enticing, the way they curved and disappeared into the undergrowth. But now, in the dark of the room, her only longing was to remain within the safety of the four walls and the warmth of the bed. She shivered, snuggling deeper under the cover, breathing in time with her friend.

The door creaked open. There in the light that spilled in from the kitchen, she saw the silhouette of Ioan Trifoi. She closed her eyes. If he found her awake, and took to comforting her, she might cry. If he put his arms around her to soothe her, she might divulge the secret. So, not trusting herself, she sealed herself into her own private world of darkness, and all that he saw were the heads of the two young girls peeping out from the coverlet, and the room, neat and orderly, with a chair where their clothes were laid out in perfect symmetry: the identical embroidered blouses, the thick cotton skirts, the floral headscarves. How innocent it all looked, he thought, and felt a pressure in his chest, where anger and guilt welled up inside him.

Moving to the bed, he kissed first his daughter's head, then Gabriela's. In the dark he could not see the flutter of her eyelashes that came, not from the flitting procession of dreams, but from the thoughts of a young mind awake, and alone with its troubles.

At the other end of the village, the night was filled with the dull echo of wood clapped against wood, as shutters were pulled tight, each dwelling closing down for the night, its occupants relieved to retreat behind the safety of doors and windows after a day of such turmoil.

Only one household remained wakeful. From the windows of Radu Surdu's home, pools of light illuminated the darkness, attracting an army of midges, who hovered and darted in a fierce geometric dance.

Inside, a scrawny young boy-man with pale skin and red hair looked around the room at the gathering, and wondered how he had come to be there. Danubiu Bratu was seventeen, and bewildered. It was all to do with the raising of hands, that much he knew. He had voted in church with the rest of them. Not that he cared so much about the expulsion of a strange young woman. He had hardly set eyes on her. Only on the night of the Lazarica festival. The little he had seen of her had not been unpleasant. The opposite, if he thought about it. Her dance was beautiful. More than beautiful. If he had had his choice, he would have kept her in the village. So he could not recall exactly why he had raised his hand. Except that it had all happened very quickly – Diaconu's sermon, the vote. There had been barely a moment to think. But he had hesitated. He knew the Trifoi family. Ioan had shown him how to plane wood to get a smooth surface. He had been at Doinitsa's christening. That Ioan's daughter should be bewitched was beyond him. He could not raise his hand.

Then someone had jabbed him in the back, and a jeering voice had said: "Are you still a boy, too young to vote?" The voice belonged to Mihai Marinescu, who throughout his short life had shown a passion for taunting Danubiu about the colour of his hair. When they were both younger, he would gather other smaller boys around him and lead a chant: "Danubiu, Danubiu, with all the carrots on his head. If we tore them out, would Danubiu be dead?"

Between the shove in his back, the sneer of the voice and the rustle of the raising of hands, Danubiu, in his confusion, had felt only the panic that comes to a lone boy isolated in a crowd, and knew vaguely, irrationally, that it had something to do with the colour of his hair. Still he had hesitated. For a spilt second. Then his hand had gone up, as if of its own accord.

Afterwards, everything had followed in swift succession: about a third of the men in the congregation, those who had not raised their hands, disappeared quickly down the road, keeping their wives and children close to them, not looking back. The others clustered around the church, excited, with a new sense of purpose, heads raised to where Radu Surdu stood at the top of the steps. He barely disguised the triumph in his voice as he announced the evening meeting, which, given the urgency of the situation, he required all present to attend.

Which they had. Looking around him, Danubiu saw the familiar faces of the villagers: Miron Corvan, Pavel Micu, the Barescus, the Illitch clan. He took comfort in the familiarity of the faces. He had grown up with their sons. He had played down by the river with them, diving half naked from the rocks in the warm weather. If they had all agreed to raise their hands, surely there could be no true harm in it? He told himself this as Radu Surdu stood up in front of the gathering and began to speak.

"Friends, I thank you for your vote. I thank you for your attendance." Surdu's eyes were bright. His voice was strong. With every sentence, he seemed to expand as his shoulders relaxed and his chest barrelled outwards.

"We have, by a majority, called for peace and order to be restored to our community, a peace and an order that we have a right to, for the sake of our health, our safety, and that of our children."

Surdu turned to Father Diaconu, who stood beside him, motionless but for the nodding of his head.

"In the last few months, we have been subject to strange forces, forces of evil." Surdu leaned on the word evil, and paused.

From where he stood, in the third row, Danubiu felt Surdu's eyes on him, as if he could see into his soul, and could read the doubt that had lodged there. In his confusion, Danubiu turned his gaze away, to the crowd. In the front row, he could see Grigore Rusu, with his square shoulders and short-cropped hair, and beside him, four of his friends, who looked as though they came from the same stock, with their thick necks, ruddy faces and pale blue eyes. Danubiu felt he was in the wrong place, at the wrong time, in the wrong company. And all because of a split second decision to raise his hand.

"We have lived through the worst flood in a decade. We have seen the invasion of rats of unnatural size. We have seen innocents in our midst possessed by the forces of darkness."

Surdu's voice filled the room, and a murmur of assent rose to meet it.

"An element that is foreign to the soul of our village has arrived like a plague to blacken our lives. Let us be brave, let us be ruthless even, in our actions to rid ourselves of the shadow that has fallen over us."

The murmur grew. From the back of the room came a shout of support. Surdu stared out over the rows of upturned faces.

"For do not be deceived. If we fail in our duty to remove the shadow, it will lengthen, even as we speak it is searching for us in the dark…"

Surdu's words reverberated around the room, and out into the night air, reaching the ears of those neighbours who lay awake in their beds:

"…and so we call for the suppression of the nefarious influence, that this woman who travels in the company of Satan be removed, along with others who are foreign to our lineage and whose behaviour is suspicious… so that goodness, and purity, and light, may return to reign in our village…"

Surdu paused, stretched out his arms to the assembly and waited. As if on cue, a cry went up. Danubiu heard it as a barrage of sound where words were like pieces of sharp rubble thrown around the room. "Yes!" "Let's be rid of her." "She means no good." "Foreign bitch!"

He stayed silent, his eyes on the floor.

The roar rose like a wave. Cresting on it was the voice of Surdu: "Any man not in agreement with the motion to drive out this shadow from our midst, let him raise his right hand now."

Every man present kept his hands by his side, Danubiu Bratu among them.

Gabriela had never walked alone in the forest before. Throughout the long sleepless night, she had prepared herself for the journey: she must not go too fast, lest she become exhausted; she must not drink the water too quickly, in case she ran out and suffered from a parched throat; she should not venture on to any of the smaller tracks, even though they may present themselves as shortcuts, for she knew how paths had a way of twisting and twining. Of all her fears, the greatest was to be lost in the forest in the dark, with the wolf's yellow eyes on her, or the breath of a bear close on her back.

So she had set out, later than planned, for Magda had kept watch over her, even though Doinitsa had played her part with conviction. It was midday before she had managed to slip away, when Magda had gone to gather fresh mint to make a brew to soothe her daughter's pains. The towpath had been easy. It was a shortcut she knew by heart; she found its familiarity comforting. With the sun overhead, Gabriela felt the fears of the night evaporate, and she rhythmed her breath to her pace. She had found the track that led up the mountain by the old moss-covered stone that marked its entrance. Up and up she walked, stopping only twice to drink from her gourd, in measured sips.

The climb steadied her mind. All would be well. She would reach Paraschiva's house by mid afternoon, deliver her warning with all the speed the day required, recover her strength, and return by nightfall. Paraschiva, she knew, would ask Pavel to accompany her back down the mountain, so the return journey held no fears.

She felt satisfied with her progress, even when the path grew steeper, and the shade of the trees darker. She noticed that their trunks were studded with the shapes of eyes. She felt they were watching her. On one side of the track, an ancient mulberry tilted towards her; its branches stripped of their bark, like arms that had been flayed, and in gashes in the rotting wood, groups of beetles had made their home.

Higher and higher she climbed, to where the bright green of beech and oak gave way to darker evergreens, to where the fronds of fir trees stretched out, bowing in the wind, like rags on old women's arms.

She remembered her grandmother, and the hush in the room where they had laid her corpse. It reminded her of the silence of the forest, and she was afraid. As she continued, she hummed to herself so that, in the company of sound, albeit her own, she should feel less alone.

Further down, a rider was making his way up the road, travelling at a faster pace, and gaining ground with every step of his horse, which he was pushing to the limits of its strength.

Mariuca waited for him in the glade, sure that he would come to meet her. Even when their appointed time came and went, she knew he would come. She sat under a beech tree. She would wait for him all day if need be, maybe even into the night. For if, as Paraschiva insisted, she must not see him again, then what was there to go back to? Her life stretched out ahead of her as vacuous as the counting out of days until she died: to live isolated there up on the mountain until Paraschiva moved on to another world, then to stay alone on the farm, walking in the hills with Pavel and Luka. For there was no place for her back in the land she came from, and none down in the valley. So where should she live but under the shadow of the mountain ridge?

Her mind searched for a way out of its despair, and found one, albeit narrow. It lay in defiance. Paraschiva had commanded her not to see Ioan. Mariuca would do anything not to anger her. Almost. But if the only way out of her impasse was disobedience, then so be it. Looking around at the play of soft afternoon light, the dance of the leaves, she resolved to be patient. With patience, she would wait for the patter of bad tongues in the village to die down. Even if she could not see Ioan for a month – two, six, a year, even – she would wait. In time, he would find a way to come back to her.

So she lay down on the moss, and stared at the leaves. If she screwed up her eyes and looked at the sun, it became a cross of light. It calmed her thoughts, which would otherwise have taken a lethal path of their own. Focus on the cross, the light, she told herself. She must not venture to a place of longing – for her own roof, her own hearth, her own children, and Ioan coming to her at night, her own husband. The futile yearning to belong, that's where the dark path would take her. Focus instead on the cross of the sun, and be glad of the warmth that had come her way – Paraschiva, Pavel, and a home, where she had never thought to find one. Then she recalled the bundle that had lain cold and blue beside her on the mountain, and tears blurred her eyes. She closed them to the light.

Footsteps in the leaves behind her. He had come. She knew he would. She sat up and turned in the direction of the sound. She saw his head and shoulders above the ferns that grew as high as a man's chest.

He stood in front of her, blocking out the sun-cross that had been her comfort. In the dappled light, she could see his face. It was her Ioan and yet not. His face had changed. It was grey, and the brightness had gone from his eyes.

He held out his hand to her.

"Come. Come quickly," he said.

Then he was pulling her away from the glade and deeper into the forest, moving too fast, so that she stumbled as she tried to keep up with him, there where the path was almost obliterated by brambles. From time to time he looked back over his shoulder at her, then beyond, in the direction of the road that led up the mountain.

They stopped in a clearing where a group of sour cherry trees grew, their red fruit an unexpected blaze in the green of the foliage. Breathless and speechless, they lay down on the ground that was thick with fallen fruit. Above them, the branches were alive with starlings, tearing at the cherries, their sharp twittering shredding the quiet of the afternoon.

He reached out for her and drew her towards him. He could feel the pressure of her cheek in the hollow of his shoulder, the curl of her scarf against his arm, the rapid rise and fall of her chest. He stroked her head with a steady rhythm and kept his voice level as he spoke.

"You must find a hiding place in the mountains, Mariuca. For a few days. They mean you no good, in the village."

He felt her breath inheld. Then she was sitting up and staring at him, her eyes filled with the fear of an animal being rounded up for market.

He searched for the right words, ones that would convey the danger and still offer hope. He told her of the banning of the girls, of the call for her expulsion. She shook her head, uncomprehending.

"Then it is my fault, Ioan..."

"No. It is the fault of no one."

"The girls, they asked me to show them the dances."

"There is no harm in the dances. I told them that. I've told them that all along. The harm was already there, Mariuca..."

She was no longer listening. Her shoulders heaving, she buried her face in her hands, and muttered words in her own tongue.

"It is no fault of yours, Mariuca. And now is no time for blame. We have no time. I came on horseback to tell you. I might have been followed. You must leave. As soon as possible."

Still she sobbed, so that he did not know if his words had reached her. He continued to speak, trying now to give her strength, telling her of Barbu's mission.

"If anyone can resolve this, it is Barbu," he said. "And when the madness has settled, I will come for you. Until then, it is not safe."

He looked again beyond her to the path that led back to the road, then at the woman who sat crying in front of him.

"You will take some provisions. And take Luka with you. Now you must listen to me. Listen." He took her hands and held them in his own.

"There is a cave directly below the highest point in the ridge. Hunters sometimes use it, but rarely…"

Now she was quiet. Now she was listening to him. She knew the cave. She had taken refuge there when the snows came. For her, it was a place where the winter wind howled like an angry animal. The memory of the black gape of its mouth froze her mind.

"You must go, Mariuca. As soon as possible. Tomorrow. Do you understand me?"

She looked at him blankly for a moment, then he detected the trace of a nod, and he pulled her towards him and held her head tight against his chest, as if he would hold her there forever.

And now there was a new quivering in her lips, as they reached up to find his, searching for a place of warmth, far from the cold dark gap in the rock face high above them.

The more the path climbed, the narrower and more overgrown it became. Gabriela's blouse was wet with sweat, her throat dry, her mind full of odd darts of thought that had no order to them at all. She stopped and drank gulps of water from the gourd. Behind her, the track she had taken had all but disappeared, hidden by the waving green of ferns. Ahead of her, the undergrowth grew so wild and high that if she dared to penetrate it, she would feel like a cricket walking through a field of long grass. Panic rose up inside her. She felt like one drowning.

"Help me," she whispered to the woods, to the trees, to the air.

The only response was the indifferent rustling of leaves in the wind, and, somewhere further off, a crow's mocking caw.

Then she heard it. She thought at first she must be mistaken. But it came again. From somewhere quite close. The whinny of a horse.

She crept through the ferns in the direction of the sound, moving with stealth, as slow and quiet as the feral cats that stole into the village at night. Through the mesh of brambles, she saw it. It was standing quietly, tied to a treetrunk, its head hung low towards the ground. She recognized it immediately by the amber sheen of its coat. It was the horse of Ioan Trifoi.

She stifled a cry of relief so as not to surprise the animal, but still it reared up as she approached, its ears back and eyes wild. Then it heard the girl's soothing voice:

"Hush now, hush. It's all right. It's all right. Now where is Ioan then, where is he?"

Looking around, she saw the gap in the foliage where leaves had been pushed aside by recent hands.

She advanced slowly, something in the strangeness of the day acting upon her like a warning, and she made no sound, not even when she saw them through the undergrowth.

Two bodies, one white and lean, the other curved and dark, interlocked on the ground. She saw the arch of the woman's back, her head tilted towards the sky, her face contorted, gasps coming from her throat as if she were dying. And Ioan Trifoi pressing down on her, his eyes closed, thrusting at her.

Gabriela didn't make a sound. She turned and ran. Stumbling, falling, then picking herself up again, she ran without heed for the direction she took, or even the path beneath her feet, until the ferns grew thicker around her, a sea of green, and closed over her head.

24

A silence settled on the house like a pall. Magda stood in the kitchen. Oppressed by the quiet, she started to make her own noise, clattering dishes, slamming down the water saucepan, chopping through the thick wads of mint with too much force, so that the floor was spotted with shreds of lacerated green.

So he had gone. In spite of her threats, he had saddled the horse and slipped away. And then the day had brought her the worry of her daughter sick in bed and no doubt missing her friend, who had insisted on going home to her mother. A gyre of emotions twisted inside her, and found no outlet. Reaching for a jug, Magda felt the impulse to smash it to pieces, and then go on smashing – the bowls, the stacks of plates, the pieces of crockery, that made up their once orderly lives.

She went to the window and looked out over the field to the fence and beyond. It was but a short walk to the village. As soon as Doinitsa was recovered from her pains, they would take the road together, closing the door behind them. She had promised Ioan an empty hearth. She owed him that. Two women were walking by. She recognized the sisters Constanza and

Aurel Avram. They often exchanged words with her at the village well. Now, as they passed her house, they lowered their eyes and hurried on. Magda drew away from the window.

She stood in the middle of the kitchen. Her limbs felt heavy, her feet dull weights at the end of her legs. Her whole body seemed too weary to remain upright. She swayed, then sank onto a chair, as if it were the only place left for her. She might have stayed there all afternoon but for the soft touch on her shoulder and the small voice in her ear.

"It'll be all right, Mama. You'll see, it'll be all right."

They lay immobile under the sour cherry trees, even as the sun dropped its light to touch the ridge of the mountain. Afterwards, she would blame herself. She had put herself first, choosing to keep him near her, to eke out what was left of their time together, when she knew that his place was down in the valley. Later, he would lay the blame on his own shoulders – again and again, down the years – and wonder how it was possible that his eyelids had closed of their own accord and his body, drained and spent, had felt as if it belonged nowhere but spilled out on the ground, and in spite of the fallen cherries whose stalks dug into his back, and the commotion of starlings in the branches, and the heavy dread that had settled in his stomach, he had fallen asleep.

So it was that when he opened his eyes to see the changed colour of the sky, he was on his feet in the speed of a breath, and the glade rustled with his hurry to be up and clad and on his way. She saw his haste, and took his hand only so that he could lead her all the faster out of the clearing.

They saw it at the same time. A flutter of white ahead of them, dangling from a bramble. It looked like a rag, a wayward fragment of cloth blown into the undergrowth. As they got closer, a gust of wind lifted it. Just for a moment. Just long enough for them to see the corollas of red and green petals stitched onto it in a floral symmetry. Ioan recognized them at once. He saw them every day, on the sleeve of his daughter's blouse.

He stopped in his tracks, his body and mind numb. Then he was crashing through the ferns and ripping away brambles until he held it in his hand. Still he refused to accept what was in front of him. There on the sleeve, overwhelming the delicate stitched-on flowers was the larger, misshapen dark bloom of a bloodstain.

"Doinitsa!" He cried out his daughter's name.

He looked at Mariuca. Her face was blank. Her mouth opened in a plea of sound.

"Doinitsa!"

"Doinitsa!" they yelled again and again, as they searched the glade, the woods and copses beyond, then a deep gulley where a stream wound its way around boulders. They called out until their throats were dry and their voices hoarse. They continued to cry out the girl's name, even as the night closed in around them.

All they received by way of an answer was the indifferent quiet of the dusk as it crept across the mountain.

Ioan rode as fast as he could. Where the path evened out, he urged the horse into a trot, but, for the most part, the rutted surface slowed progress to a lurching walk, so that Ioan's heart raced with impatience, while he tried to keep his grip steady on the reins.

Desperate, they had carried on their search by the light of a half-moon, until a wind had blown some ragged clouds down from the mountain peak, and their quest had become a futile groping in the dark, where any tree trunk could take on a human shape, and any being a rock or a bush. Even so, Mariuca refused to give up, until Ioan took her by the hands and told her, for her own safety, to return to Paraschiva's house, while he went down to the village to sound the alarm or – may God be on their side – find his daughter returned, unharmed.

Now, on his lonely ride down the mountain, he held on to this sliver of a beacon of hope. That his daughter be returned unharmed. It was his prayer, now, he who prayed so rarely.

The road curved away from the dark sweep of the mountain, turning towards the valley below, and the village. Many a time Ioan had felt the relief of the tired traveller at the sight of the clusters of rooftops, barely visible in the dark. He reined in his horse. It was as if the village had come alive and was glowing, orange, in the night. From his vantage point, he could see the flare of torches, bobbing like bright glow-worms in the dark. He dug his heels into the horse's sides and set off at a pace that endangered both rider and mount, whose hooves, clashing too hard and fast against a rock, sent sparks into the air. And all the while, somewhere in his mind, the words went round and round as if they had acquired a life of their own: Please, God, that she be returned, and unharmed.

People's shadows flitted along the main street, dark moths all heading in the same direction, drawn to the square outside the church, which was illuminated by the light of a hundred torches.

With faces distorted by the dance of flame and shadow, Ioan could barely make out the familiar features of friend or neighbour. He accosted the first person who crossed his path.

It was a young man, his face pale in the thin light of an oil lamp. Danubiu Bratu raised it above his head to get a glimpse of the strange rider with desperation in his voice, on a horse that was covered in a lather of sweat and flecked with foam that was flung from its mouth as it tossed its head, its eyes made wild by the proximity of too many flames.

When he identified the rider as Ioan Trifoi, he lowered his eyes, backed away without speaking, and, holding the oil lamp high above his head, he walked on, until his slight shape disappeared into the dark mass of the crowd.

There, on the edge of the surge, Ioan could see two silhouettes. If shapes could have spoken, these would have cried out to his soul. The rounded figure of a woman, one hand holding her shawl close around her, the other hand in that of a young girl whose head was tilted towards her, as if in search of protection. Ioan slipped off his horse and ran to them, clutching them both to him in a grip that would squeeze out all but the breath of their lives, now so dear to him.

"Magda! Doinitsa!"

He buried his head in his daughter's fine hair, and wept.

For him, time stopped, frozen in the moment of touch and gratitude. That she be returned, safe and unharmed. The prayer answered. His daughter, whole, in his arms. He felt the miracle, as he had felt it at her birth, when he had first cradled her.

Magda broke away from him. She was pale-faced, her mouth set in a thin line. She looked at him as if from a long way away, the great distance of betrayal between them.

"It's Gabriela, Ioan. Gabriela is missing."

Ioan stood, perplexed, unable to comprehend what his wife was saying. Gabriela. Missing. Not his daughter at all. One prayer answered, only to be followed by another evil. And his wife was in front of him, her face a cold white mask.

"I thought she had just gone up the road, to her home. That's what she told me."

Ioan heard the tremble in her voice that betrayed her anguish. He longed to reach out to her. But the stiffness in her body told him that she had closed herself against him. He felt for the cloth in his pocket and crumpled it into a ball. He could deal with none of it – the guilt, his absence, his deceit, the horror that now faced them. He pushed them all aside and found a new, clear point in his mind. Gabriela. Her safety. The sleeve in his pocket, with its red stain.

"Take Doinitsa home. Take the horse. Stay at home and lock the doors."

He took his daughter's head in his hands.

"I promise you, it will be all right. We will find Gabriela. But you are best out of this. Both of you."

"But – everyone is assembling in the square," Magda protested. "Radu Surdu has called a meeting to organize a search party."

"Go home, Magda."

"But I must search. We must all search. It was my fault, I –"

He pulled Magda aside, so that, in the half-light, their daughter would not see the sleeve he withdrew from his pocket, with its red and green embroidered flowers, and the deeper red of the stain. Magda looked at the cloth blankly for a moment, then put her hand to her mouth. When she spoke, her voice was barely louder than a breath.

"Where did you find this?"

"Up the mountain."

Magda nodded. Ioan looked away. There was a beat of silence between them, then the sounds of the village, roused from its sleep, rushed in to fill the space between them.

The last of the villagers were hurrying past, their faces pinched and pale under headscarves and hats. No one cast a glance at the man and woman and child who stood in a triangle on the street, as if unsure of which way to go.

Then the triangle broke apart, as the child and woman, leading a horse, moved away down the street, while the man followed the movement of the crowd towards the church square.

Torches, oil lamps, tallow candles: a mosaic of light met his eyes. The absurd thought crossed his mind that this could have been a Christmas scene, with all the closeness of a community in celebration, but for the faces. The light flickered on them, distorting cheekbones, deepening eye sockets so that pupils glinted out of dark hollows.

Ioan Trifoi paused on the edge of the crowd, caught, for a moment, between the urgency of his mission and the danger it represented. As his eyes took in the gathering, it was as if the village he had known all his life had suddenly become a stranger to him, as if the very ground under his feet was shifting, in this warp between the familiar and the strange. For the number of the villagers had swelled. There were faces, many faces that he did not recognize. He looked around, searching for allies, for friends.

He could make out the Temerus – Tunde and her daughters, their faces tight with fear – standing close to the Brumarus. The whole group stood well back from the main body of the assembled, clinging to the safety of the shadows. In the midst of them, Ioan could see Valentina, her dark eyes wide and staring.

At the front of the gathering, were the Illitch clan, Elena Barescu, and the rest of Surdu's followers from the village. They stood with torches held high and faces raised to the greater light that spilled down on them. For there, on the top step of the church, stood Radu Surdu. On either side of him were flaming torches mounted on stands. Behind him, the church doors were open wide; from within, pinpoints of light came from the multitude of candles – flickering, desperate prayers for the return of an innocent. In spite of the smallness of his stature, Radu Surdu's figure, illuminated in the darkness, took on the aspect of a divine silhouette, come to lead a community out of distress.

Under him stood Miron Corvan and Pavel Micu, and on the step below was a line of men: Grigore and his friends, and others whom Ioan did not recognize.

Radu Surdu took a breath and began to speak. His words were clear and clipped.

"Friends, followers, members of the community, we are gathered here for a matter of the utmost gravity. The darkness that has crept through our village, infiltrating our community, subtle and devious as the power of Satan, has now declared itself."

Surdu paused, and the silence was punctuated by the crackle and spit of a wayward flame leaping up into the night air.

"One among our midst, an innocent child, was touched by the hand of evil, and that hand drew her into a dance with Satan. And now we find that this evil has not one hand, but many."

The shadows cast by the torches danced an eerie, jagged dance across the portal of the church. The villagers watched, mesmerized by the wild choreography of light and dark, and the high, hypnotic voice of the speaker:

"As we stand here, we bear witness to its force. We took up arms against it. We tried to seal up its power. We banned the dance of Satan. So it comes to us as no surprise that this evil has manifested itself elsewhere. It is the nature of the battle. We were prepared for its onslaught. My good friends…"

Surdu spread his arms wide to encompass the men that lined the steps of the church. Their faces were expressionless, but their eyes gleamed.

"My good friends have left their wives, their children, their villages, to help us stamp out the cause of our distress. We thank them for their sacrifice in the fight against a force which threatens to engulf us in obscurity."

Miron Corvan and Pavel Micu murmured their agreement, which was soon taken up by the crowd.

"For this force has now acted again, as we knew it would, and claimed as its own the spirit of a young girl, has caught her in its insidious trap. Tonight, here, in this gathering, we pray for the soul of Gabriela, whose soul we fear has been drawn into the dark. As we speak, the frail body of a young girl is at the mercy of a heinous force. Let us call on our spiritual leader to lead us in prayer…"

Here, Surdu turned his head to acknowledge Father Diaconu who stood, half hidden behind him, in the shadows.

"…that we may seek out and bring back to the light a child that has been taken from us, enveloped by the shadows, and may, at this moment, as a handmaiden of the devil, be seeking a means to our destruction…"

Surdu paused again and looked out over the throng, his gaze probing the sombre space his words had created.

Ioan searched the crowd for any sign of dissent. There was none. Only Gabriela's mother, Irena, still frail from the fever, swayed for a moment, as if on the verge of collapse, and had to be held upright by two of the women who stood close to her.

Ioan's chest rose and fell with the rapid breath of anger. Clutching the ball of cloth in his hand, he pushed his way through the crowd, forcing a passage through the dark bulk of shoulders, dimly aware of the murmur that rose all around him, of the heads turned towards him, of the torchlight shone in his direction, as he made his way to the bottom of the steps and stood facing the lines of unfamiliar faces that stared down at him, and, above them all, Radu Surdu, with his black-eyed gaze, glittering yet impassive.

Ioan met his stare. A hush fell upon the crowd as he mounted the steps until he reached the impassable row of henchmen. Turning his back on them, he looked out over the mass of upturned heads, and prepared himself to speak. When he did so, his voice carried loud into the crowd.

"Listen to me, all of you. A child has gone missing. A child! Not the servant of Satan, a young girl!"

Ioan scanned the crowd for support. Looking down at row upon row of faces, he felt again that the village as he knew it had ceased to exist. Still he continued:

"This is not the time to be speaking about the forces of darkness. This is the time to send out a search party."

From the edge of the crowd came murmurs, quiet, at first, then rising.

"Whose side is he on?"

"He's never been in church this six-month."

"If anyone knows about the forces of darkness, it's him."

There was a shuffling of feet, and a ripple of movement at the back of the crowd, which set torches and oil lamps bobbing, casting haloes of light against the walls of houses.

Ioan could feel the crowd against him, with a dangerous hunger of its own. Then he thought again of Gabriela, lost, cold, afraid, somewhere in the mountains.

"I beseech you," his voice was straining now, somewhere between a cry and a plea, begging to be heard, "the girl is innocent. There are no forces of darkness. We must assemble a search party. There is no time to lose."

From the crowd, now, some new murmurs: "Perhaps he's right." "Find the girl, before it's too late." A ripple of confusion. "We should act first and talk later." The mob like a river with a divided current, swirling around on itself.

"Friends, friends…"

From where he stood above Ioan, Radu Surdu spread his hands wide in a calming gesture.

"…we will of course, of course, send out a search party. But if the child has been taken up by Satan, in what realms… where, but where, does one search for the invisible?"

Ioan's voice cut through the air.

"Enough of this talk of the invisible. Is this visible enough for you?"

He held out the sleeve. The crowd craned their heads, able to make out, in the flickering light, nothing more than a pale rag dangling from his hand.

"It is the sleeve of Gabriela's blouse. I know it to be hers, for my own wife stitched it."

There was a muffled cry. Irena's mouth was open, contorted in anguish.

"Where did you find it?" Surdu's voice boomed across the square, claiming the attention of the crowd.

"Up the mountain."

Surdu descended the steps. The row of men beneath him parted, so that he moved through them as a general moves among his ranks, to come level with Ioan.

"And what were you doing up the mountain?"

Ioan felt Surdu's eyes on him, though he kept his own on the crowd.

"What does it matter what I was doing up the mountain?"

"It matters a great deal."

"I often go up the mountain."

Ioan's voice trailed off into silence. The truth would bring nothing but shame and downfall. Surdu, seeing him falter, moved in as fast as a killer dog after a prey.

"What were you doing up the mountain?"

"I say it matters nothing to you or to anyone else what I was doing up the mountain."

His voice was met by the silence of the crowd. It was the silence of judgement. Ioan thought of Gabriela, and from the muddle of his mind, he found the lie it had been seeking.

"I was… gathering sour cherries."

In spite of the seriousness of the situation, someone in the crowd snorted with laughter. A man rarely, if ever, gathered sour cherries. It was women's work.

"You were gathering sour cherries?" Surdu's voice mocked.

"Yes, I… I, I needed to take my mind off… off the troubles of these past days."

"And these cherries, they take your mind off your troubles?"

"Yes."

"And did you find any?"

"What does it matter what I found?"

"It matters a great deal what you found." Surdu directed his gaze to the sleeve that Ioan held in his hand.

"I... I did not find any."

Ioan's mind was moving in ten directions all at once. He felt a rage sweep over him, rendering all thought silent.

"In the name of God, I will not stand here talking while Gabriela's life is at stake!"

His words rang out across the square. They reached the ears of some, then many. A murmur rose.

"He is right."

"What's all this talk of cherries?"

"Let's saddle the horses."

Caught by the current of sound, Surdu stood, uncertain, for a moment. Then, sensing he could not withstand it, he joined it.

"Organize a search party," he barked the command to the men who lined the steps, who at once dispersed to set about their task.

"Trifoi, you will take us to where you were... gathering sour cherries."

Ioan stared at him for a moment, then said, simply: "I will need a fresh mount," before he joined the men who were assembling in a corner of the square.

25

Barbu Temeru had seen the sun rise and set, and the stars come out and then hide themselves behind a veil of cloud. He felt a light but unrelenting drizzle on his shoulders and face. By his calculations, he should be no more than a few hours' ride from Birtiza. The last part of the road was the darkest, and the longest.

He thought of the day, filled with sights he'd never thought to see, and sounds he'd never thought to hear, he who had spent all of his life up in the village, cradled in the uplands, away from the traffic of mankind. Today, he had seen mountains give way to hills, and hills give way to a plain that stretched out to the horizon, its monotony broken only by the unrolling dirt road with its two deep ruts left by the passage of carts, and the meander of a muddy river that had turned golden at sunset.

He had passed peddlers, their wagons creaking and clanging with the jumbled mass of their wares: tin pots and knives, scissors and shears and billhooks, baskets, herbs and ointments and some fruit or vegetable that Barbu had never seen before, gleaming red and spiky as a witch's fingers. As the sun was setting, he had stopped to speak to an old woman bent nearly double under the weight of a basket full of hay that she carried with a leather strap fastened around her forehead. When she removed her load, he saw the welt on her skin, and guessed it was permanent, the mark of all the years she had borne her burden. He asked her how far Birtiza was along the way, but she simply waved her hand towards the horizon.

He had passed ragged tents flapping in the wind, and shacks that leaned against each other, holding themselves up in a mutual tilt that defied gravity. Around them, foraging in the mud, he had seen what he took to be young pigs, until he got closer, and saw they were children.

The rain was falling, fine but constant, when he arrived at what he took to be an inn. A farmer a few miles back had told him of its whereabouts, but in a dialect so thick that to Barbu's ears it sounded like a new tongue.

The house was dingy, low-lying, and built around a muddy yard. Barbu tied his horse to a post and knocked at the door. Through a crack in the slats of wood, he could see a dark eye staring out at him. He explained that he was a traveller on his way to Birtiza, in need of food and shelter for both himself and his mount, if their host would be so kind as to receive them.

He heard a wheezing and a coughing, and the click of the latch. The door opened to reveal an old woman dressed in black, barely distinguishable from the darkness of the room behind her. She said nothing by way of a welcome but, with a gesture of her head, indicated that Barbu should enter.

He found himself in a dank room, whose only light came from a tiny oil lap, and a listless fire in the corner, above which hung a black iron pot, whose contents explained the acrid smell that hung in the air, that of curdled milk and something rancid that Barbu was familiar with, but could not identify. Around the fire were the huddled shapes of three men. Like the old woman, they blended into the darkness of the room, for their faces were so covered in grime that the natural colour of their complexions had long since disappeared. One of them grunted at Barbu by way of a greeting, so he drew up a stool to take his place in the company of strangers.

No one spoke. No one asked him his business or where he had come from. When the old woman ladled some white liquid and some lumps of grey meat into a bowl and put in his hands, he spooned it into his mouth without speaking. The only sound was the intermittent spit of the fire as a raindrop found its way through an unfixed tile in the roof.

It was with relief that Barbu followed the woman across the yard to the stable and, having fed and watered his horse, found himself a pallet of straw on which to stretch out, thankful to be out of the presence of the unkempt silent men, and alone with his thoughts, which kept him awake with their rattling.

The search party scoured the forest throughout the night. On Surdu's orders, they lit a fire in the glade. It was their beacon, calling them back from the density of trees and undergrowth. The thirty men divided into four parties, each group fanning out to cover the gulley, the slope beyond it, the undergrowth, and the tracks that led up the mountain. Ioan Trifoi found himself with six men, none of them from the village. He noticed that while they left a space of some thirty yards between each other, two of them stayed near to him. He could hear them thrashing the bushes not more than ten yards on either side.

What did he care, so long as Gabriela was found? He pushed aside the twisted branch of a pine tree. He listened, in between the shouts of the men and the beating of bushes, for another sound – a moan or a cry – but heard nothing but the rustle of some small animal in the undergrowth. Once, some bird of prey flew past him, so close he could feel the air from the beat of its wings against his cheek. And so they searched, widening the circles, their shouts echoing through the forest, until the stars began to fade.

At dawn, they regrouped in the glade, where the fire was now a crumble of black ash and a pale plume of smoke.

Radu Surdu sat on a log, his back straight, betraying no sign of fatigue. Around him, the men, weary and silent, were slumped against tree trunks, some of them stretched out on the earth. Ioan Trifoi sat on the ground, slightly apart from the group, his head in his hands.

Not a man spoke, as if hushed by defeat, or the grey quiet of daybreak. The dying fire had ceased its crackling. A wanderer stumbling upon the scene could have been forgiven for mistaking the group for hunters, tired after the kill.

The sun rose over the ridge. Its first beams filtered through the forest as the birds started up their dawn chorus in a cascade of sound.

Above the heads of the men, starlings gathered in the branches for their early foraging. Radu Surdu looked up at them. For a long while, his eyes did not leave them, until, one by one, the men followed his gaze. There, above their heads, in the branches shaken by the birds' greedy beaks, were hundreds of clusters of ripe red fruit – a harvest of plump, crimson sour cherries.

Ioan kept his head in his hands, his eyes closed, so that Radu Surdu's voice came to him as from somewhere far away. It was as if he had been expecting it all along.

"So you found no sour cherries?"

Ioan raised his head. He saw the ground around him thick with fallen fruit, saw the circle of men's eyes on him, all as focused as hunters' eyes when their prey is surrounded. He knew why he had never hunted.

He shook his head. Truth to tell, his own fate mattered little to him. He felt like a man drowning, for whom the depths would bring a dark relief, but who had to stay afloat only for the sake of those he loved.

He said dully: "We must continue the search, now it's daylight."

"Oh, we will continue the search all day, and the next, and the one after if need be," Surdu's voice was smooth as oil. "When these men are tired, we will send others to replace them. But you, Ioan Trifoi, will not be among them."

Ioan Trifoi looked around the circle. The faces were impassive.

Surdu motioned to the two men who had not left Ioan's side throughout the night.

"Take him to the village," he said.

26

The rain had stopped. The sun shone clear and bright on Barbu Temeru's face as he rode down the main street of Birtiza. Never in his life had he seen such a coming and going: carts laden with glossy red and green peppers, bulging misshapen sacks of potatoes, unruly mounds of wild greens; donkeys plodding along, resigned to their towering loads of hay, or pieces of timber strung across their withers, wobbling appendages that threatened the safety of any inattentive passer-by. A jumble of smells assailed Barbu's nostrils: the tang of pike freshly fished from the river, the odour of curds, the sweat of the people who milled past him.

The Council of Birtiza was housed in a tall square building next to the church, at the end of a street lined with stern houses with unwelcoming stone façades. Barbu had no difficulty in finding it, for all the roads in the town - and in the whole region, it seemed to him - converged on this grey-brick edifice, with its windows so square and regular they appeared to have been the design of a mind with no time or inclination for anything resembling the lines of nature.

The massive oak doors were open, and through them passed an assortment of humankind: gentlemen in frock coats, haggard women dragging scrawny children by the arm, stout middle-aged women with headscarves fastened tightly under their chins.

Barbu tied up his horse to a waiting post, and joined the throng.

Once inside, he found himself in the biggest hall he had ever seen. Footsteps echoed on a polished stone floor, the voices of hundreds of people reverberated from where they sat on benches, row upon row.

Around them, the black-clad figures of members of the Council of Birtiza moved like stag beetles, the wide brims of their hats weaving in and out of the crowd like antennae.

Barbu stopped one of them as he hurried past. He was a pot-bellied, fleshy little man, neither of whose eyes could agree with the other, for each moved in its own direction, so that Barbu had a hard time deciding on which one to address. He settled for both, looking first at one and then at the other. When he explained that he had to see a member of the Council about a matter of the utmost urgency, the man tilted his head towards a bench at the far left of the hall, on which a dozen people sat crushed together, elbow to elbow. Barbu was about to tell the man that his business was not of a waiting kind, but the man's face had already disappeared beneath the lowered brim of his hat, and with hurried footsteps he vanished into the crowd.

So Barbu took his place at the end of the bench, next to one of the gentlemen in frock coats. The man glared at the wild-haired, mud-spattered traveller who had squeezed so close to him that the touch of his shirt was defiling the neatly pressed sleeve of his jacket.

And so Barbu sat, and waited.

Ioan Trifoi's hands felt numb and swollen, where the ropes had cut off their blood supply.

In his mouth, he could taste the salt of his own blood. The ropes. The blow. Dislocated scenes jerked their way into his mind. The ride down the mountain. Two men so close to him that their stirrups clashed against his. Other men behind. In front, Radu Surdu. The entry into the village. Streets lined with faces, pale, some blank, some disbelieving, some jeering. Women with hands clasped in prayer, men – some his neighbours, some whom he had counted as friends – staring straight ahead of them, not looking him in the eye. No one, not a soul, daring to break the line of watchers to step forward in protest. Holding, instead, their children close to them. Keeping their heads level, not looking up at the men on horseback who rode past them.

When they reached Radu Surdu's house, the burst of unexpected laughter that came when one of the men said: "Well, now we've got him, where do we put him?" For no one had ever been arrested before in the village. There were no police, no courthouse, no gaol. The black rage in Radu Surdu's eyes. For the thing Radu Surdu most hated was being laughed at.

"Take him to the woodshed."

They marched him down the long path to the shed by the stream that ran at the bottom of Surdu's garden.

They shoved him down onto a high-backed chair, tied his hands behind his back. Ioan could hear the innocent rush of water from the stream until the dull crack of wood against his skull, and in his mouth, the taste of blood.

They passed another rope around his shoulders and pulled it tight. Then another around his feet. They left him, closing the door behind them, drawing the bolt, leaving him in the half-dark of the woodshed, their prisoner.

The only movement he could make was the twisting of his neck from side to side, but this sent sharp darts of pain through his head, so he sat still, and listened.

He heard the scrape of wood on stone, the creak of two chairs under the weight of men, the mumble of voices.

They spoke in a dialect different from that of the village, so Ioan had to strain his ears to hear them. He could make out only disconnected phrases:

"…carry on the search… child killer… get rid of them once and for all… foreign scum…"

Then, as far as Ioan could discern, the conversation turned to the length of their watch, and when and what they would eat for lunch.

Foreign scum. Mariuca. They would not find her now. By now she would be gone, already making her way up to the mountain ridge, and the cave. Soon Barbu would be back with help. But in some part of his mind there was an insistent voice, a murmur that would not go away. And he saw again the look Mariuca had given him when they parted: the dark anguish in her eyes that told him she knew why Gabriela had exposed herself to the dangers of the mountain. She knew whom it was that Gabriela was trying to save. The look had told him that she would not abandon the young girl, as the young girl had not abandoned her.

In spite of the pain, Ioan twisted his head from side to side, trying to loosen the rope around his shoulders. It gave a fraction. He looked around the woodshed. There, in a corner, half hidden behind the woodpile, he could discern the wooden handle of a trowel, maybe, or a shovel. Either would do. Even if there proved to be no blade at the end of it, the handle itself would do to bang a man about the head.

He rocked back and forth on the chair, edging it, little by little, to the woodpile.

Inch by inch, he advanced towards the handle. He would put his hands on it.

He was close to it now. It was within an arm's reach. He twisted his shoulders again, trying to prise free his limbs. He rocked the chair again, too strongly, this time. It made a loud scraping sound on the floor.

The sound of the bolt being drawn back. A sudden flood of light. The man stood over him, looking down on him.

"Restless, are we? Bored?"

Ioan looked up at him, and saw the glint in his eyes.

"I had the needs of nature," Ioan mumbled.

The man sniggered. He raised a fist and brought it down on Ioan Trifoi's stomach. Ioan felt a wave of nausea as the chair rocked one last time, then toppled over. A thud, as his head hit the hard packed earth of the woodshed floor. And then the boot in his groin, and again in his ribs, and again in his stomach, and the voice, speaking in time to the rhythm of the blows:

"Piss in your pants, child killer, shit in the seat of your trousers. For that's what you are, piss and shit."

Then the sound of the door slammed shut, the bolt drawn, and him lying on the floor, dazed by the pain and the filaments of sunlight that came through a crack in the wooden door. Through the blur of broken light, he could see the man's shoulders relax, as he took out a pipe, lit it, and settled back on his chair.

Barbu had waited all morning, watching the motley mass of humanity entering and exiting the councillors' rooms. Like ants, he thought, little ants each one intent on the individual trail of its existence. A pressure was building in his chest. If he waited his turn, he calculated it would be late afternoon before his voice was heard. Too late to set out on the long day's return journey.

When the door next opened and a tired elderly couple hobbled out, he waited no longer. Striding across the floor, ignoring the voices that rose in protest from the bench, he walked into the room and slammed the door shut behind him.

A man with a puffy pale face and receding chin sat behind a desk stacked with papers. To Barbu's eyes, he resembled a worried rodent.

He looked up at Barbu and blinked nervously, startled by the huge man with wild hair and wilder eyes who had entered his office with all the tumult of a spring tempest. He was about to motion Barbu to take a seat, when he saw that he had already sat down.

Without preamble, Barbu began his tale. As he spoke, even to his own ears it sounded far-fetched, some fable invented to tell around a fire. Girls who danced at night with will-o'-the wisps, their banning by the priest, a small-minded man able to take over a whole village, a young woman who had come over the hills and whose life was in danger. When he mentioned Radu Surdu by name, he detected a flicker in the man's eyes, and noticed the way his fingers traced nervous circles on the desk. As he spoke of his suspicion of Surdu's blackmail of Diaconu, the circles got faster and faster.

Barbu finished his tale, sat back, and waited.

The thin man coughed, looked at the wall, then out of the window, then back at Barbu again.

"This is a very serious matter," he said. "And one beyond my jurisdiction. I think we shall have to refer it to the Chief Councillor."

"The Chief Councillor?"

"Yes."

"Then let me see him."

The man laughed a nervous, thin laugh.

"I will, of course, put you on the list right away."

"The list?"

The man coughed again, and a muscle under his right eye began to twitch of its own accord.

"There are people who have been waiting for two weeks to see the Chief Councillor."

Barbu's fist on the desk set the stacks of papers shaking. The man's fingers stopped their fidgeting in mid-circle.

"In God's name, there are people's lives at stake. Who knows what will have happened to them by then? It begins with the banning of young girls and the slitting open of a pet dog. Who knows where it will end? People are at each other's throats. It will not be the first time the river has run red…"

The man stared at Barbu. With the anxious shaking of his head, he looked to Barbu like a frightened rabbit. The man was out of his depth, of that Barbu was certain. He reckoned his job must be to keep trouble away from his superiors' doors. And now, Barbu thought, he is caught, for he knows this trouble will not be brushed away. In the man's agitation, Barbu saw a chink, a breach which, if widened, might be broad enough in which to wedge a hope.

He leaned across the desk.

"I have a request," he said.

The man blinked quickly, unsure of what scheme the wild man was on the point of conjuring.

"I have no need of any decision on your part concerning this matter. I understand that, given its gravity, it must be handled in due course by the Chief Councillor. I have only need of a document, with the stamp of the Council, to say that the whole matter, including the serious charge of blackmail of a member of the clergy, will be investigated."

Barbu's words hung in the air. The thin man's eyes moved rapidly from side to side. The fingered circles started again, more slowly this time. Then his face relaxed. A document that promised nothing more than an investigation. This he was authorized to write. He did it all the time, knowing full well that, for the most part, no investigation ever followed. It was a harmless enough gesture, and one that would rid him of this unruly man from the mountains.

"I… I think that would be possible," he said.

They looked at each other, both men locked, for a moment, in an expression that betrayed nothing of what either of them was thinking. Then the councillor reached out for a piece of paper and began to write. There was silence in the room but for the scratching of the quill. The man blew on it, stamped it, and handed it to Barbu, as if happy to be rid of the whole affair.

Barbu stared at it, then handed it back to the man.

"What's wrong?" The muscle under the man's eye began to twitch again.

"I can't read," muttered Barbu.

The man smiled with relief, took the paper, and read out its contents in a high monotone, like a violin stuck on one note.

Although the text was short, it was full of long words and convoluted sentences, so that Barbu felt as though his mind was a skein of wool that someone had unravelled and tied into knots. Still, he understood enough to know that contained in the document, with its spidery calligraphy, its flowery language and its official stamp, was the word blackmail. The force of it was his only chance of salvation.

Barbu took it, folded it and placed it carefully in his pocket. He was about to thank the man and leave when he paused. Spreading his hands on the desk, he said:

"I have one other small request to ask of you. It will take but little of your time."

27

Footsteps, and voices.

Ioan Trifoi had no idea of how long he had lain there, or of when he had lost consciousness. He calculated, by the dimness of the light, that it must be nearing sundown.

He could make out the rough dialect of his two guards and then another, younger voice, speaking in the accent of the village.

"We can arrange it for you," one of the guards said. The other laughed.

"No. No, thank you," said the young man. The voice was familiar to Ioan, but, with the aching of his body and the dryness in his mouth, he could not put a face to it.

Another rough laugh: "You'll miss out on the fun."

"More than fun. A right little party. Up in the hills," the other guard joined in.

"I will stay here. Thank you. I volunteered for the watch." The young man's voice quavered.

"There's plenty of other volunteers to watch over this… pigshit."

"No, I – can't."

"Suit yourself."

Footsteps receding. Outside, now, all was still. The owner of the young voice must be alone, thought Ioan. From where he lay on the floor, he craned his head forward.

In the early evening light, through the crack in the door, he could make out little more than the narrow shoulders, the head with its growth of curly hair. It was then that he knew the name of the owner of the voice. By the colour of his hair.

"Danubiu," he said, but was surprised when no sound came. His mouth was clogged with dried blood.

"Danubiu," This time his voice was a hoarse whisper. He saw the young man flinch.

"Help me. You can help me."

Danubiu turned his head.

Ioan's voice was a rasp. It was as if each word had to be pushed out of his mouth.

"Danubiu, you have seen my daughter baptized. You know I would never lay a hand on a child. You know that, Danubiu. You know it."

The young man remained silent.

"Danubiu, can you live with this on your conscience for the rest of your life? These men, they are bullies, cowards. They run in packs."

In spite of the pain, Ioan was choosing his words with care. He had seen Danubiu as a child running away from the bigger boys, bruises on his arms and the stains of tears on his face.

"Danubiu, hear me."

The young man said nothing. The silence stretched over seconds, then minutes.

The voice, when it came, was barely audible.

"I am under orders. I can't speak to you."

Ioan let out a deep breath.

"I can't disobey orders." The young man's voice was hesitant.

Ioan whispered to himself, in the dark: "You just have."

Now it would be a question of time.

Then his head fell back on the floor, and he lay there, waiting.

The drumming of hooves echoed in Barbu Temeru's head, even after he had reined in his horse to a halt as they approached the village. He had ridden at a cruel pace. A road had never seemed so long, nor time so distended.

All day thoughts had jostled for a place in his head. Doubts, too. One, in particular. The thin man in his office. The speed with which he had agreed to Barbu's demand. What if the document's words were not those that the man had read out? The spidery hieroglyphs could have been bird droppings, for all the sense they made to Barbu. He thought back to Birtiza. Three times he had stopped men in the street, brandishing the paper in front of them, asking if they could read. One after another they had shaken their heads. In desperation, he had accosted a gentleman, a learned man by the look of him, but when he saw the official stamp, he had hurried on his way, wanting no involvement. So Barbu had decided that he might waste all day trying to find a man who was both learned and kind. Instead, he had mounted his horse and gone on his way.

Still, the question irked him. He had had all day to work out a plan, in time to the rhythm of the horse's hooves. Ioan Trifoi's house, he felt sure, would be watched. No friend or neighbour could be trusted, not since suspicion had crept into the village like a rat that steals into a house in the middle of the night. He would go to Radu Surdu's directly, alone, armed only with the official stamp of the Council of Birtiza. Strange, he thought, that one circular blotch of ink on a page could yield such power, and over so many.

But first, he had to seek out another person, one in whom he could place his trust.

He dug his heels into his weary horse's sides, to quicken its pace.

Paraschiva dragged her old bones up the mound. Each step reminded her of her own mortality. At one point, out of breath, she stopped to look down at her house. There, at the portal, stood Mariuca. She had kept a lone vigil throughout the previous night and most of the day, looking out over the valley, watching the men ride up and down the mountain road below, scanning their movements for any sign that Gabriela had been found. She would not listen to Paraschiva's pleas that she should heed Ioan's warning and take refuge in the cave higher up the mountain. When Paraschiva looked into her eyes, she saw that it was the young woman's guilt that held her as fixed as a sentinel. It was then that the old woman knew that any power she had lay, not in trying to shift the will of Mariuca, but in invoking the guidance of the spirits.

So she climbed the mound, willing her bad knee not to give way under her. One step. Another. This one for Gabriela. This one for Mariuca. This for Ioan. Now this one for Pavel. These were the steps of love. They took her to the top of the mound.

She reached the broken tree trunk. The crow's feather had gone. She shivered.

Around her, the fronds of pine trees cast shadows on the ground. Closing her eyes, she called on the spirits. They came as if from afar, their sound barely perceptible, like the distant beating of wings.

With a sudden rush, they were upon her. Inside her head, she heard the whispering chaos of their voices. Then the sound died away, and in its place was the vision of something dark flapping in the wind. It came towards her, enveloping her in a swathe of black, covering her body and eyes in a shroud of darkness. Then a spot of light. The point grew to form the shape of a head. The pale face of a young girl, her eyes closed. The light extended into the body of the girl, peaceful, as if asleep, covered in leaves, quite still, but for the movement of her chest that rose and fell with her breath.

Then the girl faded away and in her place came another vision, another face, another body. It was a man lying in his own blood, his face swollen, twisted with pain. She knew the man. He was one that she loved. She swayed, almost fell to the ground, but other visions jostled for her attention. A mob that had come alive, bristling with staves and knives; they moved inexorably across mountains, and borders, and time. They were as perennial as the harvest, only their yield was blood. They vanished as quickly as they had appeared, and all that remained was the dim veil that had wound itself around Paraschiva's body, her dark companion.

She shuddered, mustered her strength to cast it off, and returned to the mound, to the broken trunk, to the late spring evening.

The stars had come out, studding a deep indigo sky.

She made her way down the mound, steadying herself, cursing the slowness of her legs. For she longed to tell Mariuca that the spirits had shown her Gabriela alive, and breathing.

Of the rest, she would say nothing.

A half moon rose in the sky, casting its light on the façade of Radu Surdu's house, with its round windows revealing nothing but darkness behind them. The front doors were shut. On either side was the shadow of a man. From where he stood, hidden behind the trunk of a beech tree, Barbu Temeru could not make out their faces, but saw that each of them held a club by his side.

He took a few deep breaths, and reached inside his trouser pocket to touch the document. Then he felt for his belt, and his hand closed around the handle of his knife. He had no wish to use it. It had not been a part of his plan. But the plan had changed, as the village had changed. He replayed in his mind the sequence of events: his return home – the house dark, the door locked, then the bolt withdrawn, Valentina's face haggard from her sleepless vigil for her father's return; the tremble in her voice as she told of all that had happened in his absence: Gabriela's disappearance, Ioan's arrest, the villagers all against him, his imprisonment, rumours of what lay in store for the inhabitants of the farm up the mountain.

"And did no one intervene?" Barbu asked, keeping his voice low and calm only for his daughter's sake. She had shaken her head. "There are many more, now. They came from other villages. From Birsata, from Vatu…" And she had broken down, and wept. He had calmed her, to make her listen to what she must do. The piece of paper taken from his pocket and carefully placed into her hand. The fear in her eyes, then her nod, her acquiescence, her hand raised in farewell as he left, as quickly as he had arrived, but not before he had taken down the knife on the wall, the one he used to cut the pig's throat in the autumn. He had not thought to use it in his lifetime on the flesh of a man, but times had changed, he thought, and it was with anger, as well as fear, that he reached for it.

He held it now, as he stepped out from behind the beech tree. He noticed how the handle slipped in his palm, which was wet with sweat.

He paused, clinging to the shadows, knowing that once he emerged from them, there would be no retreat. Then he let his arms fall to his sides, threw back his shoulders, and crossed the street to the house.

The guards saw little of his coming. He was well matched with the night, with his face and clothes covered with the dirt of two days' travel. But they heard the advancing footsteps, and in unison they raised their clubs.

Barbu Temeru stood facing them. They were illuminated by the light of the moon. He was taller than either of them by a head. He looked down on them as if they were boys and their clubs nothing but sticks to play with.

"I demand to see Radu Surdu." His voice was low, but the glower on his face left neither of the men in any doubt but that he could raise it.

"We have orders that he is not to be disturbed," said one of the guards.

"Tell him I have here a document that concerns him greatly."

The men glanced at each other. If they disturbed their leader, who had not slept these last two nights, they could look to their own skins. If they failed to wake him for a matter of some weight, they were courting an ill fate. Barbu saw their uncertainty.

"Tell him I have in my hands a document…" He raised his head to the impenetrable blank gaze of the house, and called up to the round windows: "…from the Council of Birtiza."

There was silence, as if the house had swallowed his sound.

The guards stared at him, taken aback by this man who dared to shout out at night while the rest of the village, by day, had kept their silence. Their hands tightened on their clubs.

Then the click of a window being opened above their heads. A voice, high, thin, unmistakable.

"Show Temeru into my study. I will be there shortly."

The guards' faces relaxed. The decision had been taken out of their hands. They pulled open the door and led Barbu Temeru down a long corridor lit at intervals by oil lamps that hung in the alcoves of the walls. They ushered him into the study and left, closing the door behind them.

Barbu looked around him. A flickering candle on the desk shone on neat stacks of papers. They reminded him of another desk, another pile of documents. On the wall opposite, he saw the giant shadow of his own head, its outline quivering in time to the movement of the flame.

Footsteps. The door opening. Another shadow next to his on the wall, doing its own strange dance. The voice, oily, quiet.

"I believe you have come to speak with me. Please, take a seat."

"I prefer to stand."

"As you wish."

Surdu looked up at the dark giant who towered over him. Then he turned away to sit opposite him, behind the desk. Barbu noticed the sheen of sweat on his bald head.

On the wall, the gold pendulum of a clock gave out a pale gleam. From within it came the faint hollow sound of ticking.

Barbu put his hand in his pocket, took out the document and held it up so that the light of the candle shone on the stamp of the Council of Birtiza.

The men's eyes locked in a stare.

"May I see it?" Radu Surdu reached for the document. Barbu withdrew it a fraction, so that it was just beyond Surdu's outstretched hand. Surdu reached for it again. This time, his fingers closed on the stiff paper. He grabbed it, clutching it in front of him, his eyes scanning the text. The face in front of Barbu was blank as a mask.

Then the eerie sound of laughter.

"This is a nonsense! A foolery. You have read it, I trust?"

There was mockery in the voice. Radu Surdu knew that many of the lowlier families in the village could not read, the Temerus among them.

Barbu said nothing. He stared, and waited.

"Ah, perhaps not," Surdu said. "Then let me read it to you."

He raised the paper and read, by the light of the candle:

"It says that… 'The bearer of this document has visited the Council of Birtiza, and that the Councillor who received him has decided that his case will be without outcome, given the impossible nature of his account, and the lack of his authority.'"

Radu Surdu laughed again. Still Barbu said nothing, but watched as Surdu lowered a corner of the paper to the candle. A roll of flame crept up the document, transforming it into a wafer-thin curl of black paper, which became a scattering of black flakes on the desk.

"Now what is your document worth?"

Surdu looked at Barbu. Barbu held his gaze.

"Everything," Barbu said. "For if it was worth nothing, then why did you burn it?"

Between them, the candle flame bobbed up and down, a bright tongue eager for another morsel.

"It was worth nothing, and, in any case, it no longer exists."

Barbu detected a tremor in the voice. He continued: "I had the notion to request a written copy. The Councillor in Birtiza was most obliging. It will by now be with someone I trust," he said. "If I am not back within two hours, they will pin it to the door of the church. Then the whole village will have this… worthless information…"

A glint of satisfaction came into Barbu's eyes at the same time as it disappeared from Surdu's.

"You have used the blackmail of a priest to achieve your ends. I'm sure the village will be most interested to hear of it…"

Radu Surdu stared straight ahead at the wall opposite.

"So I'd best be on my way," Barbu said, turning to the door. "But I am not leaving alone." Barbu leaned down over Radu Surdu, so that their shadows blurred and became one on the wall.

"Ioan Trifoi is coming with me. You will release him."

Radu Surdu rose without a word. In silence, he led Barbu down the corridor to the back of the house, and out to the woodshed.

When they arrived, they found two empty chairs, the door of the shed open wide, and a pile of abandoned ropes, a dark coil on the floor.

"Where is he?" Barbu growled. "What have you done with him?"

Radu Surdu's face was in the shadow, so Barbu did not see the almost imperceptible nod, the signal to the guards who were silently approaching. Before he could turn around, Barbu saw the ground rise to meet him, as he was felled by a double rain of clubs.

28

At the pressure of a hand on her shoulder, Mariuca awoke with a start.

Paraschiva stood above her, the dark silhouette of her head framed by the shape of a bat's wing full of stars. The girl had fallen asleep, hypnotized by the dance of the torches weaving in and out of the trees far below.

"It is all right." The old woman's voice was steady. "Gabriela is alive."

The young woman jumped to her feet.

"The spirits showed me."

Mariuca clutched Paraschiva's hand. "Please God," she said. The old woman looked into her face. It was thin and frightened, and had lost its lustre. Only the dark eyes shone with a belief born out of desperation, a faith in voices from a world beyond.

The two women stood, thus, holding hands, caught in something between a prayer and a plea, watching the torches flicker in and out of the trees. They continued to watch as the lights formed a curve, each one like a jewel in a bracelet of diamonds, moving out of the forest and onto the mountain road. Here, the curve straightened into a line. The women stared, expecting it to move down the mountain, willing this to be a sign that the search was at an end, that the spirits had been right, that Gabriela had been found alive. "Please God," Mariuca mouthed the words to herself. Then she held her breath and waited.

The line of light hovered for a moment then, instead of turning down the mountain to the village, it moved in the opposite direction, up the road, towards them.

They stood transfixed, watching the lights advance. Then, in a flurry of movement, they turned towards the house. Paraschiva pushed the girl in front of her.

"Run! Run up the mountain! Hide!"

The young woman would not leave her side.

"Run! It's you they are after. They'll not want my old hide!"

Still, Mariuca kept pace with her, holding tight onto her elbow, supporting her. Paraschiva pulled her arm free.

"Go!" she shouted.

The young woman said nothing, but stayed by her side. Paraschiva was struggling for breath. She stopped and turned to face the girl. Behind her, the lights were moving up the mountain, a parody of some festive procession.

"Go, please." The old woman was pleading now. "For me, for Ioan. Think of Ioan."

Still the girl would not move. Paraschiva caught her breath and shouted towards the farm: "Pavel! Pavel!"

They caught sight of him. He was already running across the yard to where they stood. He, too, had seen the lights. Behind him, like a shadow, ran Luka.

They could hear voices, now, carried up through the funnel of rocks.

"Pavel!" Paraschiva took her son in her arms, and felt his big frame envelop her. It was as if she would stay there, protected from the harm of the night.

Then she broke away.

"Take her! Take her up the mountain. Now! Go, now!"

He had understood. He took Mariuca's hand. She wouldn't move. He saw his mother's face, pleading, and he knew what he must do. He pulled Mariuca towards him, dragging her behind him as he half walked, half ran towards the path that led further up the mountain.

Paraschiva saw her struggle, trying to slip out of his grasp.

"Go!" she called after them.

Then she watched as the girl turned her head to look back at her. Her mouth was twisted. She was trying not to cry.

And then she had turned away and was running with Pavel, across the yard, over the grass, to the opening in the leaves that marked the track to the mountain ridge.

Ioan Trifoi swayed and had to steady himself on a branch that hung low over the towpath. He forced himself to inhale deeply, but with each breath he felt the pain, as if some sharp stone was embedded in his chest.

The night swirled around him. If he looked up, the grey clouds seemed to be whirling in a dance of their own around the moon, which lurched across the sky and, with his blurred vision, he saw it drift apart to form two silver discs.

He breathed. The pain grew, then subsided, then returned. He must go on. Somehow, he must reach those that he loved up the mountain. Inside him, a broken struggle of muscle and bone warred against his will to continue.

He forced his mind into a place of focus that was beyond thought, or fear, or despair. Beyond all physical pain. He put his attention into the path in front of him. His legs were heavy, he felt the trickle of sweat down his chest. He began to walk. One step, then another.

Beside him, the river flowed past like some sleek, oiled animal, mocking him with the ease of its flow.

Mariuca and Pavel ran on and up, the only sound, their own feet trampling leaves on the path. Luka ran ahead of them, with the quiet stealth of the wolf. The track narrowed. In the dark, stones and rocks and trees, familiar by daylight, became misshapen lumps, dark twisted figures. They came to a place where the track forked in two. One way led up to the mountain ridge, the other curved and dipped its way into a tunnel of darkness, framed by the branches of pine trees. They paused. There was silence, but for their quick breath and the quiet panting of the wolf-dog.

"Go back, Pavel," she whispered. "Go back now. For Paraschiva."

Her eyes implored him, but in the dark, he could not see them. He could make out her arm, raised, pointing back to the path they had taken. He shook his head.

"Go back. For Paraschiva."

The moon came out from behind a drift of clouds. He saw her look, and understood it. His heart was pulled in two, with only one beat to decide which way to go.

Then the moon disappeared. In the darkness, he heard the rustle of foliage. When the silver light returned, he stood alone on the path, looking at the dark gap in the leaves into which Mariuca and the dog had vanished.

Paraschiva lit a fire, in spite of the warmth of the June evening. She looked around at the orderliness of the kitchen. Then she walked slowly to the shelf, poured herself a glass of tuica, and sat, and waited.

She did not have to wait long.

She heard the scrape of the wooden gates being pulled back. Shouting. Footsteps in the yard. The squawking of hens. More shouting, closer, now.

She stared at the fire. A log became dislodged. She focused on the orange cavern, the space where the coal had been.

The door burst open. There were seven of them. Two of them she recognized from the village – a thin man with a sallow skin and dark eyes and hair, a bony head; a big man with a fat nose and stubble on his chin. The others she had never seen before. Two of them looked like brothers, with their short-cropped fair hair and ruddy complexions. The others she hardly had time to see at all. They moved quickly into place behind her. One of them stood at the blind side of her face. But she could hear him. He spoke loudly, in spite of his proximity.

"Let's have us a drink with the old witch. Want another drink, old witch?"

Paraschiva said nothing.

"If she tells us where the bitch is."

"Search the house and yard." One of the red-faced men barked out the order, at the same time as a hand pulled off her headscarf and caught a handful of her hair. Now he came into her line of vision. He had very pale blue eyes. There was something curious about them. Stone, she thought. He tugged harder on her hair, so that her head was dragged back, her throat exposed. When she spoke, the strangled sound of her voice was strange to her own ears.

"Shame on you," she said.

Then she heard the crashing of plates on the floor, and from the yard came the sound of a bucket overturned and the splintering of wood.

"Where is she?" the same voice, shouting in her ears.

She said nothing, not even when she felt the sharp point against the skin of her throat.

"Where is she?" The voice more impatient now. The knifepoint digging a little deeper. From close by, the reassuring crackle of the fire. It will not be long now, she thought. Quickly, it will be over. Good. Good, for the man's impatience.

Then the woosh of spittle, the wet on her face. Let him spit. Like the fire. The fire spits. Consumes. Changes. It will all be over soon. Still, the pain of her neck bent back into an unnatural arc, the ache of her scalp. Then some guffaws, the shuffling of feet, something heavy being dragged across the ground. Coarse laughter. The dull thud of something bulky thrown to the floor. Her head pushed forward, now. For a moment, the room spinning until her vision cleared. When she saw him, she let out a moan.

Pavel lay on the floor. His mouth was open. A pink sliver of blood and saliva hung from his mouth.

"Now, *this* will tell us where she is, won't *this*?"

Paraschiva watched as the thin man with the dark eyes and sallow skin raised his foot. She heard the thud as the boot hit Pavel's back. She saw him writhe. She watched as the boot rose again.

"Stop it!" One of the men with cropped fair hair spoke quietly. He made a low sucking sound and looked around him.

"Not him. Her."

He nodded to the man with the knife. This time he held her head steady, so that Pavel could see her face.

Pavel watched as he brought the blade to her throat and pressed. He saw the thin red rivulet trickle down her neck and creep along the creases of her wrinkles.

"Where is she?" The man with the small blue eyes was bent low over Pavel, speaking into his ear.

"You can save the old witch or the young bitch, but you can't save both of them."

Pavel shook his head. Watched the man nod again. Watched as the blade caused another rivulet.

Then he whimpered, as a dog whimpers, before he made his choice, before the split second that would remain with him for the rest of his days. He raised a hand and pointed out across the yard. The man took his knife away from Paraschiva's throat. Her head fell forward. She looked at the floor. Nor did she look up to see them drag Pavel to his feet so that he could lead them across the yard, towards the mountain track.

Pavel led the way. They walked in single file, the man with pale eyes close on his heels, four others following.

Pavel looked from side to side. Nothing but the thick mesh of pine trees. If he tried to run away, their branches would snare him before the men did. This part of the path offered no escape. Then his mind jumped ahead, to where the track forked. He walked with a steadier pace, in spite of the man's footsteps so close behind him.

They came to the place where the path divided. Pavel stopped. The five men closed around him. In the dark, they could not see the expression on his face. It was that of someone who had bargained with himself, and was at peace with the deal he had made. He pointed to the track that led deeper into the forest, away from the moutain ridge, away from the cave.

The men pushed ahead of him. Now, Pavel's head felt clear. His feet moved with purpose. Not a stone, not a rock wavered under them. He knew the track by heart. And he knew the shortcut through the undergrowth that led to a narrower path, one that could take him back to the farm. Even in the dark, he knew its dips and mounds. He moved quickly, without thought. He heard the cuss and yell as one of the men tripped and fell. A scuffle as others stopped to help him. His own feet ran on and on, and with every step, he put distance between himself and his captors.

One of the men hit out at a bush near his head. There was the flutter of wings, and a bird flew to the safety of the upper branches.

"We've lost the idiot," he said.

The man with the blue eyes said nothing. He looked up at the path where Pavel had run ahead into the dark. Then back in the direction where the path had forked. He adjusted his belt and shifted his weight from one foot to the other. He was angry, and he was not going to show it. It was he who had tripped and fallen, trying to keep up with the idiot man who was so slow in his thought and so swift on his feet. It was he, with his pale eyes, who had such trouble seeing in the dark. When he looked at the men next to him, he could make out only the outline of their shapes, the glimmer of eyes. His own weakness was the source of an anger that was flooding his brain.

"We don't need the idiot." He addressed the men as if they might be of kin to the simple-minded fugitive. "We need her. And what's to say he was taking us the right way anyhow? You two, carry on up this path. If you find either of them, bring them back to the house. We'll cover the other track."

He motioned to the bony-headed man to lead the way. He followed behind, so that he could stay close on his heels, and not reveal the weakness of his eyes.

Her own noise frightened her. Any step she took, however careful, caused the rustle of displaced foliage. It was as if the very leaves and branches were her betrayers. Her pace was too slow. If they were on her trail, they would catch up with her. She hitched up her skirt and trod the smallest of tracks, which led to thickets unbroken by paths of any kind.

She stood still and listened, the wolf-dog quiet by her side, intuiting the need for silence.

Then she heard it. From somewhere on the path below her, the crack of a stick breaking underfoot. Not far off. A dark panic fluttered over her, like a night curtain blown in the wind. She moved on, faster now, raising the thin arms of brambles that blocked her way, trying, at all costs, to carve herself a silent passage.

The thicket gave way to an outcrop of rock. The moon illuminated a sheer wall of grey stone, its pinnacle silhouetted against the sky. On one side, great lumps of grey boulders lay strewn on the ground, as if some pagan god had flung them down in a careless game.

The sounds grew louder. Voices, now. Footsteps, heedless of the noise they made – the crash of bodies moving fast through undergrowth.

Mariuca looked up at the rock face. The sheerness of the stone mocked her. She looked at the boulders, twice the height and girth of a man. She ran. Lifting her skirts, she ran to the other side of the rock wall. Then she stopped, and stifled a cry. For the land that she stood on sheered quite away, as if sliced away by some giant knife, leaving a huge empty vent of darkness. Far below her, she could hear the rush of water, a mountain stream flowing unconcerned on its downward passage through the rocks.

She turned in circles, then, unable to stand still and await her fate, yet knowing all the while that her movement was as useless as a random spinning top that children played with in the sand.

The wolf-dog watched her, its head bent low, its tail close to its legs.

The base of the rock was cleft, as if some angry hand had hacked at it with an axe and twisted the blade to get it free. She knelt down by the gap in the stone, and peered into the dark crack. Not big enough for a human frame, but wide enough for a dog.

"Luka!" she whispered.

She felt the warmth of the dog breath close to her cheek. Then the sounds from the thicket below them, and the dog's growl, the hackles raised on its back.

"Go, Luka!"

The wolf-dog didn't move.

"Go!" She pulled the animal by the fur on its shoulders. "If they catch you, they'll flay you alive. Go!"

But the wolf-dog remained by her side, stubborn, faithful.

"Go!" Her voice was cracking now. Her mind was filled with the flash of random images: smoke, the blades of knives, skin spread out on the ground, witness of unimaginable inventive cruelty.

"Go!"

Still he would not move.

She walked to the pile of boulders and found one small enough to lift, heavy enough to do its task. She went back to where the dog stood in front of the rock cleft. She raised the boulder above the dog's head.

The animal looked up at her. He knows, she thought. He knows what I am about to do, and still he remains.

"Go, Luka!" There were tears in her voice. Still, better this way. Better any way but their way. She closed her eyes and brought the boulder down with all her force. It hit the earth with a dull thud.

When she opened her eyes, she saw the cleft in the rock, and the dark shape of the dog vanishing into it. She rolled the boulder over so that it blocked the opening. Then she leaned back against the rock and breathed deeply.

They were shouting now, calling to each other through the trees.

The panic that had fluttered inside her stopped at the same time as she saw them emerge from the thicket. There were two of them, and a third close behind. She bent to pick up a stone and held it up, unsure of which man to aim at.

One of them had a small bony head. He was shouting to the man behind him.

She threw the stone at him. It struck his forehead, leaving a little gob of blood that gleamed black in the moonlight.

The man stopped his laughing. He was closer now, and his club was raised.

She stood still and faced him, as Luka had stood still in front of her. Her mind was dull and cold and blank. She closed her eyes.

No blow came.

When she looked again, she saw a man with pale blue eyes, his hand barring the raised club. Beside him was the man with the bony head, his mouth curled in something between pleasure and rage. A third man stood behind them, fat and witless.

The man with the pale eyes put his face close to hers. He smelt of tuica, and sour milk.

He undid the knot of her headscarf at the back of her neck. Its loosened folds fell across her shoulders and over her breasts. His hands then, on her, through the thin cotton of her dress, before he pulled at the ends of the scarf, wrenching it free from her head, exposing her skull, with its dark regrowth of hair.

Her hands flew to her head to cover it, at the same time as other hands grasped her wrists and fastened them tightly with her own scarf, then wound the cloth around her back and tied it in a tight knot in front of her chest.

"Take her down to the farm," said the man with the pale eyes. "And you…" he addressed the man with the bony head, "find the others. Tell them we've got her."

The man raised his hand in protest, as if he resented being deprived of the precious moment with the prey.

"Don't worry, we'll keep a piece of her for you," the pale-eyed man laughed, and followed close behind her, while the fat man walked in front, holding onto the ends of the headscarf, pulling her back down the mountain, as one would lead a goat or a sheep, towards the market.

29

They crowded out the kitchen with their bulk. Two of them stood on either side of Paraschiva. When Mariuca saw her, she was struck by her smallness. The two women looked at each other. Mariuca saw that there were tears in her eyes. She had rarely seen Paraschiva cry. She knew that she was crying not for herself, but for her, Mariuca. And she wanted to call out to her to stop, that her tears were not needed, that some part of her had flown off to safety up there, under the sheer rock face, that her body might undergo pain, but that part of her soul was high above the mountain ridge, way beyond the reach of predatory hands.

It was as if the old woman had heard her.

"Pah!" she raised an arm in the air. It hit the earthenware bottle of the man who stood on her blind side. There was a crash as the bottle smashed to the floor, then the crack of a fist against her cheek, another bottle uncorked, a round of laughter. The smell of alcohol, reeking from the ground and from their mouths.

"Let's give the old bitch a drink."

Paraschiva felt the bottle rammed into her mouth.

There was the brittle sound of teeth breaking, and she was choking and spluttering, the sweet liquid spattering over her cheeks, stinging the cuts on her throat.

Mariuca heard a scream and knew it to be her own, as two arms lifted her, and four more pinned her to the table. She saw the grins on their faces as they lifted her skirts. She caught sight of Paraschiva, her mouth an open maw of anger, then reshaping into a gape of surprise as she stared at the window. She saw the old woman make a last effort, raising her hands, forming the strange but familiar movement, the coil of the open palm, the ripple of the fingers in the air, mimicking the leap of flames. In the black square of the window, someone else had seen it too, and understood its meaning. Pavel, his eyes wide and focused, echoed its movement before vanishing into the dark.

Then one of the men pressed himself down on Mariuca's head, and all went dark.

"Maybe she'd like a swig too."

Then hands, a fumble of rough fingers, the bottle pushed in the fork of her legs.

She heard the screaming then. This time not her own, for another voice shouted:

"Will someone shut the old witch up?"

She heard the scream cut, a cord of sound broken. But with the darkness over her head, she did not see the man drag the old woman by her hair into the yard, nor the red spray that showered onto the ground when the man slit Paraschiva's throat from ear to ear.

She did not see the man return to the room with his hands red. But she heard the moment's silence, then a whoop of nervous laughter.

They took her in turn. Their yells and cries masked the roll of the barrel on the earth outside, the pouring of the liquid, the rush of flame as torch touched alcohol.

The fire licked around the house like a hungry hound.

It caught the thin dry thatch of the roof fringe, it swept down from the roof and up from the ground, where Pavel had poured out its trail.

The room filled with a thick, clogging smoke. In an instant, the drunken shouts of the men were transformed into choked cries. In the haze of their heated minds, in the deadly opaque air of the room, they barely saw the figure that swept through the door and lifted Mariuca and half-carried, half-dragged her through a gap in the flames and did not release her until they were at a safe distance from the house that had become a bonfire.

They slumped onto the ground. They lay there in the dust. Mariuca pressed her head against Pavel's chest, and felt the heaving as he gulped in air. She did not move. She did not look up to see the dark shapes of the men thrashing about behind a wall of flame. One of them spun himself out through the blaze and landed, a random ball of fire, rolling and jerking, a burning human log, on the ground.

Pavel watched in silence and listened as the fire did its own talking: crackling, as it consumed the wood of the walls; spitting, as it devoured the roof slats and beams of his home.

Later, with the dawn, Ioan Trifoi saw it too, from where he stood on the mountain path. The unnatural iridescence. The smoke rising into the air.

The pain left his body. He forgot the stabbing in his chest. He ran up the slope, beyond the curve in the road, towards the portal.

Through the empty bat's wings, he saw it. The house, or what was left of it: the charred remains, black twisted beams that jutted up like the ribs of a burnt beast.

A dull pulse came into his head, like the slow beat of a drum, as he approached the wreckage. He picked his way through the rubble of the yard, all the while with the throb of one thought in his head. He had arrived too late. He had not been there for them.

He was about to cry out, when he saw the bodies. He saw their black forms through the wisps of smoke. At first he thought they were pieces of wood. They lay strewn inside what was left of the house and around it, in odd poses: a hand crooked in the air, as if in salutation, a mouth open as if about to call out. Around them hung the smell of rancid fat. He felt his stomach heave. He looked around for some sign of life.

The stable was untouched. The door was open. He heard the sound before he went through the blackness of the doorway. The lowing of a cow. The reassuring softness of the sound, at odds with the destruction that surrounded it. And then another noise. A low whimper, the kind an abandoned dog might make.

He found them huddled together, slumped in a corner. Pavel, with his arm around Mariuca, who stared straight ahead and out at nothing. The odd silence but for the lowing of the cow. A crash from outside as a beam fell from the remains of the house and crumbled to the ground.

He squatted down in front of them and put his arms around them. It was as if he held two rag dolls. Then he felt the heaving of Pavel's shoulders under his touch. Mariuca did not move. When she raised her head to look at him, her eyes were vacant.

They told him that her soul was far away, somewhere safe perhaps, or somewhere back in time, before they had come for her, or further back, in a recess of her memory, before her village had resembled the charred ruins of the house outside, or further back, even, in some remote past when her people had lived down by the bend in the river and had thought, mistakenly, to have found a home.

When he looked at her face, he saw in it the expression of one who had lost all instinct – for protection, for love, for survival.

"Mariuca," he was calling her back to him.

Her eyelids fluttered. Behind them, still, the vacancy in the eyes. As if she were trying to remember who he was, this stranger with his skin discoloured by dark purple bruises, one eye swollen shut. And then a barely perceptible nod of recognition.

He held her and stroked her head, as if trying to make things better, knowing all the while they would never be right again.

She turned her head towards the corner of the stable. The distant look came back into her eyes, and he knew. He knew before he stood up and went to the bundle in the corner of the room. He knew before he drew back the blanket to reveal her face. Paraschiva's mouth half open in what could almost have passed for a smile. It was as if she were asleep, but for the gash across her throat, like a grotesque second mouth, gaping up at him.

Ioan turned away, staggered out into the yard, and retched. The drumbeat had gone from his head. He looked around, half hoping to see one of them alive, on whom to vent his rage. He breathed deeply, gulping in the air. He must stay calm. They were killers. They had killed, could kill again. The dead, the soul of Paraschiva, he would honour later. He must get them to safety, the living.

And then he realized there was no safety. Not down in the village. Not up in the mountains. He knew what had to be done. He pulled himself up, swaying as he did so, dizzy with the nausea of shock and pain.

He went to the well and filled a bucket with water. He carried it to the stable and placed it beside Mariuca. Cupping his hands, he placed them under her mouth. She drank a sip, then turned away. He wet his hand and passed it over her head. He made Pavel drink before he too felt the cool of the liquid on his own lips.

Then he smoothed out the pallet of straw.

"Be still, here."

She obeyed him like a tame animal, all will and thought gone.

He returned to the yard, and the woodpile. He chose two long thin birch branches and laid them on the ground, a yard apart. He went back to the stable to take a piece of a rope that hung from a hook. With it, he began to weave a lattice under and over the branches and the space between them. He had covered half their length when the sun rose from behind the mountain ridge, flooding the yard with light.

He looked anxiously towards the portal. The task was taking longer than he thought.

"Pavel!" he called.

Pavel appeared, stumbling across the yard towards him, turning his head away from the black ruins of the house that had been his home.

Ioan showed him how to thread the ropes, knotting them around each pole, stretching them taut across the space, then knotting them at the other side. Pavel watched him, with the stain of tears on his face and a question in his eyes. But he did as he was shown, and they both worked together in silence, concentrating on the task.

Then the shadow of the young woman fell across them. Ioan saw the dark stains on the ground near the hem of her skirt.

He looked up at her.

"Can you walk?" he said.

Her head was an outline, with the sun behind it. He spoke up to the blank of her face.

"I must go back, Mariuca. This is the only way. Pavel and I will carry her down to the village. When they see this, they will turn. It is our only hope, to have them on our side. Otherwise they will come, more of them. Do you see?"

She was still, a black statue against the light.

"Mariuca, can you walk?"

She nodded.

"We will go a little way. Up to the cave. They will not find you there. I will be back before evening. I promise."

He rose and held her against him. She was rigid in his arms.

"Mariuca, walk with me now. Pavel will finish here. Walk with me. You must walk."

He looked up at the sky. The sunlight was falling on the mountains opposite, turning their rock a pale gold.

"We must go, Mariuca. It is not safe here."

He looked back over his shoulder to the road.

"Now, we must go."

He walked away from her, towards the barn, and returned a few moments later with a blanket, a pouch of dried fruit and a gourd.

She said nothing, but bent to touch Pavel on the shoulder. When he looked up, she made a little rolling movement with her hands, and cupped them in front of her heart.

"Come, Mariuca."

When he took her hand to lead her away, she went with him, walking stiffly, like a doll, without looking back at Pavel, who was holding the cup of his hands out to her.

The cave was a half-hour's walk up a track that looped its way around the steep mountain slope. They didn't speak, saving their breath for the climb, on legs that threatened to give way under them.

The cave was shaped like a mouth, overhung by a lip of rock that had been worn smooth by time. Ioan entered it first, bending double under the overhang, only straightening up when he was in the dark vault.

Out in the sunlight, she waited. To her, the cave smelt like a grave. She heard him call out to her. And she went to him. Why not the quiet of the tomb? Still, she shivered as she dipped down to go into its darkness.

She could not see him, but felt him close to her. He was talking to her, barely aware of what he was saying, as she was barely aware of his words, but something in the sound of his voice was telling her that in spite of it all, it would be all right. He would make it all right. There would be a place for her, when the village had come to its senses. He would make a place for her, for them both. He would build a house on the edge of the village. He would find a way to make it all right.

He held her against him and stroked her cheek. She kept her head pressed to his chest. Her eyes stared straight out, looking at nothing but the dark wall of rock.

30

With every step down the forest track to the village, Ioan felt the world tilting a little more out of his reach. Nothing seemed real. Not the smoking ruin of the house on the hill behind him, not the dark place where Mariuca lay, not the prone figure they carried, strapped in between wooden poles, wrapped up in a blanket so that she looked like a little totem, a figurine, small in death, she who had seemed so large in life. She looked so peaceful, like a baby swaddled up out of harm's way. For a moment he found himself longing to join her in such a sleep.

Through a gap in the foliage, they saw the cross that marked Paraschiva's father's grave. They paused. Listened. The mountain road was quiet. There was no search party, no coming and going of men. They could dare the few paces.

From where they stood beside the grave they had a clear view of the village. The way down to it was deserted. Ioan nodded to Pavel. They placed the stretcher on the ground.

As soon as Ioan was free of his burden, he felt it. The spinning. The lightness of breath. His legs limp, as if they were made of wool. He fell to the ground.

The broad hand of the earth was under his back, the great empty blue sky above him. His muscles slack as rope on the ground. The blue dazzled. His mind a quiet bird returning to where it belonged. He knew what it was to rise into the sky. He knew what it was to die on the ground. Neither mattered. The village didn't matter. The spilt blood didn't matter. He would not think about her, lying in the cave, waiting for his return. There was no waiting for there was no time. Just the rotation of the sun, in a spinning blue.

The shadow of the cross faint on the ground, falling indiscriminately on little yellow stones, on the wood poles, on the pale blanket that hid the body beneath it. He knew then that she did not belong under the shadow of the cross, but in its wood. She had nothing to do with the place where straight lines crossed. That place was for the villagers, with their minds constantly in need of certainties. She was beyond that, he knew. She was in the whorls of wood, she was in the constant swirl of matter.

Later, he would be unable to describe, or even recall, what he had understood that morning, lying between the shadow and the great empty blue. Yet he knew it to be true.

He heard the rub of rope against wood. When he raised himself, he saw that Pavel had untied the knots that held her body in its strange cradle of hemp and wood. The ropes lay around her on the ground like dead snakes. It seemed right that she be free of them.

Pavel reached a hand to him and pulled him up. Then he bent down and scooped his mother into his arms as if she were a small child, and led the way back to the cover of the forest track.

There are as many different sounds of bells as there are voices. Ioan knew them all. He had grown up with them. The dull hollow toll with the long gap in between each chime that signified a death. The peel of joy that celebrated Easter, or Christmas, or a festival. The urgent clang that heralded a storm or flood. And the light cascade of sound, each chime like a drop of water, that celebrated a birth.

They heard it when they reached the towpath. The waterfall of sound.

Ioan closed his eyes. The sound of the bells was loud in his head. Perhaps he was imagining them. Perhaps they were bubbles of sound born out of a sickness in the brain. The jubilant bells. And Pavel behind him on the path, carrying a dead mother in his arms.

The bells called him. He followed the sound, and Pavel followed him. They left the river and took the path that led through the birch wood up to the cemetery behind the church. They hunkered down behind a tombstone, close together, Pavel cradling his mother's body.

Voices coming from the square. Loud, shrill, jubilant. Words that Ioan tried to string together to make some sense.

"They have found her."

"Alive. Just a few cuts and bruises."

"They say she fell down a gulley."

For an absurd moment, in the jangle of his mind, he thought they were talking about her, she whom he was trying not to think about, up on the mountain, in the mouth of a rock.

The voices again, snatches of phrases that rose above the peel of the bells.

"Where is she?"

"At Irena's."

"Thanks be to God."

Ioan leaned back against the tombstone.

"Gabriela is safe," he whispered the words to the stone, and to Paraschiva, as if she could hear, and to Pavel, as if he could understand. "Gabriela is safe."

Ioan motioned to Pavel to follow him. They moved close to the ground, Pavel running awkwardly, bent double under his load. They approached the surge of sound, moving from the cover of one tombstone to another, towards the village square.

They were closer now. He could recognize individual voices.

"They say she walked back into the village during the night."

"Like a ghost back from the dead."

"It's a miracle."

Then the voices gave way to a chanting prayer of thanks. It wound around him, a thread of sound. Ioan felt it weave its way into his chest, and quickly and unbidden, the tears came to his eyes. He brushed them aside. They weakened him, more than the pain in his head, more than the stabbing in his chest, for in them, he might dissolve.

Leaning forward from the cover of ferns, he watched the crowd that had gathered in the square.

They stood in an irregular semi-circle, fanned out around the steps that led up to the church portal. In front were the women of the village. They carried long white candles whose flames flickered, barely visible in the sunlight. Behind them stood the men, hats in hands, humbled before the miracle of the child returned, a prayer answered.

To Ioan, it seemed for a moment as if the village was as it had always been. As if the old woman he loved were not lying dead beside him.

The women's voices rose like water. He could swim in such a sound.

He brushed aside the ferns that hid him. He stood up slowly, his legs weak under him, and walked towards the crowd. Behind him, keeping the same rhythm as Ioan's footsteps, Pavel carried the fragile burden in his arms.

The chanting stopped. Ioan saw their faces, blurred, as if through liquid. Pale faces. Wide eyes. He saw the face of his wife. He saw her cup her hand to the open O of her mouth. He saw her arms reach out to him and then drop to her sides. The crowd parted to let them pass. He felt their whispers around him as Pavel laid down his load on the dust of the square.

Then the whispers faded into silence, but for the rustle of cloth as villagers pushed against each other to get a closer look at what their eyes had glimpsed, yet their minds not comprehended. The body, stiff and cold as a frozen bird in winter, the arc of red staining the pale wool of the blanket around her throat.

A candle dropped to the ground.

He felt a hand on his shoulder. When he turned, he saw the dark eyes bright with grief. Across the forehead, two deep purple welts. The black hair and beard matted with caked blood.

"Dear God, what have they done?" Barbu Temeru looked down at the body of the old woman. He put his hand on Ioan Trifoi's shoulder. His voice was quiet.

"It's over, Ioan," he said. "They have gone – left during the night – Surdu, Diaconu, all of them."

Ioan heard the words as a sleeper hears someone trying to wake him.

"Gone?"

Barbu nodded. He looked towards the church door. A small white square of paper was pinned to it.

"An official stamp. All of our spilt blood has not the power of one grey mark on a scrap of paper."

Somewhere in the crowd, a woman was sobbing. Ioan looked around him. Faces with mouths clenched in grief. Some turned to their neighbour, in search of solace. Many with eyes fixed on the ground, not knowing where else to look.

"It's over, Ioan. They will not be back," Barbu said.

"It is not over."

Ioan spoke first to the dead woman on the ground, then to the living who surrounded him.

"It is not over." His voice trembled. His shoulders shook under Barbu's hand. He was thinking of the cave. Of the mouth of the cave. Of the girl, in the darkness of the hollow rock.

"He's right. We will avenge this murder," a man's voice called out, shrill, cutting through the hush.

A rumble of support.

"Find the killers!" another voice called out.

"Hunt them down."

"Kill them."

The rumble grew into a growl. A circle of harsh sound surrounded Ioan. He looked at the faces. Men and women. The same faces who had watched without expression when he had been led through the town in shame. One face blurred into the other. They are the same, he thought, all part of the same animal. How quick it turns.

"They are dead," he said. "Burned, along with the house."

There was anger frozen in the air, with nowhere to go. The crowd clung to it, for it was their escape from guilt. It was their mask. If they dropped it, they would have to turn to themselves.

It had a life of its own. Ioan could feel it. Barbu could feel it. The animal in the square, with nowhere to go.

Ioan felt his legs weak under him. There would be no running away. Something had to be named.

If it cost him his last breath, he would name it. The animal would be called to account.

"It is not over," he said again. The trembling in his voice had stopped. He stood up straight and looked out over the crowd.

"Paraschiva is dead. Mariuca survived."

A candle sputtered and went out. No one spoke.

"She is hurt. She needs help. I need people to come with me, to bring her down to the village. She needs nursing. And she needs a home."

The wild animal silenced now. Now it had no mouth. A woman whispered to her neighbour. They looked at Magda, who stared straight ahead, at the air.

Their silence when he was led through the village in his shame. No one speaking out for him. Their silence now as they listened to her plight. No one speaking out for her. The anger rose in Ioan Trifoi. If the animal required the venting of rage, he would oblige.

"She needs a home."

The wild animal breathing now, preparing to pounce.

"Why don't you take her in?" The voice came from somewhere at the far end of the square.

Ioan looked at the ground.

"Yes, why don't you take her?"

"He already has."

A snort of nervous laughter. A needle of sharp sound. The animal pricked, ready to stir. The pressure of Barbu's hand stronger on Ioan's shoulder now, a warning.

The women's eyes, nervous, sharp as beads, darting looks towards Magda. The men, a group now, their faces flushed, their voices rising.

"She's a harlot!"

The wild animal bristling now.

Ioan could feel it closing in on him. If he spoke now, it would pounce. If he kept silent, it would creep up on him from behind.

"Fornicator!" The word was hurled at him, a stone, from somewhere in the centre of the crowd.

He looked down at Paraschiva. The fixed smile on the mouth. The dried arc of blood. Then his own blood pounding loud in his head. The faces swimming around him. The ugliness of the animal. He heard his own voice, defiant:

"And if I am, then she is no worse than me. Her crime is no worse than mine. It is less. For I have betrayed my wife."

Magda's head bowed. Her chest heaving. The women staring at her, while he spoke the unspeakable.

"Yet for that, you would not leave me to die in the hills like a dog. Why?"

Barbu's hand clenched on his shoulder, trying to stop up his words with his touch. But the words had a life of their own.

"Why? Because I am a man, because I am of the same colour, because you think I am of your kind." His voice cracked. "I am not of your kind."

Silence, now, in the square, but for the sputtering of candle flames, futile, invisible, in the sun.

"You were calling for justice. Do you call this justice? We have seen death at the hands of killers, while you stood by and did nothing. It is not the first time. We have seen deaths before in our village, in the land around our village. Is that what you want? Another death on your hands? More blood?"

He could hear a woman sobbing beside him. It was his wife.

"Is this what you want?"

He had no more breath. His head began to spin. In front of his eyes, the faces were becoming blurred, a mass of pale suns, quivering, as if in a heat haze.

The beast was silent. It was disappearing now, unable to answer, although he kept asking the same question, again and again, as he swayed and tried to keep his balance and failed, and fell to the ground.

31

When he reached the cave, she had made a small fire out of twigs, encircled by stones. The firelight quivered on the walls of the cave, and on her skin. Her wounds had healed. She was clean and smooth. She had rubbed a red powder on her. A healing powder. She said she had found it under the rocks. He could see it on her arms and legs. He wanted some. Some of her healing. So he took it from the pouch in her hand and rubbed it on his head, over his eyes, where the pain was at its strongest, over his chest, where the cut bone was at its sharpest. When he was done, his head felt clear, his breath felt free. They were the same colour, he and she.

The colour of healing, he wanted to say.

Just this fire, this colour, and a little time. To be healed.

And her hand, that was important too. To hold her hand.

32

The hand that held his was gentle, and patient. Its touch was timeless.

When he opened his eyes, the room swayed in and out of his vision, the angles of ceiling and walls curving, then straightening, then twisting again. So he closed his eyes, to return to the quiet of the dark.

But she was there. The soft touch. The voice that finally, one morning, called him to conciousness.

The face looked down at him, as from a great height.

"Ioan, Ioan, are you awake?"

He put the face and the voice together. They belonged to Barbu's daughter, Valentina.

"Where am I?"

"You are safe. We are looking after you. You will be well soon."

"I need you to hold my hand."

So she took his hand and held it in hers. He looked at their hands on the blanket. There was no red powder. His hand was the same colour it had always been.

The mouth of the cave is bigger than he remembers it. Still, he has to bend double to dip under the lip of overhanging rock.

Inside, he swims in darkness. Soon he makes out shapes, the dull blue of rock. The floor of the cave, the earth, for some reason threatens him. Still, he finds himself scouring it with his hands. He is searching for something, although he doesn't know what. A circle of stones? The ash of a burnt-out fire? A patch of red powder?

He finds nothing. He calls out her name, knowing that she has gone. He expects no answer. He calls out her name again, this time to anchor her name to the rock. Absence is in a way worse than death, he thinks, for there is no tomb on which to grieve. The sound is his inscription. It does not echo. There is no return of his voice. The rock swallows it.

He lies down in a corner of the cave, where he left her, and closes his eyes.

He does not know how long he has slept, or even if he has slept at all. He has been wrapped up in dreams, or memory, and now he doesn't know which is which. They are indistinguishable. They flow over him like water. He can float in them. He is on the riverbed, swimming with one arm. The other reaches out in front of him. She swims ahead of him, just beyond reach.

He wakes to a presence in the cave. He does not know if it is night or day. He cannot see it clearly, but it is standing close by. He can see its shape. An old woman? A tree? The figure of a brown girl? It bends over him. It blows on his cheek. Its breath is a word. Now, it says. Now.

He knows it is calling him. He follows. It could call him anywhere, he would go. Towards darkness or light. He is prepared for both. Now, it breathes again.

He gets up. Walks out of the mouth of the cave. Into the sun. The daylight shocks him with its glare. Now.

He looks up towards the mountain ridge. He sees them, black against the sky. Maybe they are a trick of the eye. The figure of a young woman. A dog beside her. They have been waiting, patient, for him to look up. Now he has seen them, they can go.

The glare is too strong for his eyes. He closes them. Just for a moment. When he opens them, the figures have gone.

He wonders if he should follow them, beyond the mountain ridge. He wonders if he would ever find them. He wonders, too, if he should go back down into the village, hold his daughter in his arms, retrace his steps.

He does neither. The light is too bright. He goes back into the cave. He lies down. He feels it, the presence. It is still there. If he reaches out, he could touch it. He could take its hand, he thinks.

He closes his eyes and lays his hands on his chest, in the dark, just in case it isn't there.

EPILOGUE

All day and all night the rain had fallen, pattering over fields, trees and the rooftops of houses.

Ioan sat by the fire and listened to the baby's greedy sucking on the breast. He looked across at the young woman, the tiny girl child cradled in her arms, and smiled. They were so beautiful, he thought, with wonder at the miracle that had been passed down from his loins.

Doinitsa had grown into a pale-skinned beauty who had had the choice of young men from the village. She married her first sweetheart, Mihai, the blacksmith's son, and together they had produced the pale-faced bundle that now lay in his daughter's lap.

After Mariuca had gone, he had not returned to the village. Out of the ruins of Paraschiva's farm, he had built a house. At first, just a wall to keep the wind out. Then more walls, to keep himself from the world.

For a year he lived alone on the mountain. From time to time he would walk to the top of the ridge and look over, to the land beyond. Sometimes he saw a traveller moving along the road, and he caught his breath. Until the figure got closer, and he knew, by the mass of baskets that hung around its neck and shoulders, that it was a peddler; or, by the sheep that followed, a shepherd, herding his summer flock to the richer pastures of the higher slopes of the mountains, to the south.

From time to time he would go down to the village to see his daughter. For five years, thus, he watched her grow from a girl into a young woman. Magda he had barely spoken to. A nod, a short exchange – two people who had everything to say, but no words between them.

Then, little by little, time had done its work. Their conversations grew longer. Her appeals for help, when another storm ripped away a piece of the roof. Another child born in the village, and could he build it a cradle? Pavel, who lived with her now, was in need of his company. Little by little, the pieces of their lives joined together, tiny intersections crossing, until, one winter's day, when the snows of the mountain dazzled his eyes with their vision of unending solitude, he had closed the door of his mountain refuge, and returned to Magda, and his daughter, and his house in the village.

He would nod to the villagers as he passed them in the street, and they to him. But he rarely entered into anything but the briefest of conversations, because of the memory. It was his lethal line to the past. It would never leave him. Faces, some of them neighbours, friends, and not one of them daring to step out of line, in protest, to support him. He looked away from their betrayal. They turned away from their shame.

Surdu and Diaconu had disappeared, vanished

into the dustbowl of the plain. There had been no investigation. A war had come and gone and taken with it half the young men from the village. Ioan had been spared the fight, because of his blurred vision. After the events of that night, he had never seen clearly.

A woolly-minded but well-meaning young priest had been sent from Birtiza to bring order to the troubled village. No one had complained about his lack of leadership, for people had had enough of the hard lines of leaders, and those of the battlefront.

So Ioan Trifoi lived his life as if in a shell. He lay down with his wife, and in time they resumed touch. But it was the shell of a man that made love to her, and into the shell of a woman that he left his seed.

The fire crackled with a steady flame. Doinitsa started to sing. It was not one of the village songs. It was one of the tunes that Mariuca had taught her, a song of the people who had lived down by the bend in the river. Her voice called him back to the land of memory. It was a place he went to rarely, as a walker would not go along a riverbank in the time of a spring flood, for fear of being washed away.

Barefoot, I take the road in front of me
Then shoes I make from soft leather
The soil speaks through their soles
Now all is well
I own good shoes
With the spirit of the earth beneath my feet
I can walk far

I have no fear of frontiers

The baby puckered her lips, pursing her mouth into the air.

Ioan picked up a poker, with a view to stirring the fire, on such a damp night, into a better being.

The flames gave a new heat, warming his body, the way the song kindled a forgotten core in his heart.

Perhaps, he thought, when the rains stopped, he would go to the mountain ridge, right to the top, and pass through the crack in the rocks, in search of what lay beyond.

ACKNOWLEDGEMENTS

Heartfelt thanks to all my friends for their invaluable editorial advice: Dr Dawn-Michelle Baude, Michael Burberry, Denise Larking-Costes, Martin Lewis, Steve Lockie, Bob Mohl, Tom O'Brien, Maureen Pucheu, Ray Renolds, Cynthia Savage, Murray Simpson, Roger Surridge and to all the members of my Paris writing group.

To Dana Radler, Meg McGuinness, Adrian Mathews, Suzie Dixon, Beverly Charpentier and Bernard Houliat for being such intrepid travelling companions in Transylvania.

To all my friends in Romania at the universities of Brasov and Sibiu with whom I have shared such special moments, and to the people of the Maramures who gave me such a warm welcome.

To David Grossman, for believing in the book and working to promote it.

Lastly, to my Irish mother for her poetic spirit, and to my Hungarian father and grandfather, who survived the extremes of racism under Nazi occupation of Hungary, and to my grandmother, Annushka Vermes, who did not.